saint destiny

fred stesney

Stag
Beetle
Books

For my wife, who always believed in me.

your best life 1:

You'll Never Know If You Can Fly If You Don't Jump Off a Cliff.

Go big or go home. Maybe you've read that on a t-shirt. That's because to go big, you have to LEAVE HOME. Sitting around some two-bit town waiting for something great to happen to you ain't gonna cut it. (Believe me, I've been there. Literally.) The world won't come knocking on the door of your trailer to find out how wonderful, special and talented you are. You have to go out into the world and pull on its ear while kicking it in the ass.

You'll probably have to go to a big city, like New York (or big-ish city, like Nashville) and you may not like it there. It could be crowded, dirty, noisy, expensive, and handing out parking tickets like Halloween candy. The people there might give you attitude because their city has an art museum and more than one McDonald's, but, when you're starting out, you just gotta suck it up.

And, no matter what, things will go wrong. Really, REALLY wrong. Even after getting everything you thought you wanted, you may find yourself broken-hearted over some guy you should have known better about. Or embarrassed on national television by some jerk reality show host trying to destroy you for ratings. Or in an ER clinging to life after some rando with a gun decides you're a witch. Or on the run from the Mexican government coming after you with SUVs and M-16s. But the crazy part is - when you're past all that and looking back - it'll all make a good story.

one

. . .

THE PORT AUTHORITY BUS TERMINAL doesn't make a good first impression of New York. Especially in January. The guys sleeping on the ground looked like they'd fallen off the welcome wagon and then got run over by it.

I found a Starbucks and sat on the floor with my cracked-screen phone, looking for a place to live. Leaving home felt like stepping off a cliff. The bus ride felt like falling. Now it was almost noon, and I saw the ground rushing up at me. I didn't have enough money to waste on a hotel room or a cup of coffee. If I didn't find a place to live in the next few hours, I'd go *splat!*, sleeping on the ground at the bus terminal too.

I found a listing in my price range (less than $450) in Bushwick, Brooklyn. (Wherever that was.) It was a roommate situation. I'd never lived with anyone but my mom before. Never lived away from home. I figured I could put up with strangers. Not like I had a choice, anyway. *It is what it is,* I thought. Sucky, but something I had to go through.

I called Gavin, the guy who posted the listing. He seemed cool enough on the phone. He told me how to get to the apartment on the L train. (And how to get to the L train from the bus terminal.) The subway was a whole new thing to me.

I'd only seen New York in movies and TV shows, and you hardly see people riding the subway in movies and on TV.

The subway was right under the bus terminal and a ride cost more than I could afford. I didn't know what to do about it until I saw a woman open a gate and push her stroller through. The gate just stood there, wide open, and I ducked through. Some old guy glared at me, like I'd stepped on a baby chick.

I wanted to tell him that I was an honest person. (It's not like I never stole anything. I don't think anyone can say that.) But I had hardly any money. I'd become an upstanding citizen soon enough. Then I'd gladly pay my fare.

A 3 train came by a few minutes later and I hauled my old suitcase and sleeping bag on. The car was crowded with all types of people ignoring each other. They put maps in the subway cars right above the seats. The station names were really small, and I had to lean over a lady to read them. I had to check the map again and again. She seemed annoyed. *Really, lady, if you don't want to be crowded, why are you living in a city with eight and a half million people?* Whatever. Haters gonna hate.

I didn't see any empty seats, so I sat on my suitcase, feeling everyone looking at me like some teenage girl who just fell off a turnip truck. I reminded myself that I was going to be a huge success, and I wouldn't have to ride the subway forever. (And, for the record, they don't grow turnips where I'm from, so no turnip trucks to fall off.)

———

I popped out of the subway station far from where I started, but still in the middle of the city. It was more city than I'd ever seen in my life. A lot of the streets in New York have numbers, probably because they had too many streets to think of names for.

At least the cold didn't get to me. I'd been through some below zero-degree days back home. This was easy.

Gavin lived not far from the subway station. (Thank God, because I was *so* tired of lugging my suitcase around.) The building looked like it used to be a warehouse, and it took up most of the block. I found the buzzer and pressed the button. Gavin let me in.

The inside didn't look like much. Not dirty, just harsh: concrete walls, floors and ceilings painted gray. When I got to the third floor, Gavin stood at the door. Every floor had its own door, all of them locked. It seemed like a lot of security for an apartment building. Maybe they were getting ready for the zombie apocalypse.

Gavin looked tall and thin, kinda hippy, kinda Rasta. Not like anyone I grew up with. More like someone I'd seen in a Coke commercial.

"Hey," he said. "Destiny, right?" He smiled with blindingly white teeth.

"Yep," I said. "Did this used to be a warehouse?"

"Yeah," he said. "This neighborhood used to be all industrial."

The hallway was long and windowless, with the same grey paint, like the inside of a prison, or a battleship. (Not that I'd ever been inside either.) He talked as we walked: "They started converting some of the buildings into live/workspaces years ago. Now it's a lot of artists, and people who got priced out of Williamsburg. There're still some businesses around here. You get used to the noise - y'know, trucks coming and going."

We got to the apartment, and he opened the door. Inside, it felt cramped and weird. There was an entranceway and a little kitchen, and two levels of tiny rooms made of painted plywood. Calling them "rooms" was stretching it. They felt more like cells.

"How many people live here?" I asked.

"Five. Or there will be five when we find a new roommate. This is the space we have available," he said, pointing to a dark box on the ground level, right off the kitchen.

I ducked inside and saw just enough space for a mattress and maybe a small dresser. I'm not that tall - about an inch shorter than average - and my head almost touched the ceiling. The whole apartment got its light from a huge set of windows on one wall, but my (potential) box wasn't next to the windows.

I grew up in a trailer, so I wasn't expecting luxury, but this was definitely a step down. Let me repeat that: this room was crappier than my room in my mom's trailer.

I came out and looked around the apartment again. Not the best living situation, but I didn't plan on being there long, and I didn't have time to look anywhere else. "Four hundred a month?" I asked, not believing the words coming out of my mouth.

"Yeah," said Gavin. "I know. Rents are crazy in New York, but that's actually a good deal. And everyone here is cool. Caroline works at the New School and is a Super-8 filmmaker; and Monica is a seamstress and freelance costume technician. Yusef is an Uber driver; I'm a dancer."

I wanted to know what a "Super 8 filmmaker" was. *Like, she made movies at motels?* I didn't ask. "I'd need to move in today."

Gavin looked at my suitcase and sleeping bag. I realized I should have said, "Right now, like this very second."

"I'll have to tell the others," he said. "But it's my name on the lease so if you have the cash, it'd be okay. Do you have any references?"

"I just moved here," I said.

"Where from?" asked Gavin and I didn't know what to say. I mean, I knew where I was from. I just didn't want to say. I grew up outside Billings, Montana and that wasn't going to impress anyone. "From...out west," I said. That left a lot of room for the imagination.

"Oh, okay" he said. "Welcome to New York."

That was the first and last time someone said, "Welcome to New York" to me.

"And references..." he said.

"I dunno," I said. "Everyone is...uh...asleep. The time difference, y'know?" I felt so proud of myself for thinking of that.

"That's cool," said Gavin. "You look all right to me. I just need the four-hundred dollars up front for February, and we can prorate the last eleven days of January."

"Cool," I said, even though I didn't know what 'prorate' meant. I fished every dollar I had to my name out of my jacket pocket and started to count.

"Are you here for school?" he asked.

That question annoyed me. I didn't need any more school. I already knew what I was doing. "No," I said. "Work. I'm a healer." (I hadn't really started my professional career yet, but I was determined to fake it until I make it.)

"Alternative medicine?" he asked.

"Sort of," I said. "I can heal people just by touching them."

"What's that? Like reiki?"

I'd never heard of reiki and didn't want to admit it. I still wasn't sure if New Yorkers were super sophisticated or super full of crap. "Yeah, sort of like that," I said and handed him the cash.

He counted it. "I need another $77," he said.

"Why?" I asked, because he had just said "Four hundred dollars."

"For the last six days of this month," he said. "Prorated it's about $13 a day."

"Oh," I said. Now I knew what "prorate" meant, sorta. I peeled off another $77, leaving $144 to get me through the end of February. I didn't have a budget, but I knew that, if I had, I'd just blown it. There was nothing else I could do but wing it and hope that I didn't get hit with any surprise expenses.

He picked up his phone. "Let me text everyone else and tell them what's happening."

I dropped my suitcase and sleeping bag in the cave, then took off my jacket and hung it up on a nail in the wood left by the last person who lived there. I ducked back into the kitchen.

"Let me take your picture," he said. "To send to the roomies."

I struck a pose, happy to have gotten over the first hurdle, on my way to fame and fortune. "Do you have anything that needs to be healed?" I asked.

"Huh? Uh, no," he said. He looked at his phone, only half paying attention. "I think I'm good."

I didn't want to come off as pushy, but I really had to get things happening. Word of mouth was the way to success. Just one or two customers and I'd be on my way. And I realized how ridiculous it sounded, claiming to be able to heal people. *Like, who would believe that?* Gavin had called it "alternative medicine." That sounded like a load of crap, whatever it was. I had to prove myself as the real deal.

"Alright," I said. "Just checking. If you're a dancer, you probably get some injuries."

"Stretching is so important," he said.

"Totally," I said.

———

I didn't feel like sitting in my cave, so I went for a walk around the neighborhood. I found the JavaStrip, a coffee house on the corner, and went in. All the tables were tiny and close together, and not a lot of people were there: a millennial dude on his laptop and a couple of girls with dyed hair and tattoos, sitting together and talking. A bulletin board hung near the door where people posted all sorts of stuff: yoga classes, dog walking, laundry services, etc. I took a flyer out of my bag: one I'd printed up before I left Montana. It was wrinkled from being stuffed in my suitcase. I found an unclaimed pushpin and stuck it into the cork:

HEALER AVAILABLE, CAN CURE ALMOST ANYTHING, NO MEDICINES OR DRUGS, REASONIBLE RATES.

And I had my phone number at the bottom on little tabs that I cut to make them easy to tear off. Not the best flyer, but I couldn't afford to have one professionally made. I posted one there, at the laundromat, and everywhere else in the neighborhood that had a bulletin board.

In spite of the cold, there were lots of people walking around on the streets. You could live without a car here, which was great for me because I couldn't afford one.

I got back to the apartment, sleepy after my overnight bus ride. I went into my plywood cave, unrolled my sleeping bag on the dusty, concrete floor and went to sleep as best I could.

I don't know what time I woke up. I heard someone else in the apartment. I came out of my box, achy from the hard floor and a little better rested. I looked out the window. It was already dark out. A girl had her head in the refrigerator, her butt towards me.

"Hi," I said.

She turned and popped the top of a Diet Coke. She looked maybe in her early twenties with shoulder-length, dishwater blonde hair. She dressed like she had just come home from an office job. "Oh, hi," she said. "You must be Destiny."

"Yeah," I said. "Who are you?"

"I'm Caroline," she said, looking me up and down, trying to figure me out. "Did you just move to New York?"

Is it that obvious? I wondered. "Yeah," I said. "Just got here this morning." Caroline kept staring at me, like I was supposed to say something else. "I came here for my career," I said.

"Yup," she said. "That's what they all do."

"I can heal people, just by touching them," I said.

"You can cure cancer?" she said, smirking, like she'd caught me exaggerating.

I wanted to give her the finger, but I controlled myself. "Yup," I said, totally confident.

She looked like she didn't believe me. "Have you done it before? Cure cancer, I mean."

"Yeah," I said. That was half-true. A guy at my high school had a dad with lung cancer. The family was broke and desperate so they let me try to cure him. The dad *was* getting better. Then he got in a car crash and died.

"Wow," she said, but she didn't sound impressed. She probably still thought I was talking out of my ass.

"I'll have to give you a demonstration," I said.

"Well, I don't have cancer," she said and she knocked on the wooden countertop. (Which made no sense because how could she not accept that I could heal people yet think that knocking on wood would keep her from getting cancer?)

"Do you have anything else wrong with you?" I asked.

"No," she said. "I'm fit as a fiddle."

I decided that Caroline was not going to be of any use to me. (And who the hell says "fit as a fiddle?") Whatever. On the ladder of success, you don't have to step on every rung.

That's when the snoring started. It sounded like it was coming from one of the spaces on the second level. "That's Yusef," she said. "Don't worry about him. He can sleep through anything."

"He's the Uber driver, right?" I asked.

"Yeah," she said.

"What about the other people who live here?" I asked.

"You've already met me and Gavin. That leaves Monica.

She'll roll in here, eventually," she said. "Anyway, it's nice meeting you."

"Okay," I said, and that's it, because it wasn't nice meeting her.

———

I felt super hungry so I went out to find some cheap food. I passed the subway stop. A bum sat at the entrance on a flattened cardboard box, shaking a paper coffee cup. It sounded like there was some change in it. Both his legs were gone right below the thigh, and he looked in bad shape, like he wouldn't be doing well in life, even if he could walk.

On an impulse, I went over to the guy. He looked even worse close up. His clothes were filthy and his skin was red from the cold and covered with random sores. He smelled like pee and B.O. SO gross.

"Do you want your legs back?" I asked.

He looked at me like he didn't understand what I said. "Do you want your legs back?" I said again, then added "Yes, or no?" just to sound New Yorky.

"Hell yes," he said. "And a million dollars!" Then he laughed at his own joke and I could see he was missing some teeth, too. He grossed me out, but I had to follow through. I placed my left hand on one of his stumps.

"Expect a change in your life," I said.

"As long as you're down there," he said, "I could use a rub." Then he laughed again.

SO GROSS.

"You wish," I said.

It only took a few seconds for me to work my magic, and I pulled my hand away. Thank God I was wearing gloves. Before he knew what was happening, I snatched the coffee cup from his hand. I walked off slow and calm, because what could he do? Chase me down? He yelled after me, calling me the b and c words, not realizing that it was the best money he'd ever spent.

———

I got to the corner store which I later learned New Yorkers call a bodega. It was as crappy as the mini marts_from back home, but smaller. Way smaller. Even with everything crammed in there, they didn't have as much stuff as a mini mart.

I saw that there were a couple of one-dollar bills in the cup, bringing the total to $3.15. I looked around for something to eat. A package of two Pop-Tarts only cost a dollar, so I bought three packages: Blueberry, Strawberry, and Hot Fudge Sundae.

I ate the Pop-Tarts as I walked, careful not to touch them with the hand that touched the bum.

I felt exhausted. It takes a lot out of you when everything is new and unfamiliar, like a foreign country. Everyone spoke English and took American money and all but, damn, I had to figure *every* other thing out.

When I got back to the apartment (I couldn't think of it as home yet), Monica, the other female roommate—the seamstress—came out of the one bathroom we all shared. Monica had long black hair with bangs that hid a too-large forehead. A tattoo of a mermaid covered most of her right shoulder. She looked cool and I took an instant shine to her. I introduced myself and gave her the rundown of my healing powers. I asked her if she had anything that needed fixing.

"I could use a foot rub," she said.

"Not my jam," I said.

"I was kidding," she said. "Anyway, it's good to have you here. I didn't like the last guy. He was a snob, y'know?"

"Not exactly," I said.

"I mean he thought he was, like, some sort of intellectual. He always talked about artists and authors, like he assumed you didn't understand who talking about, like he was, y'know, giving you an education just by being in his presence. And excuse me, but I know who Victor Hugo is."

I didn't. "What happened to him?" I asked. "The guy, not Victor Hugo."

"He moved in with his girlfriend," she said. "That's New York. A lot of living situations are determined by who you're sleeping with. But I mean..." She looked around the room with a what-can-you-do expression. "I can't blame him."

The front door buzzer buzzed, and Monica jumped for it. A guy's voice came out of the intercom.

"You're early," she said, sounding annoyed. She turned to me with a *WTF?* expression that I didn't totally get.

"That's my boyfriend," she said. "Could you go let him in? I have to go get ready."

I nodded and she climbed a short ladder, disappearing into her second-level space. I don't know how I got roped into being Monica's receptionist, but what the hell. I went out into the hallway to the locked door at the end. I opened it to see a good-looking guy, 20-something, tall, with a beard. He didn't look happy.

"Come on in," I said. "Monica's still getting ready."

"Thanks," he said, sounding distracted, and he followed me back to the apartment.

"I'm Destiny," I said. "I just moved in."

"I'm Josh," he said, and that was it. I couldn't figure out why Monica wanted to date a grump.

We went into the apartment, and he sat on a stool in the kitchen area. There was a small table there that maybe you could get four people around, if they all crowded together. There was no place else to sit so I sat across from him.

"Like, what do you do?" I asked, hoping for a job where he could have been hurt. I know that sounds terrible, but I really needed to get the ball rolling.

"I'm a schoolteacher," he said.

"Really?" I said. "What grade?"

"Fourth."

"Are you, like, the cool teacher who all the kids like?" I said.

"They like me," he said. "I'm still their teacher, though. I don't let them get away with anything."

"You're a lot cooler than any of the teachers I had in elementary school," I said, which was dumb because I didn't know if he was cool or not. He could have been a raging asshole.

We sat for a silent for a second.

"Sorry," he said. "But I'm having a migraine." He rubbed his temples, like that was going to help.

Just like that, the door of opportunity swung open. I heard Monica's high heels on plywood above us. I'd have to walk through that door, fast.

"I can cure that, y'know," I said, super serious. Before he could say, yes, I reached out and put my left hand on his forehead and said, "Expect a change in your life." (That was going to be my signature phrase. I thought of it during the bus ride to New York.) I held my hand on his head for a few seconds. Josh looked surprised but didn't pull away. In the awkward seconds of silence, Monica started to climb down the ladder, her back to us. I put my hand back on the table just as she turned around. Not that there was anything wrong with what I did. I just didn't want to have to explain anything. I felt too tired.

"Where do you want to go?" she asked Josh.

"I don't know," he said to Monica. "The Helium Bar?"

"Okay," said Monica and, as they left, Josh gave me a surprised look over his shoulder touching his temple again. I knew that his migraine had disappeared. Something like that, with nothing to regrow, only takes a few seconds. I winked. I don't know why I did that. Wink, I mean. It was silly.

After they left, I took a second to feel good about myself. It was the end of the day, and I was in New York, with a place to live and I'd just helped someone. (I helped the bum, too, but that didn't seem to count.)

"I wouldn't do that, if I were you," said Caroline.

I turned to see her standing in the kitchen, giving me a sour look. "Wouldn't do what?" I asked.

"You know," she said.

"Really, I don't," I said, because I didn't.

"Trying to put the moves on Monica's boyfriend," she said.

"I wasn't trying to 'put the moves' on him. I was trying to help him," I said. *And why the hell are you spying on me?* I thought.

She made an annoying laugh that pissed me off. Like this was any of her business. Then she looked at my hands. "Why are you wearing gloves? It's freaking hot in here."

I put my hands by my side and made two fists. "Gotta protect my hands," I said. "They're how I make my living."

I couldn't tell if Caroline believed me or not, and I didn't care. She shrugged. "Okay," she's said in that tone that means "whatever," and she went back to her room.

I couldn't figure out what her problem was, and I *so* wanted to punch her in the nose, then not heal her.

your best life 2:

If you Think There's Such Thing as Overnight Success, You Must Be Asleep.

When someone is super successful, it looks like it happened fast and easy - like an actor moves to Hollywood one day, gets discovered the next, and stars in a blockbuster movie by the end of the week. Really, it can take a long time to build a career because, wherever you go, there are thousands of wannabes already there, trying to get their own star on Hollywood Boulevard. The good news is that most of the wannabes don't have the talent or the drive it takes to make it to the top. You need to cut through the clutter by proving yourself day after day. And you need to be patient. (Being patient is different from sitting on your behind, playing on your Xbox, waiting for something to happen.) Patience means working while you wait. It's like planting seeds. While you're waiting for them to grow, you're always out planting more. Because you never know which seed is going to grow into a prize-winning pumpkin.

two

. . .

CAROLINE WOKE me up the next morning with her knocking around in the kitchen. It took a few seconds to hit me: I was alone, in a strange city with only $140 to my name. The jolt of fear popped my eyes wide open. I had to get up and make this city my bitch.

For a hot minute I thought about going out and getting a day job. I'd worked at Burger King in high school and New York probably had more fast-food joints than you could throw a pigeon at. But no. I needed to be out there, pushing my career. Every hour spent working for minimum wage was an hour's delay to me reaching my two goals: fame and fortune.

As I lay in my sleeping bag, looking at the knotholes in my plywood ceiling, I made a plan to scout the territory. If I got to know my ass from my L train, the city wouldn't seem so intimidating.

I didn't know who else was home, and I didn't pack a bathrobe, so I threw on an oversized t-shirt and made my way to the bathroom. The bathroom was weirdly large compared to the rest of the apartment was.

I reminded myself that this was only temporary. I'd have

my own place soon enough. I didn't have much in the way of toiletries: a tiny bottle of shampoo and a thin bar of soap I saved from the one night I stayed at a motel on the bus trip here. A big bar of soap, and a few bottles of shampoo were already in the shower and I didn't think anyone would notice if I used just a little. I helped myself to the toothpaste too. I had my own toothbrush. (Really, people, I'm not that disgusting.)

Dressed and ready, I went outside. It was cold but sunny. My phone rang with a number I didn't recognize. I took the call. It was Arlene, a woman who'd seen one of my flyers. Yes! I could hear the pain in her voice. (That's "Yes!" I got a customer, not "Yes!" I could hear her pain.)

"I hope you can help me," she said.

"Sure," I said, trying not to sound too excited. "What's the problem?"

"I have pain in my lower back."

"Okay," I said. "I can fix that."

"Bless you," she said, and she sounded like she meant it.

"Do you live in the neighborhood?" I asked. "I can come over right now."

"In the Bushwick Houses," she said.

"I just moved here," I said. "I don't know exactly where that is."

She gave me the address. After I ended the call, I put the address in my phone. It wasn't far, just a few blocks.

It was a housing project which I guessed was the New York version of a trailer park. I grew up in a trailer park, so I know where poor people live when I see it.

Arlene buzzed me in and I rode up to the eighth floor in an elevator that smelled like disinfectant. The hallway was sunnier than the ones in my building but more run down. (Could anything not be crappy in this city?) When I knocked, Arlene said "Coming," and it took a full minute for her to get to the door.

"Is it Destiny?" she asked through the door.

"It's me," I said, and she opened up.

She looked maybe fifty, but she was bent over like she was eighty-five. I could see the pain and tiredness in her face. Growing up, I'd seen that face before.

"Come on in," she said, and hobbled off. I followed her into her living room, noticing she smelled a little like pee. I didn't know what to do with myself as she slowly and painfully settled into a big armchair.

Something touched my leg, and I jumped. I looked down at a cat. It meowed and rubbed up against my leg again.

"Sit, sit," she said. "And that's Pebbles. She's friendly."

I went to the couch and sat. Her apartment could have used a cleaning, and it smelled weird, but it was a palace compared to my cave. I mean, she had a couch. "It's your back?" I said, trying to sound professional.

"Bad disc," she said as the cat jumped into my lap. "The doctors say I need surgery, but I keep getting the runaround. Either the doctor can't do it on such and such a date, or the hospital can't do it." As she told me this, she seemed only half there, the other half was with her pain.

"I can fix it, no problem," I said. "But it'll take a while, like a couple weeks, for it to heal completely. And it'll cost twenty bucks."

Arlene sat still for a minute. I couldn't tell if she was concentrating on her pain or shocked at my price.

"What is it that you do?" she asked.

"I can heal people just by touching them," I said.

"Like a faith healer?"

"Not exactly," I said.

She had a plaque on her wall with an inspirational scripture:

"Be strong and courageous. Do not be afraid or terrified because of them, for the LORD your God goes with you; he will never leave you nor forsake you." Deuteronomy 31:6

If she believed in God, the Bible and miracles then I guessed she'd believe my story. I told it like this:

"My mom died a while ago. It was tough, especially at the end. It was just the two of us and I had to take care of her. Had to drop out of high school in my senior year just to be with her, because she couldn't do anything for herself."

Arlene nodded. Pebbles settled down in my lap and I scratched him (her?) behind the ears.

"The same night my mom died, I was back in my room at home, sleeping. I woke up and there she was, my mom standing at the foot of my bed. The weird part was that I wasn't afraid. Mom looked peaceful, more peaceful than she'd ever looked in life. She looked like an angel. She told me she had a gift for me then she came to my bedside and put her hand on my forehead. 'Expect a change in your life,' she said and that was it. She never said exactly what the gift was, but I knew, I just knew, it was the power to heal."

"God moves in mysterious ways," said Arlene and she smiled for first time.

"Like, all I need to do is touch your back, the place where it hurts, and it'll heal."

Arlene nodded and I moved the cat off my lap, stood up and walked over to her. "You'll need to lean forward a little," I said. "I need to...uh...get back there."

She leaned forward as best she could, and I reached down between her body and the chair, placing my left hand on her lower back. I held it there for a few seconds. "Expect a change in your life," I said.

"I think it feels better already," she said, but I knew that couldn't be true. It would take time to get better. (But never underestimate the power of positive thinking.) "And about the twenty dollars?" I said.

"I don't suppose you take Medicaid," she said, and I didn't know if she was joking or not.

"No," I said. "Just cash."

She had me get her purse for her and she gave me the twenty.

I left feeling proud and relieved. I had my first paying customer! I was on my way!

I went straight to McDonald's to celebrate. I bought a Sausage, Egg & Cheese McGriddle. It tasted like success.

———

After I ate, I went to the subway station. I didn't see the bum, thank God. The subway fare still cost way too much so I hopped the turnstiles as gracefully as I could. The lady in the booth noticed and yelled after me to pay my fare. She sounded mad. (Not mad enough to come out of the booth and chase me though.)

The train was crowded, and I had to stand. As usual, everyone avoided eye contact. A few read. Some stared at nothing. Most just had their faces glued to their phones. I wondered where I was. When you travel underground, you have no idea.

I came up out the subway in Union Square. I could see the Empire State Building from where I stood. This was the New York I knew from TV and movies, huge and busy. All the buildings were tall and right across the street from each other, making concrete canyons with people skittering around the bottom.

I walked up Broadway. The sidewalks were crazy crowded, convincing me that I made the right choice by moving here. There were sick people everywhere in the world, so it made sense to go to where most people were, right? New York was the biggest city in America. I didn't feel like a fish out of water, more like a goldfish in the ocean, if that makes any sense.

My sleeping bag wasn't doing nearly enough to cushion the concrete floor. I passed a mattress store and stopped in to check prices. A new mattress was almost rent, including the tax and delivery charge. *Someday*, I told myself.

I thought of going to the top of the Empire State building, but it cost $34! That seemed ridiculous. I didn't think I'd ever pay that much for an elevator ride, even after I'd gotten rich.

And there were rich people everywhere I looked. I could tell from their clothes that they were loaded. Not that the men were wearing top hats, or the ladies were in fur coats. You could just tell. It was intimidating. I didn't know how to talk to people like that. It felt like they were from another planet. Planet Money. But I reminded myself that I had a gift and that I'd be one of them soon enough. As I walked, I started to dream—about how I'd buy new clothes every season, how I'd have somebody drive me everywhere, how I'd have a personal assistant to do all the stuff I didn't want to do, like return the clothes I'd changed my mind about, how I'd have a million followers on Instagram. When I had all that, then the aliens from the Planet Money wouldn't be able to look down on me anymore.

I daydreamed that way all the way up to Times Square. It was the bushiest place I had ever been to in my life. Tourists swarmed the sidewalks, and everywhere I looked giant video screens went off like fireworks. There were street performers, too, the knockoff superheroes and cartoon characters being the creepiest. Wandering around, I didn't feel like a tourist, and I didn't feel like a New Yorker either. I felt somewhere in between. Like, I lived there, just don't ask me for directions.

I still had some money left over from the twenty, so I stopped at another McDonald's, this one on 42nd Street. While I waited in line, I saw a guy in one of the booths, sitting with cup of coffee that had probably been fished out of the trash. He rambled on to the invisible person sitting across from him; I don't know about what. All of sudden he looks right at me, eyes bugling out of his head, and he said really loud, "You're already doing... You're always doing what's in your heart! You can't get away from your heart! LOVE NOW!" Then he clucked like a chicken. People were staring at me. I don't know why. He was the weirdo. I just looked at the back of the guy standing in front of me in line, hoping the crazy guy would find someone else to yell at. He went back to talking to his invisible friend and I relaxed a little. I wondered if I could fix the guy. Broken bones are one thing, but how do you fix someone's head?

I got a 10-piece Chicken McNuggets combo meal, proud of myself for staying within budget. I couldn't eat there, not with the crazy guy. I walked around some more until I found an outdoor area that probably looked a lot nicer in the summertime. By then, my feet hurt so, when I was done eating, I snuck onto the subway again and went back to my cave.

———

I knocked around for the rest of the week like that, dipping into my savings when I had to for food. If I bought Pop-Tarts at the bodega and drank water from the tap, I could eat three meals a day for three dollars. I washed my clothes in the sink with dish soap. There were a few random screws and nails in my cave, and I hung my wet clothes on them to dry. If I was going to have a rags to riches story, this was the raggiest.

The flyers didn't work beyond that one call from Arlene. I went back to all the places I'd hung them to see if any of the tabs had been torn off. A few had. I found out how quickly my flyer got buried under other people's postings. New York was a non-stop battle for everything.

I stayed chatty with Monica and got her life story. She moved from St. Louis to be a costume designer. She'd worked on some off-off Broadway plays. I guessed that off-off Broadway meant low-low pay because she also worked at a barbecue restaurant in Midtown. She went on about how they served Kansas City barbecue there and how it was different from St. Louis barbecue. Listening to her left me lusting for a big plate of slow-cooked meat. That became another thing to put on the Someday List, right below the mattress.

———

The weekend came around and Caroline had an invite to a screening of a friend's student film with a party afterwards. She invited Monica to go, because of the whole costume technician thing.

Caroline didn't ask me to go. She and I were never going to be BFFs. Monica said I could tag along with her. I was still the new roommate and Monica wanted me to feel part of the group which I super appreciated.

The party was at a downtown (Manhattan) restaurant owned by a big-time movie star. I could only imagine having that kind of money where you could open a restaurant just because you felt like it. There was a screening room (what I'd call a tiny theater) upstairs that anyone could rent.

The student film lasted only ten minutes long and I didn't get it. It started with a guy and a girl, and they seemed like boyfriend and girlfriend, but they didn't seem to be that into each other. And then there was another random guy who the girl hooked up with which could have been a big deal in the story, but the boyfriend never found out about it, so it just fizzled. The last scene had the girl walking down the street crying. The end.

Afterward I stood around with Caroline and Monica while they talked with their friends. I felt like the 19th wheel on a semi because I was younger than everyone else and because they'd all been to college. No one came out and said that. I could just tell, like they all wore diploma ink as perfume.

I gave myself a pep talk: I lived in New York, making my own way, just like all of them. Probably even more than some of them who, I'll bet, still got help from their parents. I bet that the girl who made the student film had her parents rent the screening room which is so lame.

They were talking about "film." They used a lot of fancy terms and dropped a lot of names that meant nothing to me. As near as I could tell, the difference between film and movies is that movies are entertaining and make money and films are boring and win awards.

Then, while Caroline went on about trying to find a commercial agent, this cute guy comes up to Monica and gives her a hug. He looked about Monica's age and *so* New York; not like any guys I knew in Montana.

I think Caroline had a thing for him because she looked at him all goofy. She must have known him already, because she asked about what he was working on. He said he was writing a screenplay. Writing a screenplay didn't impress me. There were people in every coffee shop in the city writing screen-plays. But coming from this guy, it didn't sound ridiculous.

I introduced myself because no one else was going to. His name was Seth and that's how we met.

Caroline quickly steered the conversation away from me toward the super-eight film she was working on. She called it "a retelling of Gulliver's Travels from a feminist perspective." Seth said it sounded "cool," but I think he was just saying that, because what could possibly be more boring?

Seth asked me if I was into film, and I said no. Then I took the opportunity to tell him about my powers. I could see Caroline making a face as I said it. What was her problem?

"She cured my boyfriend's migraines," said Monica.

Thank you, Monica! I thought.

Seth made a face like maybe he was impressed.

"If you ever hurt yourself writing screenplays," I said. "I'm your girl."

And then—I'm not making this up—Caroline stepped *right* in front of me and started talking to Seth, like I wasn't even there. Suddenly, I was standing outside the group, feeling like a total loser.

I went to get another Coke (that I couldn't afford) from the bar.

Seth found me there a few minutes later. He leaned in close, like he didn't want anyone to hear. "Can you really cure anything?"

"Sure," I said, trying to sound cool. Inside, I was thrilled to have him talking to me.

"Okay, because I had a skateboarding accident back in high school. My deck hit me in the head and now I can't see out of this eye." He pointed to his right eye and then I noticed that his pupils were different sizes which I guessed was part of the problem.

"I can fix that," I said. "We can do it right here,"

"Right here? Really?"

"Yeah," I said. "It doesn't look weird or anything."

He shrugged and smiled. "Oh, okay."

I held his head with both hands, just touching his temples. I liked touching him. It was the opposite of touching the homeless guy. I wanted to do it for, like, an hour. He closed his eyes, and I said, "Expect a change in your life."

And then I kissed him. Don't know why I did it. It just happened. His eyes popped open for a second. Then he kissed me back.

Maybe I should tell you now that guys like me. I'm an inch shorter than average but I have nice boobs.

We didn't kiss all that long, maybe three seconds.

"Uh, is that usually part of it?" he asked, pulling away.

"No!" I said, smiling. "And usually, I charge money."

"Then I feel like I should take you out to dinner some time."

No guy had ever taken me out to dinner before. Not ever. I was thrilled. "Yeah!" I said and I gave him my number.

He called a couple days later and I ignored it. That may sound strange considering how excited I was when we met but, when I thought about it, I realized that a boyfriend would only be a distraction. Relationships are complicated, and I had to stay 100% focused on why I came to New York. Once I'd hit the big time there would be time for that.

your best life 3:

Clients are People Too. (And That's Why They Can Be So Annoying.)

I saw a store that sells vegan ice cream. That sounds like the crappiest ice cream ever. I mean, why bother? Like, just put sugar on a rice cake and call that dessert. But the shop sold it because there are customers who can't stand the thought that a cow got milked to make their Salted Caramel Swirl.

See, the customer is always right. As soon as you start charging money, you need to make customers happy, and keep them that way. You need to sell vegan ice cream. And nut-free ice cream. And gluten-free ice cream. And freaking fro-yo.

It's not like customers always mean to be annoying. It's just that people are people. They've got their issues, their likes, dislikes, pet peeves, and allergies. Some people really DO need dressing on the side.

Your answer to a customer should always be, YES. Figure out how to make it work later. You'll be surprised at what you can do when pushed.

three

. . .

I WAS COMING out of the bodega with a Pop-Tart lunch when I saw Arlene walking towards me. "Arlene!" I called; it took her a few seconds to recognize me. (Actually, it took me a few seconds to recognize her, standing upright.)

"Destiny!" she said, all smiles. She came in for a hug before I could stop her. (I'm not the huggy type.) Leaning into her, I noticed she didn't smell like pee anymore.

"You look good," I said when she finally let go of me.

"Never felt better!" she said. "Girl, you have the power of God in you!"

That sounded weird to me. I wasn't the religious type either. I smiled, anyway. "If you know of anyone else with back problems, or any sort problems, let me know."

She looked at me all intense like. "Can you come to church with me this Sunday?"

Hell no, I thought. I didn't know exactly why I had that reaction. Maybe because church seemed like the kind of place where you had to dress a certain way, say "Amen" on cue, and sing songs where, if you didn't know them already, you'd have to stand there and move your mouth, just trying to fake it. No, church sounded like too much pressure. But I could see how important it was to Arlene and she was a satisfied customer who I had to keep satisfied. I'd needed her to give me a five-star review on Yelp someday.

"Okay," I said, not sure what I was getting myself into.

———

Josh came back to bite me in the butt three weeks after I cured his migraines. I ran into him in the hallway of the building. "What the hell?" he said. (And he spelled hell with an f.)

I felt a wave of fear. Wasn't he cured? Did I lose my power? "Did your migraines come back," I asked.

"No, but look at this," he said and he took off his jacket. He held out his arms which were half-covered in tattoos. I say half-covered like they were half faded away.

It took me a second to figure it out. A tattoo is a wound, even if it's pretty. When I cured his migraine, all that ink must have gone on the fixer-upper to-do list. "Oh," was all I could say.

"Did you do this?" he asked.

I wanted to deny everything but it happened too fast for me to think of a story. "I think so," I said.

"You think so?" he said, sarcastically.

I told him why I thought it happened, about them being wounds and all. "Your migraines are gone, right?" I said. "And you could just get more tattoos."

"Tattoos aren't like that," he said. He looked at his arms again. "Each one of these has a meaning for me. Specific times and places."

I didn't totally get what he meant and I didn't want to argue. "Sorry," I said. "I didn't mean for that to happen." At that point, I ran out of words. I just stood there, looking like an idiot.

"Whatever," he said as he put his jacket back on and walked off.

Mostly I felt embarrassed. At least I hadn't charged him any money. And I'd done right by Arlene so there was that. I decided to take it as a learning experience. Every entrepreneur has them. Jeff Bezos probably sent some people the wrong books when he was starting out.

I was afraid that things would be weird between me and Monica, but it was cool. Some of those tattoos had something to do with Josh's college girlfriend and she was glad to see them gone. Plus he had one of Spiderman that she thought was ridiculous.

I could add tattoo removal to my list of services.

———

On Sunday I went to the Freedom Fellowship Church on Myrtle Avenue. There's a mega church in Billings that looks like a convention center. This was a brick storefront with bars on the windows. I'm not knocking it, just saying that it wasn't like anything I'd seen before. Can't say I felt thrilled to be there, though. I still didn't know what they expected of me. What if they asked me if I was a Christian? What if they tried to MAKE me a Christian? I supposed I could just run out screaming. But that wasn't going to happen, I told myself. Everything would be fine. I opened the door and walked in.

It was nicer inside than outside. They had real pews and a stage, with a drum set on the stage along with an electric piano. The back wall had a mural of a blue sky with white clouds and flying birds painted on it.

I was the only teenager in the place. A lot of old people milled around and they were dressed up fancy. Arlene never mentioned that. Suddenly I felt out of place in my t-shirt and jeans.

Arlene spotted me in a second. She grabbed the pastor and brought him to meet me. He had gray hair and was really tall, like he could have been in the NBA when he was younger. He didn't wear any special church clothes, just a suit.

"This is the girl I was telling you about," Arlene said to him. "She has a gift from God."

My gut clenched a little, just hearing that. I smiled and the pastor shook my hand and welcomed me. I got away from him as soon as possible, before he could ask any questions about God, religion or anything. I felt like I was telling a lie, even though it wasn't me who said it.

I sat down with Arlene and a bunch of her friends, because it would have been weird to sit by myself. Arlene had already told them about me, and I felt like me being there was kind of a big deal to them, like I was a celebrity. That felt good and my confidence came back. I could do this.

The pastor gave his sermon, talking about Jesus healing the sick. He said God could still heal the sick and cure the disabled. You just needed to have faith.

I wondered where this was going. I mean, I suspected, but I wasn't sure. I hoped people didn't expect miracles, like instant cures. And Jesus raised the dead. I couldn't do that. I hoped Arlene hadn't made any promises I couldn't keep. I didn't see any dead bodies in the room so that was off the table.

The pastor kept talking, working the crowd up into a lather. People shouted "Amen!" and "Hallelujah!" These people were *into* being Christian.

Then the pastor said, "God has sent us Destiny!" I sat straight up when I heard my name. This was it, my big moment. There was a stage so stage fright. My heart was hammering in my chest.

When he asked me to come up to the front, I heard more hallelujahs from the crowd. The band, the guys up there with drums and the piano started playing and it felt like a game show or something. *Destiny Wallace, come on down!*

I got up and walked down the aisle still not sure how this

was going to happen. I stood next to the pastor and waved. I don't know why I did that. It must have looked dorky. He asked the congregation if there was anyone who needed healing. A few hands shot up in the air.

The pastor pointed to a fat lady wearing a bright green outfit. She had a miserable look on her face. "Sister Hazel!" he said and she stood up. It took a couple of minutes to get to the stage. She moved like every step hurt. "What troubles you, sister?" he asked her.

Hazel complained about her shingles. I didn't know the first thing about shingles so I didn't know where to put my hands. Of course, I didn't want to admit I didn't know so I gave her the once over, hoping I could see the problem. No luck. I leaned into sister Hazel. "Shingles? What is that?" I whispered.

"A rash," she whispered back. "It hurts real bad." I thought maybe she was going to cry.

"No problem," I said and touched her forearm with both hands, like a super handshake. I said my catch phrase, "Expect a change in your life," and everyone applauded.

Next, an old lady complaining about "terrible arthritis."

Now is a good time to explain what I can and can't do. Yes, I can heal the sick, grow back limbs, shrink tumors, all that. But I can't turn back time. If you're old and things aren't working the way they did when you were young, well that's just how life is.

I touched her and did my bit, because if she had "terrible" arthritis, maybe I could make it regular arthritis. I worried that she wouldn't get better and she'd tell everyone that I was a fake.

As I helped brother Walter, a guy missing an eye, it occurred to me that no one was giving me any money. I guess I *was* like Jesus, because he worked for free, too. But how much of an asshole would I have looked like if I started demanding cash? I'd just have to chalk the day up to self-promotion.

After all the healing, they treated me to a potluck lunch. After weeks of junk food, it felt good to eat a plate of home-made fried chicken, but I didn't want to work for food. I made a mental note: no more churches.

————

I got back to the apartment to find the electric bill had arrived, like a turd in a punch bowl. Gavin told me they split it five ways and that we all owed $25. I told him that didn't seem fair since I hardly used any electricity. Other people in the apartment had computers and TVs, and I didn't even own a lamp. He said that, even if I didn't have a lamp, I still used electricity, like for the lights in the kitchen and the bathroom. Also the refrigerator.

I didn't have anything in the refrigerator either.

"You didn't tell me that when I moved in," I said.

"That's how everyone does it in the city," he said. "It's the only way. Otherwise, we'd all be guessing how much electricity we used and that would be impossible."

Caroline stood there, looking at me like I was being irresponsible, or a deadbeat. That pissed me off. I was being responsible, not throwing my money around willy-nilly. I lived within a budget so far below poverty level that there were people on welfare doing better than me.

I paid the $25, but I wasn't happy about it. It might have made the difference between me being able to pay the next month's rent or not.

I started to dream about having my own place someday, just me, with my own electricity.

your best life 4:

Putting Bubblegum in People Brains.

I don't like it when people say, "shameless self-promotion." Bravery and confidence are nothing to be ashamed of. Get out there and show the world who you are and what you have to offer. Don't be afraid to "fake it until you make it." Greatness comes when you set your mind to it, so set everyone else's mind to it, too. When the people around you expect your best, you'll have no choice but to deliver. That's how we put a man on the moon.

But, even if you're the bomb, you still need to get people to remember you. You need something uniquely you that'll stick in their brains like bubblegum. It could be a catchphrase, or how you dress, even a unique hairstyle. Anything that'll get you noticed. But be careful. If you look stupid, that's what everyone will remember you for, too. The trick is to find that thing that you can pull off that would look ridiculous on anyone else.

four

. . .

WHEN THE FIRST of the month rolled around, I didn't have enough to make rent. Even if I spent all my savings, I'd come up short. I was mad at myself for spending the money I got from Arlene on McDonald's, and for not getting any money from the church. I wanted to be mad at New York for the rent being too damn high, but I had to take responsibility. I chose to live there, and it was up to me to get out there and try harder.

I got a lucky break when my phone rang at 5:30AM on Saturday, waking me up from another bad night's sleep. A guy named Zeus MG needed my services. I assumed that was his street name. He'd heard about what I did in church, and he needed someone with my skills, ASAP.

I wasn't born yesterday. I sensed something sketchy about the whole deal. I asked what he needed, and he said one of his "boys" had been hurt. Definitely sketchy.

Growing up where I did, I'd seen some criminal elements. When I was eleven, the cops busted a neighbor for running a meth lab out of her trailer, just like on TV. Having Naomi out of there was a huge relief to my mom, because bikers came and went at all hours, making a lot of noise with their motorcycles. I also knew about the guys who sold speed to truckers at the Diesel 'n' Diner truck stop where my mom used to work. A girl knows to avoid those types. She also knows they have cash. Lots of it.

I told Zeuss MG to meet me at Maggie's Café. It was a hipster hangout, nearby and open twenty-four hours. He said okay and told me to meet him out front.

I left the apartment and walked to Maggie's in the dark. The sun wouldn't be up for over an hour at that time of year. It was below freezing so I waited in this little tent thing the café had in front of the entrance. A lot of places had them to keep the cold air from blasting in the place every time someone came or went.

A black Escalade pulled up to the curb. Zeuss MG, for sure. I felt nervous. It was a different kind of nervous than at Arlene's church. Less "I hope they don't embarrass me," and more "I hope they don't kill me."

I put on a brave face and stepped into the freezing cold. Zeuss MG jumped out of the driver's side in a down coat, hiking boots and baseball cap. Everything looked so new you'd think he bought it on the way over. "You Destiny?" he asked.

"Yeah," I said, trying to sound like this was the one-hundredth time I'd done this.

He made a quick scan of the deserted street and waved me over to the SUV. He opened the door to the back seat, and the interior light came on. A guy stretched out on the upholstery, moaning, cursing and bleeding from around his stomach. This dude needed to go to the hospital, but I figured that he didn't want to have to explain how he got this way in the first place.

"You can fix this, right?" asked Zeuss. He didn't seem like the kind of guy who heard the word "no," that often. I reached down deep and summoned up all the confidence I had. "I can save him." Then, thinking of all the rent I owed, I said, "Eight hundred."

Zeuss MG thought about it a second and his boy made some more painful noises. "Alright," he said. "Do your magic."

Magic? Is that what he thought it was?

When I opened his jacket, it looked worse than I thought. If there was a bullet hole, I didn't see it, just a lot of blood. And I mean A LOT of blood. I put my hand in the middle of the wet spot and the guy flinched.

"It's okay," I said. "You're going to live." I didn't use my usual catch phrase because it didn't seem right for the occasion. I left my hand there for a good long time, praying that the guy wouldn't bleed out before the healing started.

When I finished, I wanted to run. Instead, I turned to Zeuss MG. "It'll take a few days for him to heal, but he'll be okay. No scar or anything. Just get him home and...uh, keep him comfortable."

Zeuss MG looked at his buddy. He'd gone quiet and was still breathing. Zeuss MG nodded, reached into his pocket and pulled out a wad about as thick around as a beer can. He peeled off eight Franklins and handed them to me.

After he drove off, I went into the café and sat in a booth.

Holy crap, I thought, *That was intense.* I looked at my hands; they were shaking, and I had blood all over my glove

Yuck.

After the sun came up, I took the subway into Manhattan on a mission to buy new gloves. I stared at the train car ceiling, hoping no one would notice my blood-covered gloves. That had to look suspicious. Like, if a cop noticed, would he start asking questions?

While I sat there, it occurred to me that, if I had to wear

gloves, I needed to own it, make them part of my image. I needed something less basic, something with more pizzazz. I found what I needed in a hole-in-the-wall shop on St. Mark's Place in the East Village. They were fingerless and knitted with hot pink yarn with little silver strands. They weren't too expensive either, just in case I got more blood on them.

When the first came around, I felt a weird pride being able to pay such a ridiculous amount. *Hey, world! Check me out! I just spent hundreds of dollars for the privilege of living in a plywood box!*

My morning spent in church started to pay off. Word spread about what I could do and my phone began to ring regularly I was clear about the money, though. And I raised my rates. I started meeting people at the JavaStrip, because it was close by.

Also, I lost five pounds. That was both good and bad. Good because I lost five pounds. Bad because I'd been eating like crap. I started to feel weird about buying my Pop-Tarts at the same store, like it seemed so obvious they were (almost) all I ate. For a few days I walked to another bodega a couple blocks away until I decided that it was too far, and someday it would probably make a good story for the counter guys, like they could say that they remembered me from before I became famous and how I used to come in a couple times a day and buy Pop-Tarts.

I was at the apartment making a dinner of ramen noodles (cheaper than Pop-Tarts) when the buzzer to the outside door buzzed. When I went to see who, it was Seth! I buzzed him in. I got all nervous as I waited for him to get to our front door.

What was he doing here? Was he tracking me down? Was he mad at me for blowing him off? When he knocked, I could either jump out the window or answer the door. I answered the door.

"Hey." He said it like he was surprised to see me.

"Hey," I said, not sure why he was surprised. I mean, I lived there.

"Is Caroline here?" he asked and, next thing you know, Caroline appeared behind me, all dressed up.

"Right here," she said. And I notice that Seth is all dressed up, too. I couldn't believe it! Seth and Caroline had a date!

They started talking, and I just stood there, like an idiot. Then the tea kettle whistled, because I forgot about the water for the ramen. I tried to ignore them as they talked about what they were going to do that night, but the kitchen is right there next to the front door so what could I do? I made the ramen and tried not to look at them. I felt like a loser.

After they left, I sat down to eat and think. I reminded myself that I didn't want or need to be dating right now. Then I imagined the boyfriend I'd have once I became rich and famous. He'd be rich and famous, too. I tried to decide if he should be an actor or a musician. If he were a musician, I could go on tour with him, staying at fancy hotels all over the world. And if he was an actor, maybe I could get a part in one of his movies. I decided I should try dating a musician and an actor and see which I liked better. Or even better, find an actor slash musician.

I was still awake when Caroline came home. I didn't come out of my cave and ask her about how it went because *I totally didn't care!*

your best life 5:

The Sixteenth Chapel.

There was this artist named Leonardo DaVinci and he lived a long time ago in Italy. He painted the Mona Lisa. You've probably seen it. But the thing he's best known for is the Sixteenth Chapel in Rome. He painted the entire ceiling with stories from the Bible, all the way from the beginning to the end. For sure, you've seen the part where Adam (looking way buffed) is sitting on a rock and is about to touch God's finger. (Hey, Adam! Pull my finger!)

Whatever you're going for, you'll get an opportunity to do the one thing that shows everybody how amazing you are. It doesn't have to be a painting. If you're a musician, it can be a song you wrote. Or, if you're an athlete, it can be a perfect game or an impossible goal. Whatever shows that you are the master.

I guarantee you'll get the opportunity, but it's up to you to step up to the plate and hit it out of the park. That means always doing your best and always trying to make your best better. Leonardo painted fifteen other chapels before he did the sixteenth. That's a lot of practice! So don't give up.

five

. . .

I MET Laura early in the evening on the first day of spring. She'd heard about me through a friend of a friend. She picked the place, a coffee house in another part of Brooklyn with outdoor seating. I was sitting at a table on the sidewalk, breathing in the (semi) fresh air, when she rolled up in her wheelchair. I think my jaw dropped when I saw her. She looked like she'd been cut into pieces, then stitched back together with whatever parts they could recover. I found out later that, when she was a teenager, she was riding in a car that got boxed in by four 18-wheelers. Something about the way the air was blowing caused the car to lose control, flip over and get run over by one of the trucks. When the EMTs got to the car, it was about half the size it started out as. She was lucky to be alive. The driver, her BFF from high school, didn't make it. I felt bad for Laura, and I knew I could fix her. She could be my special project.

Of course I didn't ask her about the accident right away, I got that story later. I bought her coffee because—business tip here—that's what you do for clients. I asked her what she did, and she said she worked as a corporate lawyer. Wow. She'd gone to college and law school like that. Shows what you can do when you put your mind to it.

That also meant she had money. I tried to total up how much I should charge her for the full treatment. I was a C student in high school and a D student in math. Adding in my head was impossible. I told her I could give her a "makeover," for $1,000 cash. She seemed stunned for a second.

"I didn't bring a thousand dollars with me," she said.

"Course not," I said, though I hadn't really thought about how ridiculous it was to expect someone to have that much money on them. "Do you want to go get it?" I asked.

"The ATM won't let me take out that much and all the banks are closed," she said. "Do you take credit cards?"

"No," I said. "I'm still working on that."

"Oh," she said, like I was a fake who planned to take the money and run.

"How about you write a contract then?" I said, because she was a lawyer. "Like you give me as much as the ATM will let you and we'll have an agreement for you to pay the rest.

"I can't just write a contract on a napkin," she said and suddenly I felt like a total amateur.

"I'm not a fake," I said.

"If I thought you were a fake, I wouldn't be here," she said which made total sense. "How about $500 cash, right now? That's how much an ATM will give you at one time."

Five hundred was only half of what I wanted. "How about I trust you to give me the rest later, when the banks open?"

"Deal," she said, and we went to a cash machine. I did my bit right there in the bank. And I know it sounds shitty, but I felt a little grossed out touching her. Then the memory of my church visit came back to me, the pastor's story about Jesus touching lepers. It was part of the job. I held her hand and said my catch phrase. Then she got out the five hundred bucks.

———

Laura, good to her word, got me the rest of the money the next day. Wow! It was more money than I'd ever had in my life! My first order of business was to buy a mattress. It arrived within a week and, as soon as the delivery guys left, I took a long nap. I forgot to order sheets and a pillow to go with it, but I didn't care. I slept comfortably for the first time in weeks.

I woke up around 5 PM and left for an appointment at a Starbucks in Manhattan. I even paid my subway fare both ways because I could afford it now. I met a group of women who all had C-section scars. A C-section is where instead of the baby coming out where nature intended, the doctor cuts it out of you. Holy cow, why would anyone think that was the easiest exit? About one in three moms do it that way, so go figure. I'd gotten better at telling the story about my mom, shortening it while making it more dramatic. And I'd gotten used to explaining the side effects. One woman backed out when I told her about how she'd lose her tattoos. I'd looked online to see where C-section scars usually were and decided to touch the woman above the belly button. That was close enough. Look it up yourself if you don't know what I'm talking about.

See, after what happened with Josh and his tattoos, I figured I didn't have to touch where the problem was. I just did it to *look* like I was doing what I was supposed to do. It's what you call showmanship.

One woman wanted to pay by credit card. I told her it had to be cash: $60. After I left, I looked into getting a gadget I could put on my phone to take credit cards. That sort of stuff always bored and confused me, but I had to get my act together. I was losing too much money.

———

I got a call from a guy who wanted me to make him taller. I asked him if he still had his legs and he said, "Of course." I had to explain to him that if he was short, even if he was a midget, I couldn't change anything. I can just make people how they were born to be.

I also had to explain to some people that I'm not a plastic surgeon. I can't make your nose smaller or point it toward the sky. I can't make boobs bigger. I can't cure male pattern baldness. That's why there's Rogaine. And I can't cure nearsightedness. That's why there's Lasik.

Sometimes people asked about diseases that I didn't know anything about, and I had to tell them I'd get back to them. Then I'd do a Google search. There are an unbelievable number of sicknesses that doctors don't know the cause of and then I'd be stuck. Do I try to cure them anyway, and maybe look like a faker? Or do I say no, when maybe I could help? It was too much to think about and sometimes I didn't get back to people.

———

I tried to ignore Seth whenever he came over to the apartment to pick up Caroline. I didn't even ask him about his eye. He never said anything about what happened between us or why I didn't respond to his phone call.

My relationship with Caroline got even worse. I couldn't stand to be in the same room with her, which wasn't easy in that apartment. I got to know her schedule and tried to be out when she was in.

I couldn't help but notice the time when she went out with Seth on Friday night and didn't come until Saturday morning wearing the same clothes. I lost some respect for Seth right then and there. I mean, getting with *her*? What did he see in her anyway? She wasn't that pretty, and she was way too full of herself. I hate-watched one of the movies she made on

YouTube. *So lame.* It started with a black screen and a quote from someone named "Dante Alighieri" that did nothing to explain anything that happened after that. I am not kidding, one part of it was just weeds next to a highway. If Seth thought she was a good movie *film*maker, then maybe he was just as lame. I couldn't believe I ever kissed that guy.

————

Word kept spreading and soon I had an appointment every day. It was an interesting way to see the real city. Even though everyone is out on the street in New York, that's just them running from what they did to what they'll be doing next. The real action is inside. You just don't know what's going on behind a closed door in New York. I got to see some shit.

I got a call from a woman named Jeanine who said she needed my help. I asked what about. She said it was personal and could I come to her office? I said sure.

I found my way up to the thirty-second floor of a skyscraper in midtown. Behind the reception desk, a sign said "Barker & Swedlow" in mismatched letters that looked like someone took them from a bunch of old advertising signs. I told the receptionist I had an appointment with Jeanine. I only waited a few minutes before she came out to meet me. Jeanine could have been in her 30s, pretty and thin. I still hadn't gotten over how skinny New Yorkers were. Back in Montana, people were WAY fatter. You could probably fit three New York women into one from Montana.

Jeanine walked me to her huge corner office with an amazing view of Central Park. The trees were still bare. It probably looked amazing in the fall. She had a shelf full of trophies and framed ads on the wall. I pointed to a poster that I'd seen in the subway right when I arrived in New York. "Did you make that?"

"Yes," she said, and she sat on the edge of her desk.

"Wow," I said. It seemed like a weird job to me, making advertising. I hadn't really thought about the people who think up that stuff.

"So..." I began.

"I want to have a baby and I can't conceive," she said.

Something I liked about New Yorkers was that they got down to business straight away.

"I can help you out," I said. "I mean I can make it so you can conceive. I can't make you pregnant."

"Understood," she said, smiling a bit, like I'd made a joke. "Is there anything you need to know about my medical history?"

"No," I said. "I don't need to know anything, except for what the problem is."

Like everybody else, she asked me where I got my abilities from. I told her my story. It flashed through my mind that maybe I should change the story to something simpler, like I'm a mutant, like the X-Men. But no, nobody would ever believe that.

"Do you have a standard fee for this procedure?" she asked.

I didn't. I had a price list in my head, but the list was getting longer, and I still hadn't figured out how much I could get away with charging for different things. Now I had to think about how much a woman would pay to have a baby with a regular doctor. I'd heard of couples paying thousands of dollars to get pregnant. (You couldn't pay me enough to have one, by the way.) She looked like she made good money so maybe I could ask for a lot.

"Five hundred. In cash," I said, because now I knew how much an ATM would hand out.

"You don't take checks or credit cards?" she asked.

"Not yet," I said. "I'm still starting out."

"How about four hundred, then?" she said. "Cash discount."

I'd had enough of the haggling. "Nope," I said. "Five hundred."

She looked at me for a few seconds, waiting for me to break. I didn't. "Okay," she said. "Five hundred."

As I walked toward her, she closed her eyes like it was going to be painful or something. "Try to relax," I said, and I put my hand on her tummy. I think I felt her breakfast moving around in there. "Expect a change in your life," I said then I took my hand away.

"That's it?" she said.

"That's it," I said. "Start picking out names."

I had to wait in the reception area while her assistant went and got the money. I felt proud of myself for not backing down.

———

Another weird story is about the cat lady. I went to see her in Queens, and it was my first time to that borough. Boroughs are what New Yorkers call sections of the city. (Fun fact: There are five of them.) She lived in an area called Astoria. Her building was an old walk-up. That's a building without an elevator. Tammy looked to be in her 60s, frumpy and friendly.

Damn, did her apartment stink! She probably couldn't smell it anymore, like when you live on a ranch long enough and you just stop noticing the stink. That was a Montana thing, for sure.

Tammy felt fine. It was one of her five cats that had cancer. I liked pets, but five seemed to be too many. If you have to own more than three of any kind of pet, get a fish tank.

I felt 99% sure I could cure a cat. His name was Oreo, I guessed because of his black and white fur. Oreo looked in bad shape lying in his little kitty bed on the couch, down to skin and bones. It made me sad to look at him. I didn't feel that bad for most of the humans. I don't know why, but it's different with animals.

I put my hand on his side and felt him struggling to breathe. Poor little guy. I said my catch phrase. Then I rubbed him a little bit under his chin.

I only charged $40 because Tammy didn't look like she had the cash to spare. I would have done it for $20 but it was a long walk to, and from, the nearest subway station.

And I heard from one of Zeuss MG's buddies. He was upfront about what he wanted: to have some "identifying" scars removed. I told him I could do that and warned him that all his tattoos would disappear too. (I just assumed he had tattoos.) He said he had some "identifying" tattoos as well. Maybe this guy was trying to get away with murder, maybe he was trying to make a clean start of things. I didn't know, I just met him in a very public place and charged him extra for the tattoos.

your best life 6:

Becoming the Next Big Thing.

The reason the media exists is to find the next big thing and make it the NEXT BIG THING. See how that works? That's how you can have people who are famous for being famous. It's a self-fulfilling prophecy.

You only need a few hipsters to get the ball rolling. Start small, like with local bloggers and work your way up the chain. At every level, there's a writer/journalist/reporter/influencer looking for something new to blow up. The beast needs to be fed with another 30 under 30, or people to watch list.

You'll be asked stupid questions. You'll be misquoted and misrepresented. That's just gonna happen. Don't forget that while you're using them, they're using you. You're the honey that draws the flies, and if they think a little orange blossom will help, they'll add it.

In *Your Best Life 17*, I'll talk about fans and haters. Just know that writers/journalists/reporters/influencers can be either of those too. The fans will write the puff pieces, and the haters will post the embarrassing wardrobe malfunction photos. But so what? There's no such thing as bad publicity, goes the old saying. But—whatever you do—do *not* make a sex tape, because I guarantee people will see it.

52

six

· · ·

IT TOOK me a while to figure out that Caroline and Seth broke up. When she went on a date with another guy, I knew something had gone sideways. Then it occurred to me that Seth hadn't been around in a while. (This new guy seemed more Caroline's type: a total douche bag.)

I thought about whether I should call Seth or not and decided that I should, because he did owe me a dinner for curing his blindness, and a deal's a deal. I called and left a message reminding him about the dinner he owed me. He called me back and we made a plan.

———

Business started to take up all my days. I felt super proud of myself when I realized that. I downloaded "New York, New York" by Frank Sinatra to my phone and listened to it every morning. I was feeling positive. Up. Up! UP!

———

I arranged to meet a woman at the JavaStrip and she brought a baby with her. She explained that she was the grandmother, and that the baby's mother had been doing drugs all the time she was pregnant and that the baby had been born with all kinds of problems. The grandmother –who didn't even look 40 to me- had the baby now and was raising it. It took everything she had. I could see it in her face. She looked spent.

Just looking at the two of them got me mad at the baby's mom. Who does that to their baby? What is wrong with some people? But it wasn't the baby's fault, and I could see that the grandmother was trying her best, so I set the baby right for free. More than free, I bought the grandmother a cup of coffee.

I know I did the right thing, and it still bummed me out. I didn't want to feel sad anymore, so I went home and counted my cash. I *almost* had enough to move out of the cave.

I got a message from a woman named Candace who wrote a blog called *If It Ain't Brooklyn...* She'd heard about me through word of mouth and wanted to write a post about me. I said, sure.

We met way out in Sunset Park, which is part of Brooklyn. They called that area Industry City, and it was a bunch of old industrial buildings where the ground floor had been turned into a food hall and the upstairs made into offices for people working digitally and sustainably. The cafe she picked out had an Asian street food theme. Lots of meat on sticks.

Candace looked older than I thought she'd be, in her 30s. She had an urban hippy vibe, if that makes sense. I liked her from the get-go. Some people are like that, they radiate good feelings.

I gave her the whole story and she asked a lot of questions about my childhood: Did I have any premonitions? Visions?

Any contact with the spirit world? I said no to all that, except for seeing my mom.

It was weird to see how people saw my powers. Arlene thought I was one of God's little helpers. Zeuss MG thought I was magic. Candace thought I was in tune with some deeper force running through the universe. She said something about "the goddess," but didn't say which one.

Then she asked if she could go with me on an appointment, and if she could talk to someone I'd healed. I was fine with both. I invited her along to a meeting with a bunch of boxers (the athlete kind, not the dog breed) and I gave her Seth's number, too.

As the day of my dinner with Seth got closer, I started to think that maybe I was wrong about him. Dating Caroline was a mistake, and we all make mistakes, right? I'd have to give him a second chance.

I still didn't have any fancy clothes, so I wore the nicest pair of jeans and t-shirt I owned, washed with real laundry detergent at a Laundromat. (Moving up in the world!)

Seth took me to La Piccola Capra, an Italian restaurant in the West Village in Manhattan. It was a rainy night, and the inside was warm and cozy. We sat at a table for two with other couples on either side of us. The tables were so close together, if I wanted to, I could have reached over and taken a meatball off the plate of the guy next to me.

"Thanks for getting me my eye back," he said when we sat down.

"Hey, it's what I do," I said, trying not to sound too proud of myself, even though I was.

"The weird thing is that I'd forgotten what it was like to see in 3-D," he said. "When it came back, I was, like, woah! And you won't believe what it's done for my Frisbee game."

I didn't know if he was kidding about the Frisbee part. He seemed so smart. And so cute.

The waiter came over and said his name was Avery. He gave Seth a wine list. I hadn't told Seth my age, but I was obviously too young to drink, at least in a restaurant. He put the list down without looking at it. That was cool of him.

He asked me about where I got my powers, and I told the story again. I didn't mind so much telling him. I added a few details that I usually left out.

"Was your mom a spiritual person?" he asked.

"She had amazing intuition about people and situations," I said. "And she could sometimes see the future."

"Can you do that too?" he asked.

"No, I just heal people," I said.

"'Just,'" he said, laughing.

That made me feel self-conscious. I didn't want to say anything stupid. I had to keep him talking about himself. Guys like that, anyway. "What about your mom?" I asked.

"She lives in Brooklyn, and so does my dad, but they split up when I was eight."

"My dad ran out when I was three," I said.

"That sucks," he said.

"It's okay," I said. "My mom said he was a Class-A asshole, anyway."

"I guess he would have to be," he said

"Is your dad an asshole?" I asked, then regretted it.

"I thought so for a long time," said Seth, not sounding insulted. "He was a college professor, and he had an affair with one of his students. Total cliche, right? My mom was understandably pissed, and I heard the whole story from her side, so I hated him for years."

"And you stopped?" I asked. "Hating him, I mean?"

"Yeah. I don't think what he did was right, but now I don't see people as black or white. Everybody's gray. As a filmmaker, it's important for me to understand that. My favorite movies have complex characters. If you have a character that is reprehensible and sympathetic, that's an accomplishment."

"Like?" I asked, hoping his answer would tell me what reprehensible meant.

"Humbert Humbert is a classic example," he said. "From 'Lolita'."

That didn't help one bit. I hadn't heard of either of them. "Did you go to school for making movies?"

"Yeah," he said. I went to NYU Film School." He said it like it was a big deal. I guessed he meant New York University.

"How could you do that with, y'know—?" I asked. I meant having only one eye.

"Film is a two-dimensional medium," he said, like I would understand how that answered my question. I pretended that it did.

"Okay, what do you do now?" I asked.

"My day job is at a stock footage house. But my main focus is my script. And once that's done, I'll try to get the money to produce it."

I didn't know what stock footage was, but I knew what a script was. "What's your movie about?"

He got excited as he talked about it. "It's about a gang of criminals who steal a valuable painting. When they go to sell it, they find out it's a fake. But what becomes apparent is that there was a double-cross. One of the gang members switched the real painting with a fake so that they could sell the original and keep all the money."

"That sounds cool," I said. "Won't you have to move to Hollywood?" (I know it sounds crazy, but it flashed through my mind that I could move to L.A. with him and be the Healer to the Stars.)

"I could end up there," he said. "But I've got my network here. Anyway, a lot of famous directors made their names in New York."

I didn't know a single one because I didn't know anything about movie directors.

Then he asked the question I'd been dreading: "Where are you from?"

"Out west," I said, because that's what I told Gavin, and it seemed to work.

"Like, where? California?" he asked.

"No, not there," I said. He kept looking at me, expecting me to say something else, so I figured I might as well tell him. "I'm from Montana."

"Cool," he said. "'They filmed 'Heaven's Gate' there."

"That's a movie?" I asked.

He laughed. "You probably don't know it. It was a flop. An epic flop."

"No, I don't know it," I said.

"What part of Montana?" he asked.

"Billings," I said. That seemed close enough. "I know, it's not as cool as New York."

"New York is overrated," he said. "Okay, yeah, it's cool. That's why you're here, right? But it's not *that* cool. I mean there are some parts of the city that are the opposite of cool."

"I guess," I said.

"And Montana has real cowboys," he said.

The conversation was hard. I didn't want to talk about myself too much and when we talked about him, I could only understand half of what he said about. It felt like he was playing tennis, and I was playing ping pong.

But the food tasted awesome. I'd been to the Olive Garden in Boise, Idaho, when we went to visit my grandma. This was WAY better. I ate everything on my plate.

———

Afterward, he walked with me all the way back to my apartment. I felt nervous, not sure what was happening. Was this a date or was he just paying me back for his eye? And, if it *was* a date, how was it going? Did he think I was stupid or boring?

When we got to the front of my building we stopped and he said, "Thank you again, for everything,"

"No problem," I said. "And if you have anything else..."

"Yeah, sure," he said.

Then we stood there looking at each other for a few seconds.

"Okay," he said. "Goodnight."

I said, "Good night," too and he turned to walk back to the subway.

I have to say that I felt disappointed and confused. Our night was over, and I still didn't know our deal. I mean, he DID walk me home, BUT he didn't even try to kiss me. Was he waiting for me to kiss him? I wasn't shy about it the first time we met. Maybe he was waiting for me to do it again. I had blown off his dinner invitation for the longest time. Maybe he was waiting for me to make a move. The ball WAS in my court. I wondered if he went home just as mixed up as I was. Was this dating in the big city? I always knew where I stood with Montana high school boys. (They were always horny.) I had a lot to learn.

When I got inside, Caroline sat in the kitchen in her PJs, drinking a Diet Coke. I so wanted to say I had a hot date with Seth just so I could have one over on her. *Arg!* I hated her even more and told myself I'd probably be moving out soon.

Candace's post came out not long after the interview and her ride-along to one of my appointments. Here it is:

NOT TAKING IT ON FAITH.

Fred Stesney

By Candace Cordray

When most New Yorkers hear the term "faith healer" their bullshit detector lights up. But Destiny Wallace seems to be the real deal. Having only arrived in Gotham two months ago, she has already built a thriving business and amassed an impressive number of satisfied customers.

I first became aware of her through fellow blogger, Mack Dean. "I heard she could grow back the middle finger I lost in high school wood shop," he told me. "I was doubtful, but I had to check it out. Two weeks after my visit with her, I could see my finger regrowing. I was gobsmacked."

When I saw Mack in person, I was equally stunned. He greeted me by flipping me the bird with what looked like an infant's finger. I called Destiny the next day and she was eager to meet me.

When I walked into YAZU in Industry City, I was surprised to see a fresh-faced teenager who looked barely old enough for a driver's license.

"I get that a lot," said Destiny in her prairie drawl.

From there she told the story of how she came to have her amazing abilities:

"My mom was diagnosed with cancer, and the same night she died, she came to visit me. She told me she had a gift for me, the power to heal people by touching them."

Not long after that, she decided to move to New York. "I want to be where I can help the most people," she said.

I asked her how she felt about the faith healer label, and she made a sour face. "That's not really me," she said. "I don't talk about God or anything." Then I asked if she believed that anyone else had the same power she did.

"Don't think so," she replied. "I'm one of a kind!"

Later that evening, I accompanied her to meet three clients, all of them ex-boxers who had lost some of their brain function from head trauma. Tye, a one-time Golden Gloves champion, said "You got a lot of fighters who don't think so good no more. Word got around the boxing world that she could fix stuff that regular doctors can't. As long as it works, I don't care how she does it." Manny Cruz, who fought as a bantam weight added, "She can fix my nose and my noggin."

The process itself is short, with Ms. Wallace placing her hand on the forehead and each time saying, "Expect a change in your life."

"It's my signature phrase," she explained.

A pair of brightly colored knit gloves complete the effect. It's clear that this young lady knows how to market herself.

Seth Greenbaum, a local filmmaker, who claims he regained sight in one eye after being touched by Destiny, said, "Her powers are truly amazing! She's a very special person."

Ms. Wallace charges for her services. "It's New York and I have to pay rent too," she says, adding, "I try to keep it affordable to most people."

She can be contacted by email at expectachange@yahoo.com

———

I didn't understand why she used the faith healer angle, because I never used that term. I don't think I have a "prairie drawl" either.

It felt good to read that Seth called me "a very special person." That had to mean he liked me, right?

She had a popular blog, and she got a lot of comments. People on the Internet can be total assholes, of course. I got called a fake, phony and a fraud. I got called a charlatan, too. When I googled that, I found it's a fancy word for fake, phony, and fraud.

———

The blog post brought in a ton more business! I had Candace list an email address as my contact because I didn't want to put my phone number out there for everyone to see. If anyone contacted me by email, I would set up the whole meeting that way. Meanwhile my phone number still got passed around by the people who'd met me before the blog article. That's how I knew who came to me from the blog post, and who was being referred by my original set of customers, by how they contacted me. In a week it was about 50/50.

I had to say no to a bunch more people who didn't understand what I could and couldn't do. Some woman wanted me to make her son a genius so he could get into a better kindergarten, and one guy wrote me that saying... Well, here's what he wrote because I don't even think I can explain it:

Dear Destiny,

The soul of Jimi Hendrix has been reincarnated in my body. Unfortunately, my body will not allow me to play guitar properly to satisfy him. I am going crazy with frustration!!!! I need you to make me able to play the way that Jimi demands!!! Please help!!!

Sincerely.

Menachem Schiff

your best life 7:

Stop and Smell the Supermarket Roses.

Life is full of hard knocks. So many that it's easy to miss the times when things go your way. When those times happen, take a moment to enjoy stop and smell the roses. It doesn't have to be a big deal; a warm spring day or a cute puppy are enough to take a second and notice that there's a lot of good mixed in with the bad.

And, if you're doing everything you can, every day, to make your life better, those good things will get bigger. A Boston Creme from Dunkin' Donuts becomes dessert at a fancy restaurant. A back rub from your boyfriend becomes a professional massage at a spa. And they'll happen more often. Imagine having a weekly massage appointment! It's possible!

And you can *literally* stop and smell the roses sometimes. They sell them at the supermarket, and it doesn't cost anything to have a sniff.

seven

. . .

I WENT out the next morning on a mission to get a fake I.D. So I could get into bars. It wasn't even that I wanted to drink. Drinking is expensive in New York. I just wanted to be able to walk in. Like if I were on a date, with Seth, say, I didn't want to have to think about where we could and couldn't go. I guessed that he was cool with me still being a teenager and I didn't want it to become an issue.

Back in Montana, I would have known who to talk to. In New York, the only person I could think to ask was Zeuss MG.

I started the call like I was following up on his buddy, making sure he was a satisfied customer. Zeuss said his boy had healed completely and dropped out of the game. Then he moved in with his mom back in Massachusetts. I hoped Zeuss wasn't mad at me for losing one of his crew when I asked about the ID. He told me about a tattoo parlor in East New York called Tatooine.

"Like in Star Wars," he said.

I went down there and left with a convincing drivers' license, all for $100. The only hitch was they didn't have a Montana license. This would have to be for doormen only, who wouldn't know that I'd never been to Vermont in my life.

———

Seth called to ask me out and I knew it was a date!

I took a morning trip to buy new clothes. I went to the H&M, nothing too fancy. I was starting to live like a normal person and all those little expenses - buying my own shampoo, paying for the subway, getting sheets for my bed, doing laundry - added up. It made me appreciate how much my mom had done for me on her small paycheck.

When the day came, Seth and I ate in a funky little place in Chinatown. Seth said the restaurant had a Chinese customer-only menu. It was written in Chinese on a chalkboard on the wall.

"Do you know what it says?" I asked.

"No," said Seth. "If you ask the wait staff, they'll just tell you that there's nothing on there you'd like."

"Like gross stuff?" I said. "Like monkey brains?"

"Maybe," he said. "Or chicken testicles."

"That is so gross," I said. "Do Chinese people really eat chicken testicles?"

"I think I read that somewhere," he said.

"I didn't know chickens had testicles," I said. "They must be, like, tiny."

"How hungry would you have to be before you ate something like that?" he said.

"Starving," I said.

"You'd have to eat a lot of them to make a meal," he said. "Like thousands."

I laughed even though the thought of a bowl of chicken balls sounded gross. I looked at the regular menu, nothing about chicken privates there.

Knowing that he liked me made it a lot easier to talk. We

joked around for a while then Seth got serious and leaned across the table. "Do you know how much money you can make with your powers?"

"A lot," I said. Believe me, it had crossed my mind.

"Cancer treatments can cost hundreds of thousands of dollars," he said.

"Hundreds of thousands?" I said. That seemed crazy to me.

"And the treatments don't always work," he said.

"Wow," I said. "I have to get in on that. Even if I charged half as much..."

He shook his head. "The medical establishment is never going to accept you. That means insurance companies won't pay you and they're the ones who ultimately foot the bill."

"I'll just have to prove them all wrong," I said.

"Maybe," said Seth, "But if you're an oncologist pulling down 400k a year, you're never going to admit that a teenage girl has you beat. They're going to disparage it every way you can. I could see the whole AMA ganging up on you.'

"No, I get it," I said. (Not the "disparage" part. I didn't know what that meant. I didn't know what the AMA was, either.) "They'll just say I'm full of shit and it'll be my word against theirs. And they'll have all the fancy degrees."

"Essentially," he said.

"Let 'em," I said. "People will figure it out; that I'm not a fake."

The waiter arrived and we ordered from the English menu. The waiter had an accent, and I thought that we had something in common, both being immigrants to New York, pursuing our dreams. I ordered shrimp fried rice.

"Do you have any long-term goals?" asked Seth after the waiter left.

"I want to help as many people as I can," I said. See, famous people never talk about making money. When they interview a football player after winning the Superbowl, the guy never says anything about wanting to get paid more or wanting to be in a Gatorade commercial. No, he always talks about the game and his team and all that. Same thing with movie stars. They talk about how challenging the role was, how great the director was, how they thought the movie would change the world. Never about the 12 million they got paid.

"That's admirable," said Seth.

"For now, I'd like to be able to live on my own," I said.

"I hear that," he said. "Or find someone to live with who I really like."

"You have a roommate?" I asked.

"Yeah," he said. "She's okay."

"You have a *girl* roommate?" I said, and I'm sure I sounded as surprised as I felt.

"It's totally platonic," he said.

I didn't know what platonic meant but the way he said it, I figured it meant that they weren't hooking up.

"It's just someone I know from film school," he said. "That's the deal with film school grads. None of us can afford to live alone. Except for the trust fund kids."

I guessed that trust fund kids were rich without having to work. "Do you have any long-term goals?" I asked.

"I want to make good films that people want to see," he said. "These days, there are good films that only a small audience sees—the ones that win the Academy Awards—and bad movies that the whole world sees, like all those superhero movies. I don't think it has to be that way. I don't see why you can't make a top-ten grossing movie that makes people think and feel. I know it can be done, because it *has* been done."

He was so passionate; it was kind of sexy. I didn't tell him that I like superhero movies. No need to kill the buzz. "I totally get that," I said.

"You're in a unique situation," he said. "You're the master of your own...situation."

"I like being my own boss," I said.

"It's an amazing gift," he said. "A lot of people would kill to have your powers."

"My mom did die," I said.

"Oh, sorry," he said, getting flustered. "I shouldn't have said that. I wasn't thinking."

"It's cool," I said. "I know what you mean."

When the food arrived, I looked at the chopsticks next to my plate. I'd never eaten with chopsticks before, and I didn't want to look stupid dropping food all over myself. But if I asked for a knife and fork, I'd look like a hick. I picked up the chopsticks and tried to fake like I knew how to use them. How the hell is anyone supposed to eat rice with chopsticks? I only got about three shrimp into my mouth the whole dinner.

Afterwards we went to a film, the kind that hardly anyone goes to. It was in French with the words written out at the bottom of the screen. He said he took French in high school and could understand a lot of what the actors said. I'm sure he was trying to impress me, and help me discover art.

I got bored with the movie and I knew the night would end up with us kissing, and I wanted to get to that part sooner rather than later, so I asked him if he wanted to make-out. That's what we did for the last half hour of the movie.

He walked me home again and there was more kissing in front of my building. I went in hoping to run into Caroline (who I think broke up with that other guy, probably because he wasn't a big enough douche bag for her) but no luck.

I went to bed that night, determined to move out of my cave. I turned on the lamp I bought at Crate & Barrel and took out my cash can. It was a thirty-two-ounce can of chickpeas I'd found in the kitchen recycling and washed out. (New Yorkers were crazy about recycling.) I had $1,200 in there. Back in Billings, that would seem like a fat stack. In New York, it still wasn't enough for me to find a place of my own.

———

It's weird how sometimes things fall together by chance. Laura called me. Remember? The one who had been in the car crash. She wanted to give me the rest of the money she owed me. I hadn't forgotten about that. I was just never in the mood to chase her down. Bugging people for money is not my idea of a good time. Back in Montana, I had neighbors who had debt collectors show up at their door. I didn't want to be like those guys. Everybody hated them.

Laura came to the JavaStrip. By then, I was a regular. I knew all the baristas and they knew me. Franny worked weekday mornings. She had bleach blonde hair and nose ring. Olga worked on weekend afternoons. She was from Ukraine. They were all cool with me hanging out all the time on the weekdays because I brought in customers during the usual slow times.

Laura arrived on crutches, which was a huge improvement. I could see how all the parts were starting to move back into place. She was all smiles, even if the smile made you notice the last of the scar that went from her forehead, across her face and down to her chin. "What's the story, morning glory?" she said, all, perky.

I had a lot of stories. I told her about the blog, and all the new business, and how well everything was going. Then, while we were talking about her life, she said her sister was moving out to take a job in Philadelphia. She complained that she had to find a new roommate.

"Really," I said. "I thought you were a lawyer?"

"Lawyers can't have roommates?" she said.

"I mean, you must be able to afford to live by yourself," I said.

"I like the company," she said. "And I'm still paying off my law school loan debt—if you can believe that—so I have to factor that in."

"I've got too much company where I'm at," I said.

"You have roommates?" she asked.

"Hells yeah," I said. "A whole platoon of them. And there's one I just can't stand. I mean, she's a pill."

"Are you looking to move?" she asked.

"Definitely," I said. "I've got the money saved." That's when I caught her drift. "Where do you live?" I asked.

"In Park Slope," she said. "Not far from where we met."

"Oh," I said, remembering it was a nice neighborhood, even if it was a little—what's the word?—bougie?

"It's a ground level apartment in a brownstone on Carroll Street. Do you want to see it?"

She was my last appointment of the day, so why not? "How much is it?" I asked.

"Your part would be $1,400 a month."

"Wow," I said. It was more than I wanted to pay.

I think she saw the expression on my face, because she said, "That's okay, if it's too much for you."

But then I thought about how I didn't like my neighborhood that much anyway. There was only one subway stop and there wasn't much around there. I had to take the subway somewhere else to buy clothes or furniture, or anything. And I thought about how business had been taking off. I could make $1,400 in a week if I only saw one client a day, and I was, for sure, doing better than that. "It wouldn't hurt to see the place," I said.

We took an Uber which she paid for.

I got out on a street with trees up and down the sidewalk. Laura lived in a nice place. The building was what they call a brownstone. It was old and fancy with a set of (brown) stone steps leading up to the front door which was already on the second floor. There were another two stories on top of that.

"The family that owns the place lives up there," she said. "I live in the basement apartment." I followed her to a door just under the stairs. Ramps the whole way.

Inside, it was even darker than my place. "Do you have windows?" I asked.

"The only drawback to living here is that there are only windows in the front and the back," she said. "Not great, but, when I moved in, I had to live on the ground floor. Every living space in New York is a compromise, though. Unless you want to spend an ungodly amount of money."

Like I didn't already know that.

"I have access to the garden though," she said. "In the summertime, it's nice."

"Where's the room?" I asked.

"Down the hall, second left," she said, pointing.

I found it and turned on the light. No window was a major minus. But it was a real room, with four times as much floor space as what I had, and a normal ceiling. It had a closet, too. Still, $1,400 a month seemed like a lot for another cave.

On the other hand, I was too busy to spend time running around the city looking at places. And then there was Laura. I know it sounds weird coming from a teenager, but I liked the idea of having an adult around. The people I lived with were technically adults, but they still didn't have their shit together. I couldn't relate to them, and I couldn't look up to them either. I could look up to Laura. She seemed like a role model.

I told her I'd take it.

———

It was a spring day, so Seth and I had a picnic in McCarren Park. I met him at his apartment. He lived nearby, in Greenpoint, Brooklyn. The apartment was a two-bedroom on the second floor, above a nail salon. It was nicer than my place with some furniture from IKEA and some things rescued from the street.

I met Mai, his roommate. She seemed cool and kind of artsy. She wore glasses with huge round frames.

"She looks like the character from *The Incredibles*," I said after we'd left. "The lady who designed their costumes."

"Edna Mode," he said. "I can see that." (Among Seth's many talents was his ability to remember everything about every movie he ever saw. And, yes, he saw *The Incredibles*.)

"Too bad I can't fix nearsightedness," I said.

He laughed. "There's nothing wrong with her eyes. She has window glass in those frames."

"They're fake?" I said.

"They're an affectation," he said.

I was starting to appreciate Seth's big words. My vocabulary was ~~getting bigger~~ expanding just by hanging out with him.

"That seems crazy to me," I said.

He nodded toward my hands. "You're still wearing those gloves," he said. "Even though it's not cold out."

"That's different," I said. "These are like... part of my image."

"That's what an affectation is," he said.

"Oh," I said, not sure if an affectation was a bad thing.

I think he picked up on that. "It's cool," he said. "I get why she wears the glasses and I get why you wear the gloves. Image is important."

"Totally important," I said.

"Can I give you some advice, though?" he asked.

"Sure," I said. "You need to make this business legal."

"I'm not doing anything illegal," I said.

"I know that," he said. "I mean you need to make it a legal entity. If you don't do that, you can't expand."

"I know," I said. "I've been thinking about it. I don't know much about that business stuff and it's all so complicated."

"It's not that hard," he said. "You can get everything you need to know from the Internet. Once you're an official business, you can set up a bank account and start taking credit cards."

"Yeah, I've been meaning to do that," I said.

"And I can give you the name of the accountant my mom used for her psychology practice."

I knew he was trying to help. I thanked him for all the good advice and told him I'd think about it. (And by "think about it," I meant "think about it for ten seconds before getting overwhelmed and pushing it out of my mind.")

Later we went back to Seth's place, and he showed me the film he made for his senior project. It was called "Software Pirates," and the basic idea is pirates who write software. It was hilarious!

———

I knew Gavin would be pissed if I told him I was leaving. I'd only been there a couple months and I knew he'd have trouble getting someone to replace me. (That's why he'd been so quick to rent me the space to begin with. Because it sucked.) So, I decided not to tell him. I had the moving guys come when he was be out working his day job, managing a sporting goods store. (Good thing I didn't sign anything.)

Moving was easy. I still didn't have much more than what I started with. I called a local man-with-a-van service. They were in and out within minutes and I was at Laura's place a few hours later.

Seth stopped by after work to see my new room. His mom lived a few streets over and his dad lived in Fort Green so this was convenient for him. I introduced Seth to Laura as my boyfriend and he didn't flinch, so I guessed that he *was* my boyfriend.

They seemed to hit it off and later Seth told me how amazed he was at how Laura looked. (I'd given him the full description of what she looked like when I met her.) He said that Laura could be my "Sixteenth Chapel." I didn't know what he meant by that, but I knew it was a compliment.

your best life 8

I'm Screaming at You Because I Love You.

You're not really close to someone until you've been in a fight with them. No serious relationship is going to happen with the both of you always being nice to each other. That's just not realistic.

You've probably gotten in a fight with someone in your family. If it's your parents, then there probably was yelling. If it was with a brother or sister, you may have punched each other. That's because you're close.

You've probably never yelled at the guy you get your coffee from in the morning or punched your mail lady. That's because you're friendly with them, not friends. No doubt, your mail lady yells at her boyfriend.

The things you fight about with the people who are important to you can be pretty major. Really, the closer someone is to you, the bigger these things can get. And little things can blow up fast. Someone drinking the last bottle of Flathead Lake soda can lead to someone setting a trailer on fire. (I've seen it happen.)

You need to settle them before you can move on. You

either find a compromise or agree to disagree. Getting there means you'll have to at least try to understand the other person's point of view. You'll have to accept all the things they've done wrong and all the things they think you've done wrong. It isn't easy but it can be done and, when it's over, you'll be closer than ever.

And don't get into yelling arguments with strangers on the street. That won't turn them into friends. It'll just make you look crazy.

eight

· · ·

I WANTED to have Seth over while Laura wasn't there so we could, y'know, do it. There was no way it could happen with Laura at home. That would have been like having my mom in the other room. It couldn't happen at his place either, because his roommate was always home. Having Mai there wouldn't have been as weird, but I didn't want to have any weirdness getting in the way. So, I thought of a plan...

"Say, Laura," I said one morning while we were both getting ready to go out. "Do you like plays and stuff?"

"Sure," she said. "It depends on the play though."

I'd never been to a play, but there were a lot of them going on in NYC and people like Laura went to them. "Totally," I said. "But, like, if I bought you tickets, would you like that?"

"You want to buy me theater tickets?" she said, like it was a strange idea.

"Yeah," I said.

"Why?"

That question threw me. Like, why ask why? They're free tickets! "I just thought it'd be a nice thing to do, that's all."

"Do you need to have the place to yourself sometime?" she asked.

Damn, I forgot she was a lawyer. She knew when some-body was trying to pull one over.

"Uh, yeah," I admitted.

"You could just ask when's the next time I'll be out for the evening."

Now I felt like an idiot. Maybe I insulted her by assuming that she never went out and did anything fun.

"I have a conference in Philadelphia next week," she said. "I'll be gone for three days. You can have the place to yourself then."

"Oh, cool," I said. "And I'm not having a party or anything."

She smiled. "Just don't wreck the place." And that was that. It felt weird being treated like a responsible person. Weird and good.

———

Laura left for her conference on a Tuesday morning and Seth came over that night. He said he'd cook me dinner. No one had ever cooked me dinner before, and it felt special. He made pecan-crusted trout with orzo and green beans. Orzo turned out to be a cross between spaghetti and rice. The green beans were fresh, not frozen. I didn't really like fish but didn't say anything, because he was trying to impress me, and I didn't want to spoil it for him. It was pretty good, anyway.

Afterwards, we went to my room.

Okay, here's where I admit that I'd never done it before. I'd fooled around with a couple guys at my high school, but I'd never gone all the way.

"Are you going to take those off?" Seth asked when we were getting ready.

I knew he meant my gloves.

"Oh, yeah, sure," I said, because it would have been really weird if I'd kept them on.

I took them off and put them in the dresser I'd bought from IKEA.

Seth took my hand and looked at it. "I've never seen your hands before," he said which was a strange thing to say because there were some other body parts he was seeing for the first time too. "This is where the magic comes from," he said, still staring at them.

"Mhmm," I said. Now that we were this close, I was starting to feel, well, naked. "Like, are we gonna...?"

I don't know what I was expecting but it wasn't as mind-blowing as I'd hoped. Don't get me wrong; it was good—and I'd definitely do it again—but it wasn't the most amazing thing that'd ever happened to me.

The next morning actually felt more special. Seth had to go to work, but we went and got coffee and bagels together. I felt like a real couple, y'know, mature.

Later in the day, I got an email from a reporter at the Daily News. The Daily News was what they call a tabloid. I don't know if they have them in other cities, but tabloids are newspapers that are a little trashy, not supermarket trashy—like, no alien abductions—just not as stuffy as the New York Times.

The reporter, a woman named Sandra Rae Stevens, had read about me in the *If It Ain't Brooklyn...* blog and wanted to write about me, too. I said sure.

We met for coffee near the Daily News offices on the southern tip of Manhattan, right near the Statue of Liberty, where I still hadn't visited.

The interview went much like the one with the blogger. Same questions. Same answers. It was a warmish day, and I wore my gloves. She asked about them and I explained they were part of my image, along with my signature phrase.

"Would you be willing to come with me up to Mount Sinai Hospital and the Upper East Side," she asked. "There's a New York City fireman up there recovering from third-degree burns over eighty percent of his body."

"Wow," I said. "That sounds serious."

"It is," she said. "Do you think you can help him?"

"Totally," I said. I didn't ask for money. I'd be helping a fireman, and everyone loves firemen. Anyway, the publicity was worth more than whatever I'd have charged.

We took the subway up to 103rd St. and walked the rest of the way. On the train ride, Sandra told me the story about what happened to Lieutenant DiPietro. There was a three-alarm warehouse fire in the Bronx and DiPietro was standing near some barrels of chemicals that exploded.

I started to worry about how gross this guy was going to look. I didn't know how they ranked degrees of burns. Were first-degree burns the worst? Or were third degree?

It was too gross to think about. I asked Sandra about her job, where she went to school, how she got to New York, all that. She told me she grew up in New York and went to journalism school at Boston University. She said that newspapers were struggling and that she felt lucky to have a job.

When we got to the hospital, we went straight to the Intensive Care Unit, so I guess that Sandra had worked it all out beforehand. A guy from DiPietro's firehouse sat with him. He looked grim.

I was relieved to see that the DiPietro was covered in bandages so I couldn't see the burns. He looked like a mummy. I put my hand on his arm, one of the few unbandaged spots, then I said, "Expect a change in your life," more for the Sandra than DiPietro who I felt pretty sure was sleeping.

"Wait a minute," said Sandra. "I should get a picture of this." She took out her iPhone and I did it again.

When I finished, I looked at his fireman buddy. "He

should be right as rain," I said, and I smiled. The guy just nodded. Maybe he didn't believe me.

Not knowing what else to do, I left the room and Sandra followed me. "Like, that's it?" I asked her. "Are you gonna wait until he heals and then write a story about it?"

"Yes," she said. "How long do you think it will take him to heal?"

"A few weeks, I guess," I said, because I wasn't really sure.

On the subway ride home, I thought about all the damaged people I would see in my life. Probably thousands. Maybe millions? I was taking on a lot of responsibility. *Success is like that*, I thought.

A guy got on at the next stop and started into his speech about why he needed everyone's spare change. I ignored him.

———

I met Seth's parents. Not at the same time, because they still had some issues and couldn't be in the same room together.

The plan was to have dinner with Seth's dad at a Japanese restaurant in Prospect Heights. Meeting Seth's dad made me nervous. I was afraid he'd think I wasn't smart enough to date his son. While we stood outside waiting for his dad, I told Seth what we could talk about and what we couldn't.

Couldn't: That I dropped out of high school. That I never went to college. That I grew up poor.

Could: That I was super good at my job. That I had a bright future ahead of me.

"I'll try my best," said Seth. "But he'll probably ask you questions about yourself. I mean, that's part of why he's meeting you, to get to know you."

"I know," I said. "Let's just try to talk about the good stuff, okay?"

"It's all good stuff," he said. "Just be yourself."

"I am being myself," I said. "I'm just being my *best* self."

"It's not a job interview," he said, and he laughed which kind of bugged me, like he didn't take me seriously.

"Just help me out here, okay?" I said.

His dad arrived and he looked older than I expected, and his eyebrows could have used a trim. We sat down and ordered our food. They both ordered sushi, so I did too. I wanted chicken teriyaki, but I wanted to look sophisticated, so I asked for the Unagi which is barbecued freshwater eel. I didn't see how I could go wrong with anything barbecued.

"Seth tells me you're a holistic healer," said Seth's dad, whose name was Gene.

I didn't totally know what "holistic" meant so I said, "Kinda like that, yeah."

"The stories he tells me are incredible," said Seth's dad and I didn't know if he meant incredible/amazing or incredible/bullshit. "It's quite a gift," he said, and I decided he meant incredible/amazing. I told him that the Daily News wrote a story about me, so he'd take me seriously. That seemed to work.

Seth had already told me that his dad had been a college professor and that his thing was 19th century German philosophers. I couldn't ask Seth's dad about that, because it hit too close to the whole college issue, and I didn't know anything about Germany, philosophy, or the 19th century.

Sometimes, when Seth and his dad talked to each other, my mind couldn't keep up with them. If I thought Seth knew a lot of big words before, I didn't know how many he really had up in that brain of his. It seemed like they were trying to use up the whole dictionary in one conversation. It made me insecure. I wondered if Seth had to dumb down everything he said to me.

Seth had me talk about Montana and I kicked myself for not putting Montana on the not-to-talk-about list. Turns out, Seth's dad had been to Little Bighorn and knew about the local history. I'd been there too on a school field trip, so we had that in common. Then we talked about me moving to New York and what that was like. After a couple of cups of sake, Seth's dad told some stories about growing top in the city and how rough the place was in the 1970's. I knew a little about that because Seth had me watch a bunch of movies from back then, like "Taxi Driver." (It's hard to believe that Robert DeNiro was ever that young!)

I was majorly relieved when it ended. I hadn't done anything to embarrass myself (that I knew of.) Seth told me it went well so that felt good. I was halfway through the whole meet the parents thing.

———

A few days later, we had dinner with his mom at a vegetarian place, also in Park Slope. I gave Seth the same rules about what to talk and not talk about. He complained that the rules made it harder to include me in the conversation and that I shouldn't worry so much. Easy for him to say. He already knew his mom.

His mom was more tense than his dad. She was thin and dyed her hair, leaving a streak of grey in the front. She only drank water and green tea, so she never loosened up like Seth's dad did.

She asked me about my work, and I said everything I'd said to Seth's dad. I told her about the Daily News , and she said she didn't read the tabloids. Then she asked me about Montana, like it was the moon, someplace faraway place she would never visit. I got the feeling that she didn't like me that much when she stopped talking to me and only talked to Seth, like I wasn't there. I sat there watching them and getting madder.

Afterward I told Seth about it.

"I thought you'd be relieved," he said.

"No," I said. "I wasn't relieved."

"Look," he said. "If you're gonna have all these no-go topics that everyone has to tiptoe around..."

"Everyone doesn't have to tiptoe around me," I said.

"Okay," he said, "If I have topics that *I* need to tiptoe around, then sometimes it's just easier to talk about other stuff."

"Other stuff that doesn't include me," I said.

"Yes," he said. "Everything isn't about you."

That made me mad because I knew part of what he said was right. I couldn't admit it, though. Instead, I said this:

"I can see why your dad screwed around on your mom."

So not the thing to say.

"Excuse me?" he said.

That would have been a good time to apologize. Or pretend that I'd never said it. Or have a hole in the sidewalk open up and swallow me. None of those things happened.

"Your mom has a way of making people feel like shit," I said.

Seth stopped walking and I kept going. I didn't want to stop and look back, because I knew that I'd totally blown it with him, so I just kept going to my apartment.

———

When I got home, Laura was sitting in the kitchen, drinking a cup of chamomile tea. She knew I was meeting Seth's mom that night and she knew that I'd been tense about it. And I knew that she knew that something had gone wrong. I didn't want to talk about it, and I wanted to talk about it, so I told her the whole story, leaving out some details, like exactly what I'd said about Seth's dad divorcing his mom. Laura didn't exactly take my side and she didn't take Seth's side either. She just listened, which was all I needed right then.

"Well, I guess that's over with," I said, feeling sorry for myself.

"Is this your first big fight?" she asked.

"Yes," I said.

"You can't really say you're close to someone until you've had a fight," she said.

That sounded wrong to me. My parents had fights and that's why they split up. I told her that.

"You can't expect to always get along with someone. All couples fight. It's perfectly normal."

"I kind of hoped not to ever get into fights," I said. "They totally suck."

"They're unavoidable," she said. "The key is learning how to fight in a way that doesn't do permanent damage to the relationship."

"It's probably too late for that," I said.

"I wouldn't give up yet," she said. "I'd say give it a couple of days and then try to talk it out."

That was exactly what I needed to hear, that I hadn't blown it completely. "Should I wait for him to call me?" I asked.

"You should call him," she said.

"Really?" I said.

"Yes," she said. "Under the circumstances."

I knew she meant I was the one who'd screwed up. "What do I say?" I asked, because I really didn't know.

"Start out by apologizing and then talk it through."

"Talk it through?" I said. I knew what those words meant but not what I was supposed to do exactly. "How do I do that?" I asked, hoping for step-by-step instructions.

"I can't tell you that," she said. "You'll just have to figure it out."

None of this sounded good to me. I told her I'd think about it.

———

The story in the Daily News made the front page. They had a picture of Lieutenant DiPietro, out of his bandages smiling, looking totally normal. The headline said THREE-ALARM MIRACLE. Inside was an article about me with the title, SAINT DESTINY. I wasn't thrilled about that. I wasn't a saint. It was too much to live up to.

I should have been jumping up and down happy. Instead, I felt pressured. Things were about to GET REAL, and I had nothing in my life to get me ready for it.

Deep down, I knew I needed Seth. I had to call him and try to patch things up, something I was dreading. Honestly, it felt like a bigger deal than moving to New York. I ran through a bunch of things I could say, trying to get the words right. I really felt sorry. I decided to go with that.

He picked up with a "Hey" that didn't sound like he hated me. I took that as an opportunity to get it all out before he could change his mind.

"I need to talk to you," I said. "I need to apologize for what I said the other night. I was nervous about meeting your parents and, I dunno, I was afraid they wouldn't like me."

"I understand," he said, and I felt a weight lift off me. I didn't know that this apologizing thing would be so easy.

"Did your mom like me?" I asked.

"She didn't say either way," he said. "But could we back up a bit? I still want to talk about what happened."

"Okay," I said, bracing myself for what was going to come next.

"I understand why you were on edge," he said. "But I don't see what would cause you to say something like that."

"I said I was sorry," I said.

'I know," he said. "It's just that if we're going to be together, we have to have a certain level of respect."

"I totally respect you," I said, which was true. "I just... I don't know." I started to feel like Seth was the grown-up and I was the little kid. For a second, I wanted to hang up and forget about Seth.

But I didn't. I pulled myself together. "I won't do it again," I said. "I promise." And there was a moment of silence while I guess Seth thought about whether he believed me or not.

"My parents and the divorce can be a touchy subject for me," he said. "You have things that you don't like to talk about, so do I. And that's one of them."

"Oh, okay," I said. "I won't mention it."

"Okay," he said.

"Can we talk about the article in the Daily News, instead?" I asked.

"Sure," he said.

Then we talked about what a big break that was for me! By the time I ended the call, I felt like things were back on track.

your best life 9:

Is That an Ice Cream Cone in Your Pocket, or are You Just Trying to Look Badass?

Lawyers speak another language. It's called Legalese, whereof parties hereunto fight over stuff. Sentences are long, words get mushed together and some of it's in Latin. Did you understand all the terms and conditions of your Instagram account before clicking the "I Agree," button? Me neither.

Even if you know what the hell they're talking about, sometimes the law doesn't make sense. Like, in New York, it's illegal to carry an ice cream cone in your pocket on Sundays. Mondays, you're cool. I guess.

When you hit the big time, I guarantee you'll need a lawyer to heretofore cover your ass. All sorts of shifty-shady types are going to come at you with *their* sharks in suits. Your lawyer has to be sharper than the aforementioned sharks in suits.

Listen to your lawyer and do what she tells you. Even if it doesn't make sense. Because who would have thought that an ice cream cone in your pocket could get you arrested?

nine

. . .

PEOPLE STARTED CONTACTING me from all over. Reporters called me, looking to set up interviews. I ignored them, because suddenly I didn't need the publicity. I had an avalanche of clients wanting to make appointments. Keeping track of all of them became impossible. Honestly, I was overwhelmed.

And I had to think seriously about making my business more legit. I was like Zeuss MG, carrying a wad of 20s, 50s and c-notes. Seth kept bugging me about getting a bank account. "There's a Chase right down the block," he said, like I hadn't noticed.

Around that time, I got robbed. I didn't tell Seth about this, because he'd freak out, but some guys took all my cash. It was a set up. A guy made an appointment to meet me, saying he had "Malaysia." Stupid me didn't run that by WebMD because, if I did, I would have found out that Malaysia is a country in the far east, not a disease. He had me meet him at the end of the day on a street corner. This was in my old neighborhood. I thought it was safe, because we were in a public place. Big mistake. While I was talking to the one guy, another dude came up behind me and said he's got a knife and how I'd better hand over my cash. I felt totally scared and I told him to take the money. Then they ran off together.

It took me a long time to calm down. When I did, I kicked myself for not yelling or making more of a scene. Like, what were they going to do? Stab me to death right there on the sidewalk? And I can heal myself, so even if they poked me full of holes, I would have lived.

Anyway, having an office and taking credit cards and all that started to sound like a good idea. Still, I didn't want to go through the hassle so, the next time I went out with Seth, I suggested he put the business part together and run it, leaving me to do my thing full-time. He liked the idea and we agreed to a 75/25 split.

He went off and had a lawyer draw up a contract spelling out the terms of the partnership. I trusted him not to try to cheat me but, when he handed it to me, I couldn't understand any of the small print. You hear too many stories about musicians signing contracts that they barely read and, years later, finding out how totally screwed they were. I wasn't going to let that happen to me, so I asked Laura to go over it.

———

Laura wanted a few minor points of the contract changed but, overall, she said it was a standard partnership agreement.

She also told me that on the day of the signing, I'd have to bring ID.

"Why?" I asked. "We all know who I am."

"You still need to prove who you are," she said. "You also need to prove that you're 18 or over. You need to be an adult to sign a contract."

That was going to be a problem. "I'm 16," I said.

"Good lord," she said, and I didn't know why she was surprised.

"It's not that big a deal, is it?" I asked.

"In this case, it is." she said. "You'll need sponsorship from a parent or guardian, someone who'll be ultimately responsible for your end of the contract."

"That'd be my dad," I said. "And he's anything but 'ultimately responsible.'"

"I don't know what to tell you then," she said. And then she thought a bit. "Does Seth know you're 16?"

"Uh, no," I said. "He never asked."

She looked grim. "If you two are having sex, that would make him guilty of statutory rape."

"He's not raping me!" I said.

"It's a legal distinction," she said. "I know that it happens all the time and nobody makes a big deal about it, but he needs to know what the situation is."

"I guess I'll have to tell him," I said. I *so* did not want to have that conversation.

————

I told Seth the next day, while we ate at the Chipotle. "Sixteen?" he said, and he looked scared.

"It's no big deal," I said.

"It *is* a big deal," he said. "I could get arrested."

"No, you won't," I said, and he knew that it was true. "Who's gonna complain? My parents?"

"Why didn't you tell me?" he asked.

"Why didn't you ask?" I said.

"I don't know," he said. "I just kind of assumed. I mean, you came to New York on your own."

"That doesn't mean anything," I said. "I'm sure lots of sixteen-year-olds move to New York," and he couldn't argue with that one. "Anyway, this only matters because of the business part. I'm not old enough to sign a contract."

"Okay," he said. "I guess we can work around that. "But we

can't be together anymore," and he said that last part real quiet, like he was afraid that someone at the next table would hear.

"You're breaking up with me?" I said. I couldn't believe it. "I told you; you're not going to get arrested."

"Doesn't matter," he said.

"Because of what other people will think?" I said.

"Well, yeah," he said. "And Laura knows about this?"

"Of course," I said, and he made a face, like he'd sucked on a lemon.

He was way overdoing it. "Don't worry," I said. "She's not going to call the cops."

"I know," he said but he still looked worried. Or maybe embarrassed.

"Look," I said, "I'm a lot more mature than your average sixteen-year-old."

"No, you're not," he said.

"What?" I said. That made me real mad.

"You lied to me," he said. "That's what little kids do."

"I didn't lie to you!" I said. "You never asked!"

"It's called lying by omission," he said.

That made me even madder. Using fancy words to make me the bad guy. "I never lied!" I said. "No one ever asked me!" The people at the next table started to look over at us.

"Okay," he said. "I should have known something was up."

"What do you mean that: 'something was up'?" I said. "Why are you still accusing me of stuff?" I got up and walked out.

————

"Okay, I told him," I said to Laura as soon as I got home, not trying to hide how mad I felt. "Now what?"

"I don't know," she said.

"What do you mean, 'I don't know'?" I said. "This was all your idea."

"What did he say?" she asked.

"He said that I 'lied by a mission' or something like that," I said.

"Omission?" she said.

"Yeah, that's it," I said. "What does that mean?"

"It means he thinks you knew you should have told him how old you were, and you deliberately didn't," she said.

"I didn't think it was a big deal," I said. "Honest."

She thought for a few seconds, that's what lawyers do. And I started to calm down, now that I had a lawyer on the case.

"He never asked?" she said.

"Nope, never," I said.

"Okay," she said. "You did the right thing."

"So now what?"

"I can rewrite the contract to get around the fact that you're a minor," she said. "But you're going to have to work things out with Seth, that is if you still want him as a business partner."

I thought about that for a second. I thought I'd be working with my boyfriend. But now... "He broke up with me," I said.

"That will simplify things," said Laura.

"So, you don't want us to get back together?" I asked. I couldn't believe it.

"No," she said.

"No, we should not get back together?" I asked. I still couldn't believe it.

"No, you should not get back together," she said. "A romantic relationship will only complicate things."

My heart fell into my sneakers. "But..."

"Trust me on this one," she said. "I'd suggest you find a different business partner."

I didn't like that idea. I already knew Seth. He was smart

and I trusted him. "I don't know," I said. "Let me think about it."

But I didn't think about it. I just knew I had to get Seth back on board.

———

I needed Seth back in my corner, so I called him.

"Laura says she can work it out for us still to be partners," I said, leaving out the part about her wanting me to ditch Seth.

"Okay," he said.

"Okay?" I said, hoping that it would be as easy as that. "Everything can go back to how it was?"

"Not everything," he said. "We still can't be together. Like that, I mean." I was too stunned to say anything, so he kept talking. "It's probably better if we're not romantically involved. That can screw up a business relationship."

I wasn't happy about him taking Laura's side. I still didn't see what the big deal was. But I needed to put my career first. "Okay," I said. "Strictly business."

———

I told Laura that Seth and I were over as a couple, and she worked out a new deal. Seth would be the sole owner of the business, with an agreement that he'd hire me, as an employee. The money would be split, 60 for me and 40 for him. At first, I didn't sound like a very good deal and Laura reminded me of how much work Seth would be doing, like everything. The agreement lasted for a year and a half, until I turned eighteen. Then we'd use the first contract she wrote. That way, the money wouldn't be wasted.

Seth signed the agreement at Laura's office in Manhattan, a little before noon. Then Seth went to the stock photo company and gave his two-week notice. I would have just walked out, but he said he didn't want to burn any bridges.

Seth registered *Hand of Destiny LLC* with the state of New York. The name was his idea and I liked it. Within days of that, I was taking credit cards with the money going straight into a business account. I felt like an entrepreneur, a word I have to look up every time I write it.

The next step was finding office space. Seth said it was more efficient to have people come to me. "Travel time is a waste," he said. Sounded good to me.

He found a place in Park Slope, on the second floor, above a children's shoe store. It had been a comic book shop before. I heard all about the process of negotiating the rent and I felt glad that I didn't have to do any of that. It sounded complicated and boring.

The place needed to be fixed up. I found a Starbucks in the neighborhood that I could use as a home base until it was ready.

———

It took me a while to get used to the breakup and I'd be lying if I said it didn't make me sad. But as time went on, I realized that I liked Seth, but I didn't love him. He was good guy. He was smart and funny and all that, but there's more to love than that.

I wasn't sure how I felt about love. I'd never seen it work out in real life. Not with my parents. Not with Seth's parents. My mom's parents are still together, but I don't even know if they love each other. I think they've just gotten used to each other and past a certain age you're stuck with someone because, like, what are you gonna do? Go on Tinder?

Don't get me wrong. I want to be in love. It looks great in movies. I just need proof that it exists in the real world.

your best life 10:

Your Best Life 10: Waiting to Get Punched in the Face.

There will come a day when you have to deal with tough situations. Sometimes you'll see them coming from a mile away, like a thunderstorm. Sometimes it'll hit you before you know it, like an air conditioner falling out of a fourth-story window. There are four things to know before the shit hits the fan.

1. DON'T RUN. Stand your ground. If you run, your problems will catch up with you and you'll have your back turned when they do. That'll just make it easier for them to take you down.

2. OWN IT. This is your life and your story. Don't apologize for who you are and what you've done. You had your reasons and, since no one can stand in your shoes, nobody can completely understand them.

3. KEEP PERSPECTIVE. Think about other situations in your life where you made it out alive, like a bad breakup, or a serious illness. And even if whatever you're going through is the worst thing that has ever happened to you, it won't seem

like such a big deal ten years from now. (Unless it kills you, obviously)

4. LEARN SOMETHING. Make sure you get something out of your battle, besides scars. Find the life lesson to take with you so you don't make the same mistake again. And learn from the mistakes of others. Here's a life lesson from me: never trust a reality TV host.

ten

· · ·

CARDINAL MULCAHY, the Archbishop of New York, wanted to check me out. When I got the invite, my first thought was, hell no. Thinking about it a little more, I figured it was more publicity, so I decided to go.

We met in his office at the Roman Catholic Archdiocese of New York in midtown Manhattan, which is an office building, not a church. He called what I did for DiPietro "miraculous." Then he asked a bunch of questions about my life, including my religious background. My guess was he was feeling me out for sainthood. I mean, the Daily News had already called me that.

I have to admit, the idea of being a saint sounded kinda cool. How many people could claim that? It's a bigger title than Dame Judy Dench or Sir Paul McCartney. But the Archbishop shot that idea down pronto.

"The road to sainthood is a long one," he said. "It doesn't even begin until after the person is dead. And it's not only about performing miracles. All saints lived lives of heroic virtue."

I knew right then and there that I would never be a saint. I wanted a Ferrari and a house the size of a city block—in *this* life—thank you very much.

The weirdest part was, at the end of our little chat, he warned me that Satan could also perform miracles in order to deceive. What was he getting at?

"Don't worry about me," I said. "I'm one-hundred percent Satan-free."

———

Laura looked better and better as the days went by. Watching her body heal was amazing. The day she walked without crutches, or a cane felt like a BFD. She cried, and I cried too. Then we hugged.

Seth called her my "Sixteenth Chapel." I saw him every day. He would check in with me before going off to do all the things he had to do to get the new space ready. Since the breakup he was all business. When we were dating, he would call me sweetie, or honey. Now I was Destiny. (He even called me Ms. Wallace sometimes.) And he wouldn't touch me, no matter what. It felt like I had Ebola or something.

I hung out with Laura instead. She became my BFF. We would have dinner out once a week. We had our favorite burger place and they treated us like queens. We always got a good table. It was great. BUT...

We were at a burger place on Seventh Avenue when we had an incident. While we looked at our menus, this guy came up to our table. He looked like he was forty-something, pudgy, and wearing a New York Yankees cap.

"Sorry to bother you," he said to me, "But I need your help." Then he tells me about his ulcer which I didn't need to hear about right before dinner. I didn't know what to say to the guy so I looked at Laura. She was my lawyer after all.

"Sorry," she said. "But we're having dinner now. If you'd

like to make an appointment, you can call tomorrow during regular business hours."

The guy glared at Laura and said, "I wasn't talking to you."

I felt bad for putting Laura on the spot. And mad at this guy. I wanted to yell, but I didn't. Instead, I said, "I've got time tomorrow. Give me a call then and we'll squeeze you in." See, I was trying to be nice.

"I can't wait until tomorrow!" he said, and by now the whole restaurant was watching. Maribeth, the hostess came over to the guy, telling him that he'd have to leave. The guy started yelling and he called me the c-word. Jose, one of the chefs came out from behind the grill and got in the guy's face. I thought a fight would break out, but the guy backed down.

After he was gone, I felt proud of myself for keeping cool, but inside I was in knots. Like, what if the guy had gone ballistic, y'know?

————

I went with Laura to watch the fireworks over the East River on July Fourth. She'd never been before, because massive crowds were difficult when she was in a wheelchair. It made me happy knowing I'd made it possible for her to go. We bought red, white, and blue snow cones from a street vendor and found a spot on a highway overpass they'd shut down for the event.

Watching the rockets' red glare made me appreciate that this is the Greatest Country on Earth. I stood surrounded by people from all over the country—all over the world, even— who still believe in the American Dream.

————

And get this, the guy from the burger place called two days later and made an appointment. When I met him at a Starbucks, he didn't say anything about the incident, like the whole thing never happened, like he'd never even seen me before. People are weird sometimes.

———

We got another call, this time from a reality TV show called Hoax Busters. The host of the show was Craig Hanson. He'd gotten a little famous as a hoaxer. His biggest stunt was convincing people that a Fijian Navy ship had attacked one of our ships and we had gone to war with Fiji. It was all over the news until someone found out it was a lie. The idea behind Hoax Busters is that you can't fool another hoaxer so every week, he would find another fraud to shine a light on.

Of course, he thought I was a fraud. Seth and I saw a huge opportunity for publicity. I was going to bust the busters!

They shot the show in L.A. And I felt pretty excited. I'd never been there before, and the show was going to pay for my (economy) plane ticket, but I told them I was afraid of flying and had to go by train. I know that sounds dumb, but having a few quirks is good for a celebrity. And everyone I told about my cross-country train trip said, "I've always wanted to do that."

I rode on two trains—one to Chicago and another to California. It was better than the Greyhound bus, for sure. I had my own room to stretch out and relax in. The food was pretty good too.

The trip was going to take four days and I brought a book to read. I'd never been a reader. I never read the books I was supposed to in high school. I'd just go online at the library and read the summaries. It seemed crazy to read an entire book when you could get the whole thing in a few paragraphs. After being around Seth, I started to think I needed to become more educated. I picked "1984" by George Orwell, one of the books I got assigned to read in school. Wow, it was a bummer! But it made me think about the government and how you have to be careful about giving them too much power. That's how a lot of people in Montana felt, anyway.

I also read Eminem's autobiography. I instantly felt like he and I had a lot in common: He grew up poor and was the child of a single mom. Like me, he used his amazing talent to lift himself up. The book left me feeling inspired and ready to take on the world!

Looking out the window on the way into L.A. reminded me of when I arrived at the bus terminal in New York. A lot of what you see along the railroad tracks doesn't make a great impression. It's like the tracks spread rust, graffiti and garbage to everything around them.

Union Station in L.A. looked a lot nicer than the Port Authority. Someone from the production company picked me up and took me to the fanciest hotel I'd ever been in. (Up until then, that was a Holiday Inn.) I wished Seth could have been there. They had a swimming pool on the top floor, and I went up there to see if there were any celebrities lounging around, sipping drinks under umbrellas. I didn't see any. I looked out over the city and thought about being on TV. A part of me felt excited, and another part of me wanted to just get it over with.

The weird thing is that (aside from the fancy hotel) the people at the show weren't nice to me. They said I'd have to be down in the hotel lobby the next day at 5AM, but the car from the production company didn't come until 7, leaving me sitting there, like an idiot. Then they drove me out to the Mojave Desert. You've probably never been there, because it's a desert, hot and empty. It took four hours to get there. We didn't stop for food either. They gave me water, that was it. For sure, they were trying to psych me out. Like, if was tired and hungry, I'd crack up on camera and do something stupid.

That's how reality shows work. Seth had me read an article about it online. That wouldn't work on me. I'd been through worse—sleeping on the floor, and eating Pop Tarts in the freezing cold—back in New York.

They'd set up in the middle of nowhere. I mean, NOWHERE! From the car they took me to a trailer that – thank God – had AC. It was hot as hell in the desert. It reminded me of the time me and my mom went to visit the Badlands over summer vacation. (That's when we stayed at the Holiday Inn.)

I changed into the outfit I'd brought for the occasion. If I'd known we'd be in the middle of the desert, I'd have worn something lighter. The makeup artist put some powder on my face. Then they kept me waiting around an hour after that. As I sat there, I realized the trailer was about the same size as the one I grew up in. *Look how far I've come,* I thought. That made me more determined to show this Craig Hanson douche that I wasn't a fake.

The sun was still high in the sky when they called me out of the trailer. They set me up under a tent for an interview. A woman, named Jenny, had me tell the story about how I got my abilities. Then she asked me a lot of questions about my mom. Then she asked them all over again, and then a third time. I wasn't sure if they were trying to get better answers or if they were trying to trip me up. That made me paranoid. What sort of dirty tricks would they stoop to?

I asked Jenny a question. "Why are we all the way out in the desert?"

"We always pick a far away, open space so guests can't prearrange anything," she said.

"You could have saved yourself a long drive," I said. "I wasn't going to prearrange anything."

I met Craig for the first time on camera. I didn't like the looks of him. He looked weaselly. He smiled and shook my hand. "Kind of hot for gloves," he said.

"It's part of my image," I said, super self-conscious.

He looked at my hands, suspiciously. "Can we get a shot of this?" he said, and his cameraman zoomed in for a close-up. I resisted the urge to give the finger to the camera.

From there we went to meet Adam, a boy with brain cancer. He looked around 10 years old. He was bald under his Cleveland Indians baseball cap. It was sad. That he had cancer, not that he was an Indians fan.

We shot a whole bit where they showed me the MRIs of his skull. You could see one big tumor growing in there. I looked at him, wondering how he could still put two thoughts together. I got queasy thinking about the tumor.

"We can sit here looking at tumors all day," I said. "C,mon, let's do this." I hoped they'd use that line. It sounded like something from a movie.

"But first," said Craig. "There's someone here who wants to see you."

A cameraman got right up in my grill.

"Destiny?" said a voice behind me.

"Mom?" I said, turning around. "What are you doing here?"

She rushed at me and gave me a hug. "The show contacted me," she said. "God, I've been worried about you."

I gave Craig a mean look. That WAS a dirty trick.

"Why didn't you answer my calls?" asked mom. I felt bad because she had been paying my phone bills all these months.

"I was, y'know, busy," I said. "Getting all this happening." I waved my hand toward all the cameras and tents and trailers and stuff.

Suddenly, Craig got in my face. "You told our interviewer your mother is dead. Three times."

My stomach clenched. I wanted to run away. But no, not after coming this far. Literally. I stood my ground. "Uh, yeah," I said. "But that was just...uh... a story."

"A lie, then," he said.

"I always said it was a story," I said. "I had to... y'know... people wanted to know where I got my abilities and I had to tell them something."

"And you lied to them," said Craig, like he was a TV lawyer, and I was the killer he'd nailed to the wall.

"I told people something they'd believe," I said. I felt frustrated. I wanted out of this. I turned to Adam. "Hey, kid, do you care where I got my abilities?"

"No," he said.

"C'mere," I said. I was going to work my magic right then and there and hope it would screw up Craig's plans. Adam walked over and I put my hand on his head. "Expect a change in your life," I said. Then I turned to Craig and said something that they'd have to bleep out before it went on the air.

I stormed off and my mom followed me, so did the video crew, like toilet paper stuck to my shoe.

"Why didn't you answer my calls?" asked my mom again. "Did you listen to any of my messages? The only reason I kept paying your cell phone bills is in case you called me back. Do you know how much it cost me?"

"I told you; I was..." I looked into my mom's eyes, and she looked hurt. "I'm sorry, Mom. I REALLY was busy." I knew the camera was getting all of this, so I had to keep it together. "And I'm making it now," I said. "I've got a good business going. I'm an entrepreneur. You should be proud of me."

"I just don't understand why you ran away," said Mom.

"I didn't run away; I ran *to*," I said. "I knew you wouldn't let me go and I had to leave. I needed to get my life started. And I did. And it's great. That boy is going to get better and..." I pointed to the camera. "These a-holes are going to look like... like a-holes."

After I calmed down, we shot a segment where I met Adam's parents. They were nice to me. I found out they were already planning brain surgery. They were desperate.

When we drove back to L.A., I rode in the same car with

my mom. I wanted to talk to her, but didn't want to say anything more in front of the TV crew. I'd given them enough.

Mom did all the talking. She told me what she'd been up to, which was the same old same old. It freaked me out listening to her, because she had the life I would have had if I stayed in Montana: working a boring job that pays nickels and dimes, watching TV, and playing the lottery, hoping to get lucky. It was scary. And sad. Thank God I got on that bus for New York.

Mom came up to my hotel room and we both ordered thirty-dollar hamburgers from room service, because up yours, Craig Hanson and up yours, Hoax Busters. While we ate, I told her about my life. I told her about Laura, how she was a lawyer, and how I cured her. I told Mom about Seth, but left out the part about him being my boyfriend. I just said I met him through a friend and that I trusted him to hold down the business end of things. I told her about healing the fireman and meeting the archbishop. I also said I'd saved a gunshot victim, but left out the part about him being a drug dealer. I didn't say anything about the time I got robbed.

We watched a movie and Mom stayed in my room that night. It wasn't how I wanted to be reunited with her, but it felt good having her there and treating her to a fancy hotel.

your best life 11:

The Media Are a Bunch of Angry Leeches Swimming in a Cesspool Waiting for Someone to Step In.

In Your Best Life 6, I talked about working the media. There's a second part to that - the media are not your friends. They can be useful, and they can help you, but amigos they ain't. If they're kissing your ass today, I guarantee they'll be kicking it tomorrow. That's just how they operate. Build you up to tear you down. That's what gets eyeballs. And it doesn't matter if you're winning or losing. Your star-studded wedding is worth as much as your bitter divorce. Superbowl MVP award = Stage 4 Lung Cancer. No wonder everybody hates them.

eleven

. . .

THE NEXT MORNING, I asked Mom if she wanted to go to Mexico. It was an impulse idea. I needed a vacation and so did she. And I felt bad about what'd happened.

Mom rented a car (that I paid for) and we drove down to Monterrey to stay in a hotel for a week. Mom had a good time. We mostly slept late, ate, and hung around by the pool. Mexican food in Mexico is different from Mexican food in America. They eat goats there. And ant eggs. We had to be careful ordering. Mom had worked as a waitress, so she knew some kitchen Spanish. That was a big help when ordering.

After a while, my mom started getting on my nerves. Her life is pretty boring and, after a couple days, I'd heard everything she had to say about everything—stories about work, trailer park drama, all that. I think she told me about her neighbor who was cheating on her live-in boyfriend with another guy from the trailer park about three times. I tried not to show it when she bugged me. I just talked less. Like, if we were out by the pool, I'd close my eyes and pretend to be asleep.

I took a day off from my mom and spent it alone in Monterrey. I just needed to be by myself. Mom wanted to go buy souvenirs for all her friends back home anyway, so it all worked out.

When our vacation ended, I had to send her back to Montana. She got weepy when we said goodbye at Union Station back in LA and said that she'd pray for me. I felt a little sad when I got on the train home, and I felt bad about being annoyed with my mom. I knew I'd been kind of shitty. The feeling started to fade when we crossed the Rockies, and was completely gone by the time I crossed the Mississippi.

———

It felt good to be back in New York which had started to feel like home. NYC has that energy.

Seth was still waiting on the contractors to finish up the office space. Contractors are the only New Yorkers who don't do things in a hurry. I had a huge backlog of clients. So, I set up in the unfinished space, with a few folding chairs and the smell of fresh paint.

I ditched the gloves too. They *were* too hot and after being on the TV show, I saw that they weren't the trademark that I'd hoped they'd be.

I didn't tell Seth about seeing my mom, because I COULD-N'T. Before I went on the show, I signed a paper saying I couldn't talk about my episode before the premiere. It was all for the best anyway. Seth had finally gotten over the whole age thing and I didn't want to get into another case of him accusing me of lying. At least not so soon. You can imagine how much I dreaded the day when the episode would air.

What I liked about Seth was he was always thinking. He created Ten Dollar Tuesdays as a way to help low-income folks. It became a huge hit. When word got out there a line formed down the block. The problems began when people started camping on the sidewalk on Monday nights. The neighbors complained. Sometimes you try to do a nice thing and it bites you in the ass. My bright idea was to get a truck and drive it to wherever. I even had a name for it: HealMobile. Seth said the cost of the truck would be too much. We compromised by having Seth schedule me to visit different areas on Tuesdays where the neighbors weren't so uptight.

I had made a crazy amount of money and didn't have much time to spend it. I knew the city had awesome nightclubs, but I couldn't go to any of them, because of my age. I could've afforded to live on my own too, but Laura's place was right around the corner from the office, and I liked hanging out with her.

Eventually, the contractors got off their butts and the office space got finished. I had to think about decoration. I didn't want it to look like a doctor's office. We settled on it being more like a spa. Not wind chimes and incense, just comfortable and classy.

I got lots of what they call medical tourists, people who wanted to combine getting healed with a trip to New York. Seth had a map of the world framed and hung it on the wall. We put pins in it to mark all the places our clients had come from. One guy brought his wife all the way from Saudi Arabia. He said witchcraft is punishable by death there and the Saudi government would consider me to be a witch. Note to self: STAY THE HELL OUT SAUDI ARABIA!

———

I stubbed my toe. I was at home, in the kitchen, when I heard my phone ring inside my room. Of course I wanted to see who was calling. When I ran to get it, my little toe hit the leg of a chair. "Ow!" I said, for obvious reasons. It hurt so bad, I thought I'd broken it.

That's when I heard someone say something. I didn't understand the words, even though it sounded like it was coming from someone standing right next to me. But no one was standing next to me. I was home alone. Maybe it was Laura's computer which she'd left on the kitchen table. Or maybe it was Alexa. I stood there for a few seconds, listening. When I didn't hear anything (besides my phone ringing) I forgot about it.

———

The other surprising thing about that September is that I met Ray Benitez, the shortstop for the New York Yankees. When he came into the office, I didn't recognize him. Not a sports fan, y'know. I only found out who he was when I asked about his injury.

"Pulled groin muscle," he said. "Got it when we played the Brewers." Then I noticed that the Yankees team jacket didn't look like a fan jacket.

Ray was a chatty guy. He told me about his grandmother in the Dominican Republic who used to take him to a local healer when he was a kid. Then he told me all about the play-offs (I guessed that the Yankees didn't make it to the World Series that year.) He also told me about how some of the other guys were playing with injuries, yadda yadda yadda. The whole time he was talking, I thought about touching his groin. I wasn't sure how I felt about that. On the one hand: not bad looking and famous. On the other hand: I'd just met the guy. As I've said before, I didn't have to touch him *right* there. It was part of the show. I gave him a squeeze a little south of his bat and balls. Then I charged him up the yin-yang.

———

September 12 was my birthday, and it was easily the best birthday of my life. Laura took me to dinner and then to see *Spinal Tap: The Musical* near Times Square. I'd never been to a

Broadway show before and I had a lot of fun. (I must have been the youngest person in the theater.) My mom called me earlier in the day which felt nice. And Seth bought me a present—the pricey handbag I'd hinted at wanting.

I was seventeen. Still not an adult but pretty close. I couldn't wait to turn eighteen. I so wanted to be an adult and not have to rely on other people for things. I was getting tired of having to ask permission for things, like I was still a little kid.

———

The night of my Hoax Busters episode came a couple months later. Laura, Seth and I watched the show together at home. Laura made popcorn and Seth brought soda, like it was a party. I didn't feel that festive. My stomach was in knots. I could have warned them at the last minute, but I didn't. I just couldn't find the right words.

The first part was Craig talking about faith healers, with random clips of people getting up out of their wheelchairs the second the preacher touched them. It was all totally fake. No one heals that fast.

After a commercial break, they had my interview. I didn't like the way I looked on camera. I looked more nervous than I remembered feeling at the time. Of course, they made a huge deal out of my story about my mom. It was all a setup. Before they went into the next commercial break, they made a big deal out of a "shocking revelation," and they had a shot of me when I first saw my mom. I did look shocked.

During the commercial, Seth asked me about the "shocking revelation." I wanted to run out of there, screaming. But I didn't. Run out screaming, I mean. I told him it was just some BS the show came up with to try to make me look bad.

The show came back, and they dragged out the "shocking

revelation" for a few more minutes. I swear my heart was pounding. I got up to go to the kitchen for another soda.

When my mom appeared, I actually heard Seth gasp. Then he turned to look at me. I just shrugged. What else could I do? We all went back to watching but I knew what was coming.

Hoax Busters tried their hardest to make me look bad. They used every shot of me being pissy and swearing at them. BUT they had to admit that Adam's tumor shrank. The last part was where they talked to Dr. Yee, Adam's oncologist (an oncologist is a cancer doctor) and he was amazed at what he saw on the PET scan.

"Do you believe in faith healers?" Craig asked Dr. Yee.

"No," said the doctor, like he was insulted just being asked that question.

Craig showed the doctor the video of me touching Adam. The doctor had his arms crossed. I could tell he didn't believe any of it. All the doctor could say was, "There's much that medical science doesn't know."

"All publicity is good publicity," I said as soon as the show ended.

Seth was majorly pissed. "I can't believe we're having this same conversation all over again."

I explained why I couldn't tell him earlier, about the paper I signed. I looked at Laura. She was my lawyer. She would understand that. But she didn't jump in to defend me, like she wanted to stay out of it.

"That doesn't matter," he said. "It's that you told the story in the first place!"

I explained what I said to Craig, that I never said the story about my mom was true, and that I needed to tell people something.

"Didn't you think people would find out?" he asked, like I was crazy.

"I don't know," I said. "I never thought I'd be on TV like

that. Anyway, now it doesn't matter why I can do what I do. All's well that ends well."

Seth still looked mad. "It matters if people can trust you, and I can't trust you anymore. First about your age. Now this." He threw his hands into the air. "I don't think I can be your business manager anymore."

That gave me a jolt. "You have to!" I said. "We have a deal!" I looked at Laura. "Right?"

"Legally, it's his business," she said. "He can shut it down any time he wants."

I couldn't believe that my lawyer (and BFF) wasn't taking my side. "I don't care!" I said to (yelled at) Seth. "I'm the one with the superpowers. I can make it on my own or get someone else to be my manager. Now that I'm famous, there'll be a ton of people waiting to work with me."

"Well go find them!" he said. And then he stormed out.

There was a moment of silence, just me and Laura. "Can he really shut down the business?" I asked. I had to admit that the thought of doing this without Seth felt scary.

"Legally he's in his rights," she said. "But he signed the lease on the office space so he's responsible for the rent, no matter what. If he doesn't want to go into debt, he'll have to work something out with you."

Hearing that was a huge relief and it felt good having Laura back on my side again. "Would you explain that to him then?" I said.

"I can talk to him about the business side, but you need to patch things up with him first," she said.

I didn't want to have to do that. Seth and I had made up a couple times before and it was stressful. I made a face.

"Let's give him some time to cool off," said Laura.

That sounded good to me. "Okay," I said. I didn't ask her if she thought I was wrong about telling that story about my mom. I didn't want to know.

your best life 12:

Shipping.

We all need someone to love and someone to love us. Finding love is harder when you're a celebrity. That's why movie star marriages are revolving doors. You would think that two people who have everything going for them could live happily ever after. So, what's the problem?

First off, a celebrity's dating pool is smaller. Sounds weird, but it's true. There aren't many people who you can relate to when you're famous. That's why celebrities date other celebrities. Can you imagine Taylor Swift dating the manager of a Costco? Like, what would they talk about? She'd say, "They added Australia to my world tour schedule," and he'd say, "We had a cleanup on aisle six."

And the part about adding Australia to the world tour - celebrities are busy. You always have to be somewhere doing something. And so does your famous flame. You can spend time together, if it fits into *both* of your schedules. That's why actors hook up with people they're in a movie with.

Another thing is that your careers have to be headed in the same direction. Two TV stars might meet on the same level, but what happens if her series has 8 seasons and wins a ton of awards, and his series is cancelled? I'll tell you what happens - she starts thinking about cancelling the relationship.

I haven't figured out the whole dating thing yet. But I'll tell you this: Your most important relationship is with your audience.

twelve

. . .

I DIDN'T CALL Seth that night. Or the next day. I tried to get Laura to do it, but she refused.

Seth hadn't officially closed the business so I went to the office as usual and did the best I could. Wow, did he do a lot of the work! I got behind in my appointments and I got snippety with some of the clients. So not a good day.

I hadn't been on social media that much since leaving for New York. I wanted to be 100% focused on making it and didn't want the distraction. (You can waste a lot of time on Snapchat, believe me!) Also, I didn't want anyone in Montana to know what I was up to. Not just because they might tell my mom, but also just in case I failed. I knew I would make it big and everything, but y'know, just in case... Of course, it blew up after I was on TV and everyone from my past life sent me messages, even people who didn't know me that well, even people who'd been mean to me. It's the price of fame. I got back to some of them, especially my guinea pigs – the people I tested my abilities on back in Montana.

Orin, this kid from my high school badmouthed me on social media, trying to make #destinythefake at thing. Orin has dyslexia and, before I knew what my powers were exactly, I told him I could cure him. I remember sitting down with him in the school cafeteria. He was surprised I did that (because I'd never sat with him before) and happy (because he was hot for me). I didn't have any trouble getting him to let me touch him. Anyway, nothing changed for him because he was born dyslexic, and he was mad. I responded to some of his posts with an explanation of my powers and I told him I was sorry I couldn't help him. That didn't do any good, probably because he thought he could make himself King of the Haters. There's a lot of that online. People I'd never even met called me a fake. Like, how could they know? After a while I just stopped responding to the haters. It seemed too much of a waste of time. If they wanted to be broken and miserable, that was their problem.

Another person who reconnected with me was Ray, a rancher who I helped after he got his hand mangled by a posthole digger. His hand healed up. Now it was his lower back giving him trouble. I told him to come to New York, and I could fix it.

That gave me the idea of doing a tour, just like a rock star. I could have a bus take me all over America and, wherever I went, I could help people. The only problem was that it would take a lot of organizing that I didn't have the time or talent for. Seth would be great at that. I had to call him.

———

After a week of struggling at the office (and Seth not closing it) I called him in the middle of the day.

"Hey," he said.

"Hey," I said. "I need you to come back."

"Really?" he said.

"Yeah," I said. "I'm a little overwhelmed."

He sighed. "I don't know..."

"We have to make this work," I said. "We need each other."

"I think I'm okay on my own," he said.

I told him what Laura had said about him being responsible for the rent.

"Is that how it's going to be?" he said. "You're going to blackmail me?"

"I don't think that counts as blackmail," I said. (I looked up the definition of blackmail later, and I was right.)

"Okay," he said. "Arm twisting, then."

"We've got a good thing going here," I said. "And we're just getting started. This could be huge."

"Without trust, I don't see how that can happen," he said. He went quiet for a minute. "How *did* you get your superpowers? For real."

"I think I'm done talking about that," I said. "I don't want to cause any more trouble."

"More trouble?"

"Yeah," I said, "Everybody's waiting to jump all over me as soon as I say the wrong thing."

"I don't think you're the victim here," he said.

"Aw, c'mon, Craig Hanson was totally out to get me!" I said.

"Okay, you're right about that," he admitted. "But you set yourself up."

"I know," I said. "That was dumb." And we had another minute of silence. "Did you get your old job back?" I asked.

"No," he said. "I spent the last couple days working on my screenplay. I hadn't touched it in weeks. I needed to get back to it. I've thought about it, and I want to be a filmmaker, not a business guy."

"But you're such a good business guy," I said, and meant it.

"I'm a good filmmaker, too," he said.

After another long, awkward pause, I said. "Okay, so I'll just go back to working out of the coffeehouse while I find a new business partner. You still owe me some money so..."

"I'll get you what I owe you," he said, and I believed him. Then we said our good-byes.

I woke up in the middle of the night thinking about that phone call. It took me while to work it through, but here's what I thought was going on:

Seth couldn't understand all my decisions because he doesn't know everything I've been through. My life has been A LOT rougher than his. He still sees both of his parents; his parents have a lot of money; and he got to go to college.

Having gone to college is one of Seth's problems. In college they teach you how things work IN THEORY. You can read a million books and still not know anything about life. The School of Hard Knocks doesn't have any books, lectures or term papers. It's all tests.

The other thing is Seth can't understand what it's like to have my abilities. I found that scene from the Spider-Man movie on YouTube. As Peter Parker walks away from Uncle Ben's grave, he says, "Whatever life holds in store for me, I will never forget these words: With great power comes great responsibility. This is my gift, my curse." I can totally relate to that. If it's my responsibility, then it's my decision what I tell people about it.

———

A guy came into the office not long after I opened, wearing jeans, a trucker cap and fake smile. "Destiny!" he said.

I kinda knew who it was and braced myself. "Yup," I said, my mouth going dry. "Do you have an appointment?"

"Uh, no," he said. "But does your own dad need one?"

I knew he would turn up sometime and I hadn't been looking forward to it. I had thought about what I would say to him. How pissed I was for him running out on me and mom. For not paying child support. For not contacting me on birthdays or holidays. For not even checking to see if I was alive. I had so much I planned to say but, now that he was standing there, my stomach went into a knot, and I could barely get the words out. I just wanted him gone. "What are you doing here?" I asked, even though I knew the answer. He came here because I was famous, and he thought he could get something from me.

"Just saw that my little girl is blowing up," he said. "And I wanted to come tell you how proud I am."

That was total BS. "Okay," I said, trying to stay calm. "Good to know."

"Look," he said, "I know you're probably mad at me, and I can understand. I'm sorry. Really, I am. Your mother and I... Well, we just weren't right for each other. I tried, really, I did. But in the end... It just didn't work out the way either of us wanted it to."

"That's not how mom tells it," I said. Mom had always told me that he was unreliable and untrustworthy.

"Your mother has issues," he said, and that's when I stopped listening.

"I have to get back to work," I said.

"That's what I'm here about," he said. "I thought maybe you could use a manager."

"What?!" I said.

"A manager," he said. "Someone to run the show while you... You know..." He waved his hand in the air. "Do your thing."

"I know what a manager is," I said. "I already have some-one." It was a fib that needed to be told.

"You're better off working with family," he said. "Family are the only people you can trust."

That was total BS too. This guy was a complete a-hole. Maybe he did us a favor by leaving.

A client walked in, and I turned away from him to say hello. She asked if I could save her the time and trouble of a hip replacement. I said I could and kept talking to her, ignoring my dad.

Dad stood there like an idiot for a couple minutes before getting the hint and leaving. But I knew he'd be back.

———

I knew Seth would be back too. He *was* on the hook for the rent, and he had to realize that I was still his best job option. He contacted me and we had a make-up lunch at a burrito place on Fifth Avenue. (There's a Fifth Avenue in Brooklyn too.)

It felt weird seeing him again. I had to admit that I'd missed him, and not just for his business skills. Even if we weren't together, we were still close. He and Laura were the only people I thought of as being in my inner circle.

"Is there anything else I need to know about you?" he asked, while we ate chips and guac.

"I don't think so," I said. "I think I told you everything."

"You *think*?" he said. "Is you real name Destiny Wallace?"

"Of course!" I said.

"And you're really from Montana?"

"Yeah!" I said. "What kind of crazy questions are those?"

"Just making sure," he said.

"C'mon," I said. "You know me better than anyone."

"You still have the capacity to surprise me," he said.

"A girl has to keep a little bit of mystery about her," I said.

"This will only work with complete transparency," he said.

That sounded crazy to me. I couldn't tell him everything. Nobody does that. "Sure," I said. Complete transparency."

By the time the waiter asked if we wanted another basket of chips, he was my manager again.

———

I was in a good position. I had Seth back, taking care of business and, now that I was (semi)famous, I could jump back into dating. I just needed to find someone closer to my age, another teenager. And I needed someone less uptight.

I met Bran (Short for Branford, not Brandon) at a house concert he performed at. I was invited to the show by Bethany, a client who I cured after a bungee cord hit her in the eye. She was a musician and knew about cool shows around the city, ones that other people didn't have a clue about. This one was at a house in the West Village. There were about forty people there, sitting in a living room.

Bran came out with his guitar, and I was immediately smitten. He was tall, and thin, with dark wavy hair that hung down over his fabulously blue eyes. AND he had an amazing voice. AND he was an amazing songwriter. After the show I went up to him and told him how much I loved his music. Bethany talked me up, telling him about my "superpowers." I could see that he was impressed so I asked him out on a date. He said yes. Ka-boom!

————

I wanted to wow Bran, so I took him to a four-star restaurant in Manhattan. We exchanged life stories. Turns out, his mom was a big deal in the entertainment biz as a concert organizer. She'd put together world tours for some huge name acts. He totally had the inside track on his career. He was only nineteen and he was going to be huge.

I'm going to be huge, I thought. We could be great for each other.

He talked about his music the whole time and I was impressed by his passion. I asked him where he gets his ideas for the words, and he told me he writes straight from the heart. I totally believed that. Here's a sample:

• • •

Fred Stesney

I'm a victim of truth,
   A survivor of reality,
   A possessor of youth,
   An American hyperbole
   A speaker of words,
   A singer of songs,
   A vessel of pain,
   A writer of wrongs,
   And that's how it's *supposed* to be—"writer of wrongs," not "righter of wrongs." It's so clever. That's from a song called "Figment of My Immolation."

After dinner happened like something out of a movie. We took a cab downtown and walked across the Brooklyn Bridge. It was the perfect night for it, clear and warm.

We were standing halfway across the bridge, looking out at the harbor, when he told me about his ex-girlfriend. Not the sort of thing you bring up on a first date, but he felt he had to tell me, because he was an artist, and artists don't hold things inside. The story was that he had been in love with her, and she had said she was in love with him, and then she dumped him. (That seemed crazy to me, but her loss.) Then - like right out of a movie – I put my hand on his chest, and I said, "I cure broken hearts, you know." Then we kissed. It was the most amazing date of my life.

your best life 13:

How to Be a Good Person Even If You Don't Drive a Trolley Car.

Some people think a lot about doing the right thing. You'd think it was simple, like "do unto others," etc. But no. People argue about it, and by "people", I mean philosophers. They do things like make up crazy what-if situations about trolley cars speeding down tracks towards crowds of people. (And there's another one called the Prisoner's Dilemma that's not so crazy if you and a buddy are thinking of robbing a bank.) For those of us who aren't ever going to be trolley drivers, here are some basic ways for how to be a good person:

Altruism (Had to look up all these words.) says that you should do what's best for most people, even if it's bad for you. Like, if you have a million dollars, you should give it all to the poor, even if it makes yourself poor.

I say this doesn't work in real life because you can't expect people to give away all their money. That's just not the American way.

Ethical Egoism is the opposite. The idea there is that you should always do what's best for you. Like, if you have a million dollars, you should buy yourself a new house, if that makes you happy. Or give it all away, if that makes you happy.

My guess is that most ethical egoists are going to buy the new house.

Utilitarianism is somewhere in between. It's like altruism except that you include yourself when you think about what's good for the most people. Like, if you get a million dollars, you can buy yourself a new house as long as you invite everybody over for a party every once in a while.

I think I'm a utilitarianist. I help people, while I'm helping myself. I think most people are utilitarian. It's just human nature.

thirteen

· · ·

BRAN WAS WAY MORE fun than Seth. Bran liked to go out at night. He had musician friends all over the city and, through his mom's connections, we went to all the biggest tours when they came to New York.

I shifted office hours so that I didn't start until 11AM and I worked until 8PM. That was better for people who had to work, and better for me so I could go straight from work to whatever fun thing I had planned for the night. And I could sleep in a little the next morning. Win-win!

I'd get to the office, and I couldn't tell Seth about what I did the night before. He got all frowny when I'd tell him about hanging around backstage with superstars. Whatever, party-pooper. Our relationship was strictly business anyway, so I didn't have to care what he thought.

Weird story: Bran and I were watching a band play at Madison Square Garden, and it took me a few songs to notice that the drummer only had one arm. I asked Bran about it, and he said that the dude had lost it a car crash. Bran had to throw some names around to get us backstage, but we got to meet the one-armed wonder and I did my bit on him. Months later, I saw a picture of him on vacation and I could see the new arm growing out of his shoulder. It looked like a baby's arm because that's how it works—it's like that one part of you grows up on its own, but faster. (I thought maybe an old person could cut all her skin off and, while it was growing back, it would look a lot younger. Not a bad plan, but first you'd have to cut all your skin off and who wants to do that?)

I liked being in Bran's crowd, but I never felt totally a part of it. I couldn't talk shop with the other musicians who would go on about amps and guitars and all that sort of stuff. I realized that there was no crowd for me to hang with. I was unique—which was great—but it made me an outsider wherever I went.

Like Seth predicted, the people who really hated me were doctors. I went to a party Bran's mom put together for some charity. It was fancy-schmancy, with servers walking around with trays of tiny food. Everyone there was older, and college educated, so I stuck to Bran like glue. Bran had to go to the men's room, and I was left standing all by myself feeling like a fish out of water on Mars. I guess Bran's mom was trying to be helpful because she pulled me aside and said, "There's someone you should meet." Then she introduced me to a heart surgeon. The guy looked like a heart surgeon, maybe? I don't know. I'd never met one before.

He asked me where I go to school, and I told him I don't. I could tell he thought I was too young to be out of school, like I was a dropout, which I was. I felt embarrassed and irritated. Why did Bran's mom think I should meet this guy?

We stood there for a second, not saying anything, and I got the bright idea that I don't know much about hearts and how they go wrong. Maybe heart patients were a whole other type of customer I could connect with. "Like, what kinds of problems do you fix?" I asked.

"I performed a coronary artery bypass today," he said, and I could tell he thought that made him the bomb.

"That's, like, what?" I asked.

"It's where the blocked portion of the coronary artery is bypassed with another piece of blood vessel," he said.

Did I mention that I'd been drinking? Bran had made friends with one of the bartenders who was slipping us drinks. That might explain what came out of my mouth next:

"I could have done that," I said.

"I highly doubt it," said the heart surgeon.

"Well yeah," I said. "I wouldn't have needed to cut the guy open."

"It wasn't a guy," said the surgeon.

"Guy... Girl... Doesn't matter," I said. "I could have healed her just by touching her." And when I said this, I held up my hand.

The heart surgeon looked at my palm for a second then said, "Ah, well, I don't put any stock in any of that new age nonsense."

Now I was pissed. "It's not new age nonsense! It's not new age at all! It's..." I didn't know how to explain it to this guy. "I saved a guy who got shot," I said. "Want me to call him?"

"That will not be necessary," said the heart surgeon.

Luckily Bran showed up before I lost it on this know-it-all dickhead. I think Bran could tell things were not going well. He stood there, looking back and forth at me and the heart surgeon, trying to figure out the deal.

"If you'll excuse me," said the stupid heart surgeon and he peeled off into the crowd.

"What was that all about?" asked Bran.

I told him what had just gone down. He sighed. "I think my mom was trying to help," he said.

"It was the opposite," I said. I felt so mad. I thought maybe his mom didn't like me and was trying to embarrass me or get me to do something that would make Bran not like me. If she was, it worked.

"It's a party," said Bran. "Let's just try to have fun."

"This isn't fun," I said. "This is a bunch of snobs who think they're better than everyone else because they have a piece of paper with fancy writing all over it."

We left right after that and went downtown to hear his friend's band play. So much better.

A couple nights later, Bran took me to a Halloween party. I didn't have a lot of time to get a costume together, so I went as Saint Destiny (A Virgin Mary costume, really.) A girl in a sexy cat costume (one of many) came up to me.

"Saint Destiny!" she said. "I need you to heal me."

"What's the problem?" I asked, not sure if she was serious or not.

"I hurt my knee in my kickboxing class. It's been a couple weeks, and it still hurts. I need a doctor's referral to see a specialist - which is a total pain on the ass – so, like, maybe you can save me the trouble."

I said what I always said when people approached me outside office hours. "Call my office tomorrow and make an appointment. I can probably squeeze you in later this week."

She didn't like hearing that. "But you're dressed like a saint, right?" She said. "Aren't you supposed to be performing miracles?"

"You're dressed like a cat," I said. "So, I'll tell you what – You take a shit in a litter box and I'll heal your knee."

That got rid of her. (Sometimes it's fun to tell people off.)

And there was the time I got a call at 1AM from a woman who I'll call "Lia," and she said she got my number from a friend of a friend of Bran's. She sounded scared. I had a hard time understanding her German accent, but it sounded like her boyfriend had taken something that had made him sick, and she was afraid he would die. She wanted me to come over right then and there.

I was at a party at a photographer's loft and having a good time. I told her I needed a thousand to get me there. She said okay and gave me an address in Greenwich Village.

It wasn't far from the party, and I got there in twenty minutes. When "Lia" answered the door, I saw it was a famous supermodel. She looked different wearing sweatpants and without all the makeup, but it was definitely her. As she led me to the bedroom, I remembered who her boyfriend was. It saw it on TMZ.

Sure enough, stretched out on the bed (in his underwear) was a movie actor I'll call "Miller Hickenbotham" to protect his career. He looked paralyzed. His eyes were wide open staring at the ceiling. The sheets were soaked in sweat. I put my hand on his bare chest and thought *OMG, I am actually touching (real name of actor)*! His heart was going a mile a minute. I touched his head too, just to be sure. His sweat on my hands felt gross so I went into the bathroom to wash up.

"He'll be okay," I said to "Lia." "I should stay here for a while, until he comes out of it."

That was not necessary. It just wanted an excuse to meet "Miller."

"Lia" said that was okay. "But you can't tell anyone."

"I understand," said. "I keep all my celebrity clients confidential."

When "Miller" came back from the brink, he felt lucky to still be alive. "Lia" introduced me and told him I'd saved his life. He thanked me and shook my hand. He was still in his underwear when he did it.

———

Laura became my BFF when it came to boy stuff. We'd have dinner once a week and I'd fill her in on every fabulous thing that'd happened since last time I saw her. Sometimes I'd drop a name that she couldn't catch. I had to explain to her who a lot of celebrities are. It wasn't just that she was older, it was because she wasn't that into movies and music and social media.

I got the funny feeling that she wasn't crazy about Bran. When I'd gush about him, she'd just listen and nod. She never said anything *bad* about him. It's just that she never said anything *good* about him either.

It was at one of those dinners that Laura told me that she had had sex for the first time since her accident. TMI was my first reaction, because I still thought of her as my second mom. But I was also totally happy for her. She'd met Peter online – another lawyer – and they'd hit it off. I'd met him a couple times when he came over to the apartment to pick up Laura. He seemed like a good guy. Not a hunk, but Laura wasn't a babe, so they were a good fit. (If you want to know how attractive you are, just look at who goes out with you.) I wondered if Laura had ever shown him a picture of herself before her makeover. Probably not. That would definitely have killed the mood.

————

Bran picked me up at the office for the first time. I'd hoped to keep Seth and Bran away from each other, but it was super convenient for Bran to pick me up after work and I couldn't tip-toe around Seth forever. (And Seth broke up with ME anyway.)

"What's that dude's problem?" Bran asked me as soon as we got out on the sidewalk.

"What do you mean?" I asked, even though I knew what he meant.

"He looked at me like... Did you used to go out with him?"

I was shocked that it was that obvious. "Yeah," I said. "But he broke up with me, so I don't know what his deal is."

"And you're still business partners with him?" said Bran, like that was a weird idea.

"Yeah," I said. "Because of my age, I need someone to run the business part." (I had already told Bran that I was seventeen and he was totally cool with it.) "But don't worry. That's all over. It's strictly business now."

Bran never mentioned it again. He was *that* cool.

———

Thanksgiving came and I hoped to spend it with Bran's family— BUT he said he, his mom, and his sisters were going to visit their uncle in Chicago. He didn't invite me, and that was okay, because of the whole flying thing. He promised that we'd spend Christmas together here in NYC.

So, I flew my mom out for Thanksgiving. Laura was in town, so it was the three of us. Mom and I watched the Macy's Thanksgiving Day Parade on the TV, just like we did when I was a kid. Laura spent most of the time in the kitchen, cooking. She was excited to make a turkey. She'd never done it before.

My mom was SO embarrassing. All she could talk about at dinner were the TV shows she watched and the people she worked with at the diner, none of who were at all interesting. She went on and on about how Brenda—another waitress— was trying to teach herself Italian. Or that Gus, one of the short order cooks, plays in a bluegrass band. Like who gives a rat's ass? Not me.

And then she farted and thought that no one else heard it. I wanted to crawl under the table and die.

Laura didn't come out and say it, but she must have thought my mom was annoying. Seeing them together. I couldn't help but see that Laura was the better mom. I know that's a crappy thing to say, but it was true.

―――――――

Another celebrity on drugs story: I got an offer to go on tour with a singer named Puma Silva. She had a reputation for being a garbage disposal for drugs and alcohol. Like, she couldn't walk past a line of something without snorting it, or see an open bottle and not empty it. My only job on the tour would be to save her if she put something in her body that would kill her.

It sounded like a good gig to me. They offered a hefty amount, and all my living expenses would be paid for. I'd get to travel the world, stay in fancy hotels, and hang around backstage while meeting a ton of celebrities.

Seth didn't like the idea. He said that we were still building my brand and that doing the tour would take me off the map for almost a year. "You're not nationally famous yet," he said. "You need to stay in the public eye."

I didn't entirely trust Seth's advice. He hated Puma's music and probably would've been okay with her dying.

I asked Laura and she said it was a moral decision.

"You have an amazing gift," she said. "You have to ask yourself how you can use it that will most benefit society." Then she looked at me, expecting me to think it through.

"Well," I said. "You mean putting aside what's going to make me the most money, and be the most fun..."

"Yes," she said. "Putting your self-interest aside.

I had to think hard about this. "I don't know," I said. "Can you give me some clues?"

"Think through all the possible outcomes," she said.

"Okay," I said. "Let's say I go on the tour and Puma OD's and I save her. Big win."

"Big win for whom?" she asked.

"For her. And for her fans. Also, for all the people who're counting on that tour to earn their paychecks."

"Okay, good," she said. "What's another possible outcome?" she asked, and I felt like I was back in high school, getting grilled by one of my teachers.

"I don't go," I said. "And she OD's and dies."

"Isn't it possible that, if you don't go, and she OD's, they'll have a doctor there to save her? Or that she may not OD at all?"

"Yeah," I said. "Those are both possible."

"And what if you stay?" she said.

"I'll help a bunch of people," I said. "That's for sure."

"And just those people?" she asked.

"No," I said, thinking about all the parents I saw with their children. "It also helps the people around them."

"It's more than that," she said. "When you make someone's life better, they send positive ripples out into the world, ones you'll never know about."

I had to admit she was right. I had to turn down tour offer. Morality can be a buzzkill.

But I thought about it some more and realized that Seth was right. Why should I spend my time living in the shadow of a celebrity when I can be out there making *myself* into a celebrity? And the tour would take me away from Bran.

But working at the office turned into a grind. Seth hired a receptionist/assistant to help speed people in and out. Tiara would check people's names against the appointment list, take the money and explain a million times that we didn't take medical insurance.

Having Tiara there left me with almost nothing to do. Healing people was easy. I could literally do it with my eyes closed. I could have done it while watching a movie or texting. But for appearances' sake, I had to look like I was making an effort. So many people came through the door, they all became a blur. I tried to keep up my signature phrase, but it wasn't easy saying the same six words a dozen times every hour. Some days I would mix it up. Sometimes I tried out movie quotes:

"There's no place like home. There's no place like home."

"We're gonna need a bigger boat."

"Sweep the leg, Johnnie."

When Tiara noticed what I was doing she started to giggle. Then it became a game of trying to make her laugh. Like when I said "Do you feel lucky? Well, do ya, punk?" to a kindergartener.

I kept reminding myself how much money I was making. I could see at least a dozen clients in an hour, and I worked eight hours a day. That comes to (for people who are as bad at math as me) $2,400 an hour. Multiply that by 5 and you get $12,000 a week. Even after Seth took his percentage. I added up. And that was without "freelance." (Like the time I saved "Miller Hickenbotham.") I spent more money, too. It's amazing how much money you can spend when you're not looking at price tags. I couldn't believe how I'd survived when I first got to NYC.

———

Seth scheduled a trip to a town in upstate New York. Upstate New York is what you call anything outside of New York City. You can find farmers up there. Also hippies. We were going up there to visit an entire town that'd been poisoned.

I felt a little sleepy that morning, because I partied the night before and stayed at Bran's afterward.

"Late night last night?" asked Seth when we went to pick up the rental car.

"Mmm-hmm," I said. I was wearing the same clothes I wore the night before. The boots were high on the thigh and the top cut way low, not exactly appropriate for the occasion.

"How's it going with... Brad?" he asked.

"Bran," I said, annoyed because Seth knew my boyfriend's name. "And it's going good," I said. "He's really cool."

Seth looked at me weird.

"What?" I said.

He shrugged. "Nothing, I just asked how it was going."

"And I said it's all good," I said.

"I heard that," he said.

He sounded sarcastic and I didn't want to deal with that, so in went the earbuds and I didn't say anything during the three-hour the car ride.

———

When we got to Cobblesville, it was grey, and the trees were bare. East coast winters were a bigger bummer than Montana winters. Grayer, I guess. The town had some Christmas decorations up which helped a little.

No one looked sick. The deal was that lead had gotten into the town's water supply. Seth told me what a big deal that was. Lead can mess with your brain and it's especially bad for babies and kids. Cobblesville was still arguing with the state government about who to blame, and who should get the lead out of the water, when they called me. I saved an entire town before the sun went down just like a superhero. I got paid too. The town raised the money online.

On the car ride home, I thought about all the towns across America that could use my help, all those folks who weren't important enough to get their problems solved by the people in charge. And I felt glad to get out of there too. Depressed little towns gave me flashbacks. And that got me thinking about my mom still working at the truck stop. I decided to send her $1G a month. I could afford it and it meant a lot to her. When she got the first check, she was so happy because her car needed a solenoid replacement, and it was going to cost $850.

Wow, auto mechanics charge almost as much as I do!

————

Two weeks before Christmas, Bran told me that he and his family were going to Antigua (which is an island in the Caribbean). I got SO MAD.

"When were you going to tell me this?" I asked him.

"I'm telling you now," he said.

"You said we were going to spend Christmas together," I said. "In New York."

"You can come, if you want," he said.

(Mind you, this whole conversation happened backstage, right before he was supposed to go on.)

"You know I can't fly," I said.

"Take a boat then," he said. "We'll pick you up at the dock."

"That's ridiculous," I said.

He shrugged, then picked up his guitar and slung it over his shoulder. I wanted to grab it and break it over his head. "The invitation stands," he said and walked on stage.

I ended up back in Montana to be with my mom for Christmas. I thought about having her out again, like I did at Thanksgiving, but I didn't want to have my mom and Laura in the same room again. It felt too awkward.

A blizzard hit the Midwest and I almost didn't make it. Halfway through the train ride I wondered if it would have been easier to sail to Antigua. Mom picked me up at the train station in Billings and drove me to the Hampton Inn, the nicest hotel in town.

It felt weird being back home. Everything looked the same, but I was different. Again, I had that creepy feeling knowing that I'd barely escaped all of this. When we checked into our suite, I looked at the people working behind the desk and thought, *there but for the grace of God go I.*

Mom and I exchanged presents. I gave her a necklace I

bought at Bloomingdales. She bought me a sweater. I thanked her, even though it didn't go with my new look. Now that I was the rock star of what I did, I started to dress like it. More black leather and taller shoes.

Seth called to wish me a merry Christmas. That was nice.

"What are you doing today?" I asked since I knew he was Jewish and didn't celebrate Christmas.

"I had Chinese food with my mom last night and I'm doing the same with my dad tonight."

"Chinese food?" I said. "That's weird."

"It's the traditional Christmas dinner for New York Jews," he said.

"Don't order the chicken testicles," I said.

"Testicle on Thirty-Fourth Street," he said, and I laughed. I'd spent enough time with him that I could get most of his movie jokes.

I made it back to New York just in time to spend New Year's Eve with Bran. A band he was friends with got a gig on a round-Manhattan cruise and we went as "stowaways."

Damn, it was cold! Too cold to stand out on deck and look at the city. I hid below deck the whole time, drunk off my ass hoping not to vomit. Bran and I kissed at midnight while everyone blew horns and shouted, "Happy New Year!" It was the best New Years Eve of my life.

———

Bran played a showcase in Manhattan. (That's a concert where anyone can come but it's supposed to be for people in the music industry to check out new acts.) This one was a big deal. He was inches away from getting signed by a label. We were both super excited.

Being with Bran became the perfect way to sneak into bars. I just said, "I'm with the band," and no one ever asked me for ID. (I still carried my fake one, just in case.)

A good-sized crowd turned out, and Bran was being his usually phenomenally talented self, when he said he had a new song.

I'd never heard it before, so I listened carefully. About halfway through, I realized it was about his ex-girlfriend, the one who'd dumped him right before we started dating. And it wasn't a "I hate you, now go die" kind of song, more like a "I still miss you" song.

WTF?

I spent the rest of his set feeling weird.

I didn't ask him about it right after the show A.) Because I didn't want to seem insecure. And B.) because he needed to schmooze with the industry people. Instead, I pulled out my fake ID, and ordered myself the first of three Moscow Mules.

I asked him about it when we rode in a car (that I paid for) back to his place.

"Yeah, it's about Miranda," he admitted.

I felt the rug come right out from under me. "Are you still in love with her?" I asked, even though I didn't want to know.

"Yeah," he said.

"And that's how you let me know?!" I asked.

"I didn't write the song to let you know," he said. "I wrote it because that's what I'm feeling."

"What about my feelings?" I said, pissed.

"I can't second guess myself that way," he said. "I can't not write a song because it might upset you."

Suddenly, I felt like a hick again, like I was just some dumb girl from Montana who didn't know about art, or artists or relationships.

"Okay," I said. "I guess that makes sense." But it didn't.

I arrived at the office the next day still feeling confused about the previous night. Seth was there and he saw something was wrong, but he didn't ask about it.

As my clients came in and out, I felt better. I could save lives. I had superpowers. I was a goddess. Other people would write songs about me. Books. Screenplays. I was going to rule the world!

That night, I thought about the Bran thing some more and realized that my ex was also my business partner and Bran seemed cool with it so maybe I'd overreacted about him writing a song about his ex.

I decided to be mature about it and let it go.

your best life 14:

The Magical Land of Success.

After you've slept on floors, lived on junk food, worn the same pair of underwear three days in a row, and made every other sacrifice for your career, the day comes when you take the golden key, unlock the golden door and walk through to the Magical Land of Success.

It's amazing and strange when it happens. The Magical Land of Success is wide open and full of possibilities. Mountains become mole hills and, what once looked like the Great Wall of China, now looks like a waist-high cyclone fence. The cold wind that always blew in your face is now a warm breeze at your back. Money grows on trees there, and swag bags jump into your lap like kittens. And there's less gravity in the Land of Success so you can go bouncing along like an astronaut on the moon.

That's all cool. But without guardrails and speed limits, it's super easy to drive off the cliff no one told you about.

fourteen

. . .

SETH MADE a plan for us to go to the Global Wellness Summit, a holistic medicine conference at the Florida Hotel & Conference Center in Orlando. It was still the dead of winter and Orlando sounded like heaven.

Seth tried to talk me into flying just to save time. "Statistically speaking, flying is by far safer that driving," he said.

"I guess," I said. "But I don't like the idea of being trapped in a metal tube so far off the ground."

"You can watch a movie, if that'll take your mind off it," he said.

"No, that wouldn't work," I said.

"But..." he said, and I cut him off.

"Drop it, before I go full diva on you." That shut him up.

We drove down in a rent-a-car, staying at Ramada Inns along the way. Seth said that it paid to always stay at Ramada's because of their membership program. He was so practical, which is what you want in a business partner.

Orlando delivered on the promise of warmth and sunshine. It felt good walking around outside in a t-shirt.

The hotel was jammed with acupuncturists, herbalists, psychics, etc. And there was stuff I'd never heard of, like

146

Craniosacular Therapy, Matrix Energetics and Pranic Healing. (I'm not making this stuff up. You can google them.)

My being there created a lot of buzz and Seth had set up a string of interviews, one right after the other. I met with a reporter from the Journal of Alternative and Complementary Medicine and one from Alternative Medicine Magazine. (I'd never heard of either.) There were also some bloggers and YouTubers who were supposed to be a big deal.

After what happened on Hoax Busters, I needed a new story about how I got my powers. On the drive down I came up with a story that would sound true and be impossible to disprove. This is how it appeared in the Journal of Alternative and Complementary Medicine:

Ms. Wallace tells a tale of driving home from a party late at night and seeing a man hitchhiking by the side of the highway. "It was near freezing out," she says, "and the guy was wearing just a jean jacket." She pulled over to offer him a ride and the man accepted. He claimed he was a Crow and that he was on his way back to the reservation. Out of kindness, Ms. Wallace made the hour-and-a-half trip to Lodge Grass.

When they arrived the man - "who had said only two words the entire drive" according to Ms. Wallace - turned to her. "I've been searching for you for many moons," he said. "You have a great spirit within you." Ms. Wallace didn't understand the message and forgot about it by the time she drove back to Billings.

Only weeks later did she start having dreams filled with Native American imagery. "I didn't know much about Native American culture at the time," she said. "I did some research but still couldn't put it all together."

She says the answer came to her while she was at home washing the dishes. "I knew what the great spirit was. I knew what I could do."

I'd warned Seth that morning at breakfast that I was going to tell a bogus story to the press. I'd learned my lesson. I knew better than to lie to him.

"Why not tell them the truth?" he asked.

"This is more interesting," I said.

"This is going to blow up in your face, too," he said, shaking his head.

"How?" I said. "It's just me and the hitchhiker in the story. There's no one to contradict me."

"The Crow people aren't going to like it," he said.

"How do you know?" I said.

"I just do," he said.

"Bet you're wrong," I said. "This story is foolproof."

I took a bunch of photos with random people, and I think I was the only teenager there. It was a lot of grey hair, tie-dye, bare feet and body odor.

I sat up in my room, waiting to go downstairs to do what Seth called a showcase. I was on after the Radical Feminist Pregnancy Seminar and before the headliner, Dr. Ming Tao, acupuncturist to the stars. He was a real doctor who—if you believed the hype—cured cancer just by sticking needles into people.

Seth came to my room to walk me downstairs. "Is that what you're wearing?" were the first words he said to me when I opened the door.

"Yeah," I said. "Obviously." It was something I'd bought back in New York right before we left. It was high at the thigh and sparkly.

Seth made a face, and I knew he thought it looked either too sexy, or too bling, or both.

"What?" I asked. "I saw a dude in the lobby wearing a diaper!"

"It was a loincloth," he said.

"Same thing!" I said and that shut him up. He knew I was right.

———

I walked into the main ballroom and stopped in my tracks. It was packed! "Did you know about this?" I asked Seth. "I mean, all these people?"

"I didn't think it was going to be this big," he said, and I could tell that he was surprised too.

The Conference Director went up on stage to introduce me. *Queen of the Quacks*, I thought as I stood at the side of the room, feeling nervous. The Conference Director talked me up, listing all the amazing things I'd done. As he went on, I felt my confidence build. I *was* all that!

"Would you please welcome to the stage, Destiny Wallace!"

That was my cue.

I crossed the room to loud applause, feeling everyone's eyes on me. I was glad I wore the sexy, sparkly outfit. When I got up on stage, the lights were so bright, I could hardly see anyone. There was a podium with a microphone on it. I leaned into the mic.

"Hi," I said.

I really should have rehearsed what to say earlier. Now I had a room full of people staring at me, expecting to be wowed and I had nothing. I looked over at Seth. He just stared at me, too.

Right when the silence became awkward, an old guy came down the aisle waving a white cane in front of him. "Destiny!" he said, real loud.

"Yeah," I said.

"Destiny!" he said again, getting closer.

"Yes!" I said, not sure where this was going. I mean, I could guess, but I wasn't 100% positive.

The guy reached the stage, and someone jumped up to guide him up the side steps.

"Destiny!" he said when he got up on stage. "I traveled

two hundred and fifty miles to meet you!" He didn't have a mic, but he spoke so loudly, I'm sure they could hear him in the back row.

"Wow," I said. "Who are you?" I asked.

"Curtis," he said. "Curtis Turner."

I liked this guy. He was saving my ass in front of all these people. "Hi Curtis," I said. "What seems to be the problem?" It was a dumb question. I knew it. Curtis knew it. And the audience knew it. They all laughed. But it wasn't a totally dumb question, because I needed to know if it was something I could fix.

"Been this way my whole life," he said which wasn't what I wanted to hear. "Retinopathy from prematurity is the technical term."

"Retin-What?" I asked.

"Retinopathy from prematurity," he said, this time slower.

I looked over at Seth who already had his phone out. I had to keep the guy talking while Seth checked WebMD. "That sounds complicated," I said.

"You don't know the half of it," he said.

"You're right," said. "I'm still trying to get the Retin part." That got another laugh. We were winning over the crowd, I could tell that. But my stomach was still in a knot. If I couldn't help this guy, it would be an epic fail. "Where are you from?" I asked.

"Tallahassee," he said.

"I hope you didn't drive yourself!" I said. The got another laugh.

"My daughter drove me down. She's out there," he said, and he pointed toward the audience. I looked for her, but the lights were too bright.

Finally, Seth appeared at the side of the stage. He gave a nod that said I was good to go.

"Okay, Curtis," I said. "I can help you. Now it'll take a couple of weeks before you see a difference."

"I'm fifty-seven years old," said Curtis. "I think I can wait a couple weeks."

I touched his head and whispered, "Thanks Curtis, you really saved my ass up here." Then I said, "Expect a change in your life," loud enough for everyone to hear.

Curtis wasn't the only one in the room that needed my help. A line formed in the aisle. I had a chat with all of them and Seth had to look up a few more medical terms. Because it was Florida, I heard some crazy stories about people's injuries. One woman had a piece of her arm missing where an alligator had taken a bite out of it. The crazy part was that her ex-husband had *thrown the alligator at her*. Another guy had buckshot in the head from when he and his buddies got drunk and decided to "shoot down a hurricane."

I don't know whose idea it was, but about 15 minutes into it, they started playing new age music over the room speakers. I called Seth over while I waited for a man on crutches to make his way to the stage.

"This music sucks," I said.

"I know," he said.

"I need you to get them to change it," I said.

"To what?" he asked.

"I don't know," I said. "Anything but this."

He hurried off and the music stopped. A few minutes later, something else started. It sounded a little new agey, but cooler. Afterward, I asked Seth what it was: The soundtrack from *Braveheart*.

I still had a few people waiting when Seth stepped in and told me I was over my time limit. Wow, the time did fly. The Conference Director said a few more words and I headed for the exit. I passed Dr. Ming Tao on the way out. *Try to follow that, dude*, I thought.

A crowed followed me out of the room into the lobby. What I didn't know is that there were people outside the room who hadn't gotten in. I got swarmed with fans. Fans and weirdos. Some guy asked me if I would come up to his room and give him a chamomile tea enema. Um, no.

I didn't get back to my suite until close to midnight. I saw a bottle of champagne waiting for me, a gift from the people who ran the conference. I guessed they didn't get the memo about my age. What the hell, I earned it! I cracked it open and started drinking.

That's when I heard a voice. The one I heard when I stubbed my toe. This time it was weirder because I *knew* I was alone. I still didn't understand what it said. For sure it wasn't English. I checked the bathroom and the closet just to make sure. Both empty. Then I poured the rest of the champagne down the sink.

———

I thought my head would explode when Seth told me: I was invited to be on "Jas!" Jas! was the top-rated daytime star! She had her own media empire. People read the books she told them to read, watched the movies she told them to watch, bought the things she told them to buy. She was inspiring! (And when you wrote her name you had to include the exclamation point. It was part of her name. It was even on her birth certificate.)

"This is huge," said Seth.

"No kidding," I said. I felt so excited, I was already thinking about what to wear.

Seth got all serious. "We can't let our guard down," he said. "Remember what happened on Hoax Busters."

"Jas! isn't like that I said. "She doesn't yank people's chains."

"I know," he said. "We still need to be careful. This is make or break time."

I knew what he meant. If you became part of Jas!'s posse, you had it made. People had become stars themselves just from her say so - Doctor Scott, "America's GP"; Perry Pringle, the President's interior decorator; Beulah Lee, Queen of Soul Cuisine; and Guru Veer Nusbaum. I couldn't help but think maybe I could get *my own* tv show out of this.

I tried to calm down, but it wasn't working.

"We should watch some episodes of her show," said Seth.

"I already have," I said. "My mom watches her all the time. I know the drill."

"Then I need to watch some episodes," he said.

Some of Seth's worry started to creep in. It was big deal. It was the Global Wellness Summit times a million. I needed some emotional support. "I want to bring Bran along," I said.

"That's a hard no," said Seth.

"Why not?!" I said.

"He'll be a distraction," he said.

"I need the support," I said.

"I'm here to support you," he said.

"It's not the same," I said. "He's a performer. He understands what it's like to be in the spotlight."

"I've done some performing, too," said Seth.

"Really?" I said. "Like what?"

"I took acting classes at film school, so I'd know what the actors were going through, their end of the creative process."

"I didn't know that," I said. "You were in movies?"

"Movies and plays," he said. " I played Mettelus Cimber in Julius Caesar."

"That sounds like a Star Wars character," I said.

Seth laughed. "True."

"Anyway, it's not the same," I said. "Bran is... Well, it's different. Obviously."

"That's what I want to avoid," said Seth.

"What do you mean?" I asked.

"I mean, this is about the business and your career," he said. "Bran is extraneous."

"He's a part of my life," I said.

"For now," said Seth. "You have to think more long term."

"You think we're going to break up?" I asked.

"No. Yes... See, this is exactly what I wanted to avoid," he said, "getting your personal life mixed up with the business."

I didn't want to argue about it anymore either, so I let it drop. "Okay, fine," I said

———

We found out that they wanted to shoot some segments ahead of time where I heal people and then have them come on the show, y'know, before and after. Great idea! Jas! was a genius!

They taped the show in Atlanta, just a couple days drive from New York. Seth came with me. Laura too. It was that big of a deal. When we got onto I-95, they were in the front seat, and I sat in the back which made me feel like a little kid. When we got to Richmond, I asked for the shotgun seat.

We arrived in Atlanta around 10AM and went straight to Jas!'s studio. It was buzzing like a beehive. And it was the opposite of Hoax Busters. From the get-go they treated me like a star. I had my first experience with cucumber water. I felt super nervous and excited to meet Jas! She was fabulous. The first thing she did was hug me and tell me how happy she was to have me there. I told her how happy *I* felt to be there. She said hello to Seth and Laura (no hugging) and took me to meet the people I'd be healing. I said hello to Connie, a woman with breast cancer; Emma, who got wounded in a school shooting; and Jamal, a guy whose lungs got damaged during 9/11. Jas! left me to do my thing while she ran off to take care of something else.

The show's producers had a clear idea of what they wanted so I just went along with it. I drank more cucumber water while I did my bit and I finished before I knew it.

"That went well," said Seth as we walked back to the car.

"I know," I said. I could tell this would put me over the top. My Big Break. "I want to buy a car," I said.

"A what?" said Seth, like he didn't know what a car was.

"A Porsche," I said. "And I want to drive it back to New York."

Seth and Laura looked at each other like they didn't think that was a good idea. That made me mad.

"You can't stop me," I said.

"You're too young to get a car loan," said Laura.

"I'll pay cash," I said, even though I didn't know how much a Porsche cost.

"You can't get insurance," said Laura. "You're still underage."

"Then Hand of Destiny can buy it for me," I said.

"I think we're getting ahead of ourselves," said Seth. "We still have "Jas!" two weeks from now. Let's just concentrate on getting that right."

"This sucks," I said.

"Seth is right," said Laura. "Let's not get ahead of ourselves."

I still thought it sucked, but Laura was my lawyer and I had to listen to her.

———

Two weeks later we were back on the road to Atlanta. I didn't want to make the rookie mistake I made at the Global Wellness Summit, going out there unprepared, so I thought of a few things to say—and what not to say. I also practiced my story about how I got my powers. That part had Seth the most worked up.

"You're really going to lie to Jas!?" he said and that made me think. I wanted to be part of her inner circle and I didn't want to do anything to piss her off. She'd promoted a book called "Swimming on an Empty Stomach" that was supposed to be the writer's true, life story, but the whole thing turned out to be made up. It became a huge embarrassment for her, and the writer had to go back on the show and apologize to Jas! and the whole world. I SO did not want that to be me. I asked Seth if we could ask Jas! to skip that question and he didn't think that was possible. "That'll really call attention to the situation," he said, and he was right. I just hoped she wouldn't bring it up.

The day of the show was amazing. Jas! hugged me again and I drank more cucumber water. Her team totally knew their business and I felt like I was in good hands. Again, the opposite of Hoax Busters.

Right before I went on, I reminded myself that I was the real deal and how hard I'd worked to get to that point. I had this. When I heard my name, I walked out into the bright lights, smiled and waved to the crowd.

I sat down and Jas! told everyone how amazing I was, which was true. Then they showed the segments where I met Connie, Emma and Jamal. I thought I looked kinda dorky, but whatever.

Then they brought Connie, Emma and Jamal out onstage, and everyone applauded. Connie and Jamal looked the same. Emma wore a halter top so you could see the places where the bullet holes had been. They sat down and told their stories. When they showed Connie's PET scan, the audience oohed and aahed. Jamal blew up a few balloons and made a balloon animal which was kinda goofy, but the crowd loved it.

Then Jas! asked me how I got my powers. I froze for a second. "I don't know," I said. "I mean not exactly."

Jas looked a little confused. "You've told a couple different stories," she said.

"I know," I said. "I think I'm still trying to figure it out."

"I think we all have amazing powers inside of us," said Jas!

"Totally true!" I said.

"We just have to discover what they are," she said.

"Yes," I said. This was great. Jas! was answering the question for me. I loved her! "We all need to find our secret superpowers," I said, and the audience started cheering and applauding.

Gotta say, I nailed it!

———

Seth and Laura wanted to take me out to dinner, but I told them I was too tired and wanted to stay in and order room service. After they left for dinner, I went downstairs and met Bran. He flew down from New York that day so we could celebrate together. Atlanta's biggest rapper, Il Ponzi, was doing a secret show in a warehouse downtown and Bran used his connections to get us in. After that, we walked a couple blocks to an all-night taco stand everyone was raving about. It wasn't in the best part of town, but there were a bunch of other people from the show there, so I felt perfectly safe.

While I waited for Bran to get us our tacos, a guy in a wheelchair rolled from car to car in traffic, asking for change. I was in such a good mood I thought that I'd help the guy for free. Like, give back to the universe, right? I called him over to the curb and introduced myself.

"I'm Destiny," I said. "The girl that heals people. I'm gonna be on 'Jas!'""

"No shit?" said the guy. I didn't know if the no "no shit" was for being able to heal people or for being on television. "Look, I usually charge but I'm just hanging around here and I thought I could help you walk again, y'know, for free."

"He can walk!" said a woman's voice.

I looked over and saw an older lady sitting at a bus stop, waiting for a late-night bus.

"He's here every night begging for change and I know he can walk. I've seen him."

"Why don't you mind you own damn business?!" yelled the guy.

"It's the truth!" she said.

"Mind you own damn business!" yelled the guy.

"What are you gonna do?" said the lady, sarcastically. "Kick my ass?"

Then the guy called her a bitch and told her she'd better shut the f up.

I didn't want to get in the middle of it, so I backed away slowly.

The guy seemed to have forgotten about me, he was so mad. He glared at the old lady, grabbed the wheels of his chair and gave them a huge push backwards. He rolled backward into the street just as a pickup truck came around the corner, hitting him. I looked away before I could see what happened next.

I heard screams from the other people on the sidewalk, followed by a whole bunch of "Oh, my God"s and "Holy shit!"s.

I finally looked to see the guy sprawled out on the asphalt. His skull had split open, and his brains oozed out onto the asphalt. The driver of the truck jumped out and dialed 911. I thought I would puke.

I so did not need that kind of bad publicity. It was exactly the kind of dirt that would get me bounced out of Jas!'s inner circle which I technically still wasn't in. I went and pulled Bran out of line. "Let's get out of here," I said.

Bran stayed in my room that night, but nothing happened. I wasn't in the mood. I couldn't get the image of that guy's brains out of my head.

My episode of "Jas!" aired the day after we got back to New York. Seth came over to my place to watch it. Bran came too.

It seemed like there was a force field around both of them so that they couldn't get within ten feet of each other. I don't think they said more than two words to each other the whole time.

I felt less, and more, nervous than Hoax Busters. Less, because I knew it was going to make me look good. More, because I knew how much of my career was on the line.

I swear, my phone blew up while the episode was still happening. Seth's too. I didn't take calls from any number I didn't recognize. My mom called to say the diner was packed and everyone was watching the show.

I felt so excited; I didn't know what to do with myself. Everything that I'd worked for was coming together! I knew that my life would be completely different from then on. I would be a star, with everything that comes along with it.

————

"You're going on tour," said Seth. "It's going to be a little seat of our pants, but we already have some big venues lined up."

"Madison Square Garden?" I asked. That would have been a dream come true.

"More like Forest Hills Stadium," he said.

I didn't know Forest Hills Stadium. Still, it was a stadium. "When do we go there?" I asked.

"That's not on the itinerary. At least not yet," he said. "I'm just using that as an example. Our first stop is in Philadelphia."

Philly didn't sound like the big entrance I'd hoped for.

"I want a tour bus," I said.

"That's an unnecessary expense," said Seth.

"We need to be comfortable," I said. "My days of sleeping on floors are over."

"I'm planning it so we can stay in hotels along the way," he said. "It's just the two of us. We can fit in a car just fine."

"There'll be more than two of us," I said. "I need to bring a makeup artist and stylist."

"A makeup artist and a stylist?" he said, like he couldn't believe it. "Two more people?"

"Why not?" I said.

"That will more than double the cost of the trip," he said.

"So?" I asked.

"So, we still have to pay rent on the Brooklyn space while we're gone," he said. "I have it planned out, so we'll still be in the black even with the tour overhead, but if we start adding people..." Then he made a gesture with hands like an explosion.

I could see that "tour" meant something different to me than it did to Seth. From dating Bran, I knew what made a tour: buses (plural), stage crew, lighting crew, security team, catering...all that. This sounded more like a road trip.

"Okay," I said, trying hard to hide my disappointment. "How about we have just one extra person, a makeup artist slash stylist?"

"Okay so that'll increase our expenses by fifty percent," he said, and he sounded annoyingly sarcastic.

"I can't believe you're telling me no," I said. "We're blowing up here!"

"We are blowing up, and I'm trying to keep things manageable. Too many moving parts means more things that can go wrong. Let's keep it simple," he said.

"Having to do my own hair and makeup sounds compli-cated," I said. "I'll have enough to think about." Seth didn't come right back at me, so I guessed I'd made my point.

"Do you already know who you want to bring?" he asked.

"This guy named Juan," I said. "I met him through Bran. He's amazing. And super funny."

Seth sighed. "What's his day rate?"

"I don't know," I said. "But I can probably get a deal."

"Okay," said Seth. "I'm not promising anything but ask him his day rate."

So, no Madison Square Garden, no bus, no entourage. But I got a makeup artist slash stylist. It was a start.

———

On January 25, I realized that I'd been in New York for exactly a year. I was amazed at how far I'd come in such a short time. I went from sleeping on the floor and eating Pop Tarts to having my own business and being on national TV. I had a boyfriend *and* an ex-boyfriend. I was making it. And, if I'd come this far in just one year, where would I be at the end of the second? The sky was the limit!

———

Right before I started my tour, Bran left for a mini tour of Holland and Germany. I offered to go with him to the airport, but he said he didn't want to inconvenience me. I told him I would miss him and that those euro chicks had better keep their hands to themselves. I thought it was cool that we would both be on tour at the same time, like a celebrity couple!

And I got a passport. When Bran said he was going to Europe, I started dreaming about my own world tour. We were already planning a U.S. tour so why not?

your best life 15:

Hitting the Road and the Road Hitting Back.

Going on tour may sound like a long vacation where you get paid to go to a party every night, but that's not how it goes. Here's why:

1. It's work. Every time you get off the bus (or get out of the van) people will be expecting something from you, like any job. You're like the UPS guy, as soon as you're there, you have to deliver the goods.

2. You're on a schedule. Being on the road costs money so you have to be efficient. A day off is a day when you're just spending money, so you don't want to have those. You need to arrive places on time and leave on time. This doesn't give you much time for sight-seeing so, as much as you want to see the Doll's Head Trail (real thing), you'll have to skip it.

3. You never know what's around the bend. Traffic jams and detours come out of nowhere, no matter what the app says. And everywhere you go is a bunch of question marks, like where's a gas station? Or a nail salon? Or a bathroom? Unexpected things happen too. Tires get flat. Bags get forgotten in hotel rooms. People get shot. The list goes on.

4. It's not that luxurious. Maybe if you're taking a private jet to stadiums, it's nice. But when you're starting out, you'll probably be driving a van, staying in cheap hotels, and eating a lot of fast food.

But you should totally do it. It's a life experience you can't get any other way. You'll go places you've never been before and meet people you never would have otherwise. You'll collect a ton of stories, photos, and memories. It just might be the best time of your life.

fifteen

. . .

JUAN CAME over to my house to help me pack the night before we left for Pittsburgh. He had a few bags of clothes he'd bought that day for me to try on. I loved most of it. He totally knew my style. By midnight, we'd made the final selections.

I felt like going to go to bed, but Juan knew of a party in Manhattan that he said was going to be amazing. I put on an outfit that didn't make the cut (because it was too skimpy) and took a car into the city. It was a little weird going out without Bran and a ton of guys hit on me. I came home at 4AM and realized that we had to hit the road at seven. No biggy. I could sleep in the car.

Somehow, I was up and ready to go at 7AM. Seth made a sour face when he saw my six suitcases, but I ignored him. I'd compromised enough.

The big moment came when Seth handed me a company credit card with my name on it. *That* seemed like the big time.

Seth had rented a mini-RV which we drove to pick up Juan. Seth grumbled about having to drive all the way to Bed-Stuy to do that. He was really mad when we got there and Juan was still asleep. I cured Juan's hangover, but we still didn't get Juan and his stuff into the van until 10AM. We didn't get out of the city until 11:30AM. I thought we still had plenty of time to make it to Philly, but Seth wouldn't let it go. Juan kept me entertained with stories about some of the crazy clients he'd had. Seth just kept his eyes on the road, not saying anything.

———

We arrived at the Penn Music Hall with time to spare. The main hall was downstairs and there were no seats. Chris, the sound guy, asked me what I needed, and I said I just needed a microphone.

Are you a stand-up comic?" he asked, and I guessed he hadn't seen me on "Jas!"

"No," I said. I didn't feel like explaining the deal to him.

I walked up onto the stage and looked out, while he set the mic up. Then we did a sound check which was basically making sure the mic worked. It took less than ten minutes.

Then I went and checked out my dressing room. It was big and all the walls were covered in stickers and graffiti. One of the walls had mirrors with lightbulbs all around it, like you would expect. Juan was already in there with some outfits for the evening. The white leather suit with the fringe seemed right for the occasion. With that decided, Juan started on my hair and makeup. He said he had some new ideas.

Seth came in about an hour before I was supposed to go on. "They're moving us to the upstairs room." He explained that, because the room was downstairs, they couldn't get some people with disabilities down there.

That threw me. "But what about my sound check?" I said. Now that I knew what a sound check was, I wanted one.

"It'll be okay," he said. "It's just one microphone. Also, they want to know what kind of music you want them to play right before you go on."

"*Exploding Heart* by Damsel Gloria," I said. I didn't even have to think about it.

Seth nodded. "Okay, I think we can get that going."

———

The upstairs room wasn't nearly as big as the downstairs, and it was packed. I walked out on stage with my new theme song pumping and a spotlight following me the whole time. When I got to the microphone, I pulled it off the stand and said, "Hello, Philadelphia!" (The microphone worked just fine.) I got some cheers and applause. So far, so good. Next to the mic stand, a tall stool had a bottle of water on it.

The deal was your ticket bought you the cure for whatever. (Laura had written up an agreement that everyone had to sign, terms and conditions, all that legal stuff.)

I looked out through the glare of the spotlight and saw what looked like a wheelchair traffic jam right in front of the stage. There was no way they were going to get to me, so I jumped down off the stage. When I hit the floor, the crowd pushed forward, like everyone wanted their time with me immediately. The mob pushed the wheelchairs forward and people started to fall over, and in between them. I stepped back and two burly guys rushed in to try to control the crowd.

"Woah! Woah! Hey, people!" I said. "Take it easy!"

No one listened to me. A fight broke out and some guy hit a lady in the head with his crutch. More security guys ran in, but they couldn't stop all the people coming at me, yelling my name. I kept backing up until I ran into the stage. I had nowhere else to go. All the house lights came on.

Next thing I knew, a middle-aged lady was on top of me. She looked scared.

"Help me," she said.

I put both hands on her to keep her from getting any closer. "Expect a change in your life!" I yelled.

Two huge hands grabbed me under my arms and pulled me up on stage. It was one of the security guards surrounded by some members of the stage crew. Somehow, I'd lost a shoe. They hustled me backstage while I tried to keep up wearing only one high heel.

————

"That was a learning experience," said Seth as we drove away.

I felt terrible. Now all those people who had paid for a ticket hated me. The venue hated me. And what if Jas! heard about what happened? She'd hate me too!

I glared at Seth. "You should have seen that coming."

"Why?!" he said. "It didn't happen last time!" And by "last time" he meant the Global Wellness Summit.

"That was different," I said.

"How so?" he said, and he asked it like I was some kind of idiot.

"You tell me!" I yelled. "You're the manager!"

While Seth huffed and puffed, I glanced back at Juan who looked so embarrassed, like he'd rather get out and walk.

"Look," said Seth, trying not to act mad. "It's the first night. Mistakes were made. What matters is that we learn from those mistakes and don't make them again."

"Sounds good to me," I said, and I was only half sarcastic.

————

We all felt hangry, so Seth drove us to Geno's for Philly cheesesteak, the city's signature dish. I still wore the white leather outfit and Juan warned me to be careful to keep the cheese sauce off it. "Don't make me clean *that* up, honey," he said. He said it like he was being funny, but I knew he meant it. After we'd eaten (and I didn't drip anything onto my clothes) everyone calmed down. A couple pounds of meat and cheese can do that.

Then we drove to a Ramada outside of Philly. Seth explained that staying outside the city would save us money and make it, so we didn't have to fight city rush hour traffic in the morning. That all made sense, but I wanted to stay more in the middle of things.

———

We drove to D.C. the next day. It took only a couple of hours to get there so we had time to do a little sightseeing. Juan and I took pictures of ourselves in front of the Washington Monument, the Lincoln Memorial and the Jefferson Memorial. We posted a bunch of them to our official Instagram account. Then Juan insisted that we go to the Smithsonian Museum of American History so Juan could see the ruby slippers from "The Wizard of Oz."

Seth didn't go with us. He was at the Ramada preventing another riot.

The show that night wasn't in D.C. It was in Maryland at an old theater with seats. Seth thought that would help to keep the crowd from rushing the stage. He hired extra security too, just in case.

———

I did an interview for the Washington Post before I went on, and I told the story about the Native American hitchhiker. It was just some random newspaper, so I didn't mind bending the truth.

———

The show went much better than the night before. We didn't sell out and Seth said it was because it was Superbowl Sunday. That didn't make sense to me because, if you had to choose between watching a football game and getting healed, there's no contest! I think the bad publicity from the Philly show kept people away and Seth just didn't want to tell me that.

I don't know why but the night was all about broken noses and bullet holes. (Later on, I would see that that would happen sometimes; I'd get a whole cluster of one kind of weird injury for no reason I could see.)

I met a guy who wanted to be "erased." He was one of those dudes who was covered in tattoos—even on his face—and he'd done that totally gross thing where you put big hoops in your earlobes until they're stretched out like rubber bands. I told him to send me before and after photos for my Instagram.

Fun fact: I can't pierce my ears. I mean, I can pierce them, but the holes will fill back in in a day or two. I'm a clip-on gal for life!

———

Afterwards Juan and I told Seth that we didn't want to go back with him to the Ramada; we wanted to go to D.C. and have fun. He didn't like the idea, but he couldn't stop us. "Just do me a favor and stay out of trouble," he said. We promised we would.

Juan had some friends, Charles and Alexander, who lived near Dupont Circle, so we took a cab to their place. From there they took us to a club where no one cared about football. I used my fake ID, no problem. None of the guys there were interested in me (if you know what I mean). That was cool. I was dating Bran.

Alexander asked if I wanted some Ecstasy. I had never been a druggie in high school. (Back in the small town I came from, we just drank beer.) My first reaction was no. I'd heard too many stories of celebrities whose careers went to hell when they started using drugs. Then I realized that I wasn't like most celebrities! My curing abilities included being able to cure myself! I would never OD. (Not that I'd ever heard of anyone OD'ing on E, anyway.) I took it and I felt amazing! I loved everybody!

————

When we got back to the Ramada Inn the next morning, Seth was pissed. A little after 7AM, we rolled into the lobby to find him sitting there.

"Where the hell have you two been?" he asked.

"We told you," I said. "In D.C."

"You should have texted me," he said.

"We thought you were asleep," said Juan.

"If I'd known you were going to be out all night, I wouldn't have wasted the money renting both of you a room."

"Well, we didn't know," I said.

"And I'm still going to need my room," I said. "I need a shower."

————

From there we drove back up to Baltimore. It was in the wrong direction. I wanted to go further south where it was warmer, but Seth said that's when the space was available. It was only an hour's drive. Juan and I slept in the RV. When we got there, we had lunch at the Blue Moon Café. It was fantastic!

After we ate, Seth went down to the harbor to see the

historic sailing ships. That would have put me to sleep, if I wasn't still sleepy, so Juan and I crashed in the RV.

————

The show that night was at an American Legion Hall which worried me a little. Shouldn't the venues be getting bigger? I asked Seth about it, and he said the Baltimore Warehouse, the place we were supposed to be at, pulled out because of what happened in Philly. He said we were lucky to have someplace to go and not have to give everyone their money back.

"This sucks," I said to Seth while we were in my "dressing room," which was really just a storeroom.

"Don't worry," he said. "We're bouncing back."

"Doesn't feel that way," I said. I felt like we were just going splat.

————

Afterwards Seth took us to a Super 8 motel. I asked him what happened to the Ramada, and he said we had to cut back on travel expenses to make up for what we had to spend on extra security. I told him that Juan and I could share a room if that would help. (It wasn't like Juan was going to try anything with me.) Seth said he'd think about it but, for that night, we had to make do at a Super 8 out near the airport. That was a major bummer for Juan and I, because we were hoping to be closer to the action.

"Oh my god," said Juan as soon as we got to our room "Seth's like our dad. Did you really used to go out with him?"

"Yep," I said. "I was young then."

That made Juan laugh. "Let's trash the room," he said.

"It would only be an improvement," I said. Then I checked Bran's Instagram feed and saw some pictures from his last show. The stage lights turned him purple and pink, making it hard to see him. He posted some shots of him on a boat in the middle of Amsterdam. It wasn't a selfie. I wondered who was holding the camera.

"What do you think Bran is doing right now?" I asked. "Do you think he's as bored as we are? "

"He's in Europe," said Juan.

"What's that supposed to mean?" I asked.

"I mean," said Juan, "that anywhere in Europe is better than Baltimore."

I wondered if he was having more fun than me. I imagined him going from his gig to some hot club. I also worried that he would hook up with some girl he met at the gig, but I didn't want to admit that to Juan.

"I should call him and see what he's up to," I said,

"What time is it there now?" he asked.

"How the hell should I know?" I said.

He looked at his phone. "It's 6 hours ahead so that's... It's 8 in the morning there."

"Do you think he'll be up?" I asked.

"Not if he's having a good time, he won't," said Juan.

"I'm calling him," I said. I took my phone and went out into the hallway, down toward the vending machine. He didn't pick up and I didn't leave a message. I guessed he was having a good time.

———

We drove back past Washington D.C on our way to the next stop, Richmond, Virginia and the River Club, another concert hall. Seth and I were both on edge, not wanting this to be a repeat of what happened in Philly.

The article about me came out in the Washington Post in the Lifestyle section. The reporter described the outfit I wore as "millennial Stevie Nicks."

Okay, boomer.

Seth gave me a hard time about telling my "origin story" as he called it.

"It's the Washington Post for chrissakes!" he said. Okay, millennial.

————

I had to hand it to Seth, he had it all figured out when it came to security and organization. They had the room set up with barricades to keep everyone from rushing all at once. I did my mic check and went to pick out my outfit for the evening.

Juan was doing my makeup when he leaned into my ear and said, "I have some DMT," he said.

"Oh," I said, not sure if I should know what DMT was.

"It's a hallucinogen," he said.

"Oh," I said again, because I didn't know what else to say.

"Wanna try some?" he asked. "I got it back in D.C. I've been holding onto it for a special occasion."

I'd never done anything like that before. It was like acid, right? Was I going to see little green men, or something? "It'll mess up the show," I said, wanting to say no and not sound uncool.

"It'll only last for five to fifteen minutes," he said.

"Five to fifteen? Then what's the big deal?" I asked.

"That's enough time to completely change your life," he said.

That hit me: Here I was suddenly changing everybody else's life, and here was a chance for me to change mine. I said I'd try it.

————

If it was five to fifteen minutes, it felt longer. Suddenly, I went from sitting in the RV to floating through colored shapes and it was like my body just disappeared. I was me, but not me.

Like, I still existed, but I wasn't Destiny. Time didn't mean anything anymore. For all I knew, I had always been there. But that wasn't the freaky part. The freaky part was when I went back into the RV, but it wasn't like when I left it. Everything was there but...different. And I wasn't alone, and it wasn't just Juan. There were these tall creatures circling around me and their "faces" were shifting and changing. It felt like the harder I tried to see what they looked like, the harder it became. Then they started talking and I could see what they were saying, like voice balloons in a comic book. And it wasn't English. It was an alien language, like if Hebrew and Chinese had a baby. Holy shit! This was the language I heard when I stubbed my toe! And when I drank the champagne! I knew they were trying to get me to understand what they were saying. When I couldn't, I got the feeling they were mad at me.

Then—just like that—I dropped back into the dressing room, the real dressing room. Seth was standing in the doorway, looking a little worried and totally pissed.

"Wow," was the first thing I said when I landed.

"You okay?" he asked. He leaned into my face, looking from one of my pupils to the other.

"Uh, yeah, sure," I said.

Seth looked at Juan. "You're fired. Really. Out. Now."

Juan didn't say anything. He just made a face like Seth was overreacting and he started throwing stuff in his makeup bag.

"No, really, I'm okay," I said. I wanted to talk to Juan about what I saw.

Seth kept glaring at him. "She's a minor. I could have you arrested."

Juan didn't have an answer for that. He threw up his hands in surrender. Seth kept an eye on Juan until he and all his personal stuff was out of the room. (I paid for the clothes, so he didn't take them, thank God!)

After Juan left, Seth looked at me like I was an idiot. "What the hell?!" he yelled. "I'm busting my butt every day to make this happen and you're pulling this bullshit?!"

"I'm fine, okay? It's not going to affect the show," I said.

"That's beside the point," he said.

"No, it's not," I said. "I can heal myself, remember?"

"You absolutely do not want to go down that road," he said.

"I'm not 'going down that road,'" I said.

"Don't become a celebrity cliché," he said.

"I'm not!" I said. What more did Seth want out of me? "Who's going to do my makeup?" I asked.

"You don't need makeup," said Seth.

"Oh my god! Have you ever even met a girl before?" I said.

"Can't you do it yourself?" he asked.

"I guess I have to," I said. I grabbed a mascara wand and turned to the mirror, to let him know the conversation had ended. He got the message and left.

I wanted to tell Seth about the message from beyond, but I knew he would just think it was the drugs talking. I looked around the room, wondering if the creatures were still there, watching, even if I couldn't see them.

I did the show that night, distracted. Juan said the experience would change my life. Did it? What was the message? And why couldn't those things just have talked in English?

———

We both slept until checkout time the next morning, then we drove to Raleigh-Durham, just the two of us. Juan did a lot of the talking and, without him, it was quiet. Too quiet. I knew Seth was still mad at me, and I was still mad at him, for calling me a "celebrity cliché." I was unique. And I wasn't going to "go down that road." I was blazing my own trail. I'd show him. I'd show everybody. I popped in my ear buds and ignored him.

We'd just crossed the border into North Carolina when we started talking again. We'd known each other too long to stay mad forever, and we'd been through bigger fights. He said he was sorry for blowing up at me, and I promised not to do DMT again. And that was a fact. It was just too freaky. I wanted to talk to Seth about what I saw and figured I'd give it a few hundred more miles before I mentioned it.

your best life 16:

What to Do When Someone Mistakes Your Heart for an Old Tire and Dumps It by the Side of the Road.

Breaking up with someone is always shitty and when it happens—don't kid yourself, it'll happen—it'll seem like the zombie apocalypse salad with Christmas is cancelled dressing. And you'll have to eat it without a fork.

Here are some things you can do for the heartache:

1. Be okay with feeling sad and mad. There's no point in keeping your feelings bottled up. Cry. Scream. Throw things. Let it all out until there's nothing left.

2.Get your ex out of your social media. Block, unfollow and unfriend. Delete photos, if you have to. This person no longer exists to you.

3. Don't contact your ex. Unless it's to get back house keys or your dog, your ex is off limits. Don't think that you can be friends, either.

4. Do not get a breakup haircut. Don't get a tattoo either. And if you like boys, don't decide that you like girls or vice versa.

5. Don't jump into a new relationship. That's like dancing with the snake that just bit ya.

6. Don't obsess over what went wrong. There was nothing you could have done to save the relationship, other than have been a different person.

7. Find something to keep you busy. Lots to see and do here: Hang out with friends, take up a new hobby, start working out, take a trip, or focus on your career. Really, this should be fun.

8. Become a better person. "That which doesn't kill you makes you stronger," as they say. You'll come out the other end of your heartache knowing a little more about who you are and what's right for you. Use that experience to make sure you don't end up with another loser like the one that dumped you.

sixteen

. . .

WE WORKED our way down the east coast, until we had our act down. Seth became the master organizer. He booked a show almost every night of the tour. Things ran more smoothly and I was becoming a pro. Of course there were always snags and glitches. Once I had a dressing room that smelled like dead fish and another one where I walked in and there was a used condom taped to the dressing room mirror. We arrived at one venue to find that they'd brought in a gospel choir to be on stage with me, kind of like my backup band. I don't know if that was a good or bad thing.

Spending almost every waking hour with Seth started getting to me. Thank God we weren't dating anymore. I wondered, *is this what marriage is like? Spending every day with someone until they shred your nerves?*

While we drove, I listened to music on my headphones. Seth had to be on the phone. He would either be talking to the organizers of our next gig or checking in with Tiara who was still running the office and helping out with the tour. I made lemonade by making my own makeup tutorial videos. Tiara did most of the work. I'd just send her what I had on my phone and she'd make it look like a (semi) professional video and post it.

The best part was that we were making money. (With Juan gone, Seth could talk about money while we were driving. And we went back to staying at the Ramada.) I just tried to stay focused on that. Money on my mind and my mind on the money.

We were cruising down Interstate 10, headed for Pensacola when Seth got off the phone. "We've got a problem," he said. He looked serious. "It's your dad."

"He called you?" I said.

"No," said Seth. "He sent... Well, a lawyer he hired sent a letter to the office. He's bringing a legal action against the company."

I knew my dad was going to pull some shit like that. I just knew it! "Legal action?" I said. "Is he suing us?"

"No, not suing," said Seth, and he took a deep breath. "He claims that, because you're a minor, the deal you have with the company—me—should be invalidated. And that one of your parents –and that would be him– should be part of any agreement you have with *Hand of Destiny*."

"That is obviously B.S.," I said.

"I agree with you," said Seth. "I'm calling Laura."

It took a few minutes to get her on speakerphone.

"We'll have to deal with this," she said when she heard the situation.

"How can he even say that?" I asked. "I mean, it's just ridiculous. Doesn't he have to have some sort of... I don't know real reason?"

"Anyone can file a suit," said Laura. "It's up to the court to decide if it's a valid claim."

"It's not valid," I said. I felt pissed. There was no way in hell I'd let a guy who'd been a stranger my whole life get his hands on one penny of my money.

"Give me some time to look this over and draft a response," said Laura.

I felt better knowing Laura was on the case. I knew she was smarter than whatever lawyer my dad had hired. She was going to KICK HIS ASS.

———

On Valentine's Day, I was sitting in a Daytona Beach Ramada, missing Bran. I sent him a photo of me in my bikini with hearts on it (Nothing too sexy. I was smart enough to know what happens to celebrities when those kinds of pictures fall into the wrong hands.)

While I waited for a response, I scrolled through his Instagram feed.

I swear my heart stopped.

I found a shot of him on stage with his guitar, and right next to him—like they were performing together—WAS HIS EX! The caption said: *Me and Miranda together again at the Torhaus Nord in Bremen.*

I must have stared at the picture for ten minutes. Five minutes to get over the shock. The other five trying to rationalize it.

So they performed together? Big deal. They were both musicians.

BUT he never even said that she would be on the tour with him!

BUT what if they aren't on tour together? What if she was on a separate trip and they just crossed paths?

I realized I could go in circles like that all day. I tried to FaceTime him. He didn't pick up. I left a message:

"Hey, Bran, it's me Destiny. I need to talk to you. Call me. And happy Valentine's Day." I didn't quite mean that last part.

Seth had scheduled a little beach break for us and I'd been looking forward to making Bran envious that I could lay out in the middle of winter.

Seth came by and we went to the beach.

"What's the matter?" he asked, as soon as he saw me.

"Nothing," I said. "I'm fine." I don't think he believed me.

I felt a little better when we got outside. I'd never been to a beach that nice before. I'd gone to New York beaches but they were pretty crappy. Florida beaches were cleaner and I swear the people were better looking. I'm a seven but, on a New York beach, I'm a ten.

I tried to relax and enjoy myself, but I couldn't while waiting for Bran to get back to me. He finally called a couple hours later while we were still at the beach. When I saw who it was, I walked down toward the water, away from Seth.

"Hey," I said. "How's it going?"

"Oh, you know," he said. "Life on the road."

"I hear you," I said. "At least here, everyone speaks English."

"Everyone here speaks English too," he said. "It's amazing. And it makes me feel kind of stupid. I only know, like, three words in German."

I desperately wanted to know why he was with his ex on the other side of the ocean. "How was the show?" I asked. "When was it? Last night? The one in Bremen?"

"The show went brilliantly," he said. "The audiences have been incredible. Really supportive."

"That's good," I said. "I've had some good crowds myself. I think there were three-hundred last night."

"Wow," he said. "That *is* good!"

"Yeah, so..." I didn't know how to ask the next question without sounding like the jealous girlfriend, but I HAD to. "Is Miranda there with you?"

"Yeah," he said, just like that. "She was a bit of a last-minute addition."

"And you're what? Touring with her?"

"Yeah," he said and there was a pause that I knew meant something unbelievably shitty was coming. "I'm sorry. I didn't want to have to do this now but..."

"But you're breaking up with me," I said, trying to keep it together while my world fell apart.

"More like taking a break," he said. "Being away from the states has changed my perspective. I'm seeing a bigger picture now, and I need this time away to really think things through."

I didn't have time to bullshit myself. I snapped. "There's no 'taking a break,' Bran," I said. "You're breaking up with me!"

"If that's how you want it," he said.

"I don't want any of this!" I shouted so loud it scared away a seagull.

"I think you need to calm down," he said.

"I think you need to shut it," I yelled and I wasn't done yet. "You know what? I don't give a shit about anything you're about to say." I ended the call.

Then I stood, staring out at the ocean for a while, trying to pull it together.

Next thing I knew, Seth appeared next to me. I guessed he'd heard me. "What's the matter?" he asked.

"Nothing," I said.

"Okay," he said and he went back to his beach blanket. What is it with guys? Don't they know what "nothing," means?

I went for a walk up the beach. I replayed my relationship with Bran over in my head and saw all the clues I'd ignored. Clues? What was I talking about? He flat out told me he was in love with his ex on our first date. How could I have been so stupid? What the hell was wrong with me?

On the walk back down the beach, I realized there was nothing wrong with me. Miranda had smaller boobs than me, a bigger butt and a resting bitch face. I was a goddess. I had power. I could replace Bran with a dozen guys who were better looking AND more talented. Why was I dating a wanna-be rock star anyway? It was time for me to start dating guys more in my league.

When I got back to our beach towels, Seth looked up from his book. (Seth actually read books at the beach.) "Feeling better?" he asked.

"I'm fine," I said.

"Okay," he said, and went back to reading. Guys don't know what "fine," means either.

———

I hit the show hard that night because I had something to prove. The temperature hit sixty-eight degrees and we were outside in an amphitheater. I wore my sexiest outfit. The crowd loved it. They loved me. And we made a ton of money. And I didn't think about Bran once (unless it was to notice that I wasn't thinking about Bran.)

I got in Seth's face in the parking lot, after the show. "I don't want to stay at Ramadas anymore."

"What's wrong with the Ramada?" he asked.

"It sucks!" I said. "I want to stay someplace nice."

"Like where?" he asked. He was pissing me off. I felt like he was trying to outsmart me by asking a bunch of questions.

"Like someplace nice!" I said, pretty loud. "I know how much money we're making!"

Seth looked around to see if anyone heard me say that. "If you want to talk money," he said, lowering his voice, "we can talk money, but let's do it in the RV."

"Fine!" I said and we got in the RV.

"I've worked out a budget for the whole tour," Seth said as soon as I sat down. I could feel him trying to head me off at the pass.

"Then we need to change the budget." I said.

"So that we stay in fancier hotels?" he asked.

"Yeah," I said. "We can afford it."

"I agree, we're making a considerable amount of money on this trip. What I need you to understand is that travel expenses come out of ticket sales before we get paid."

"Okay? So?" I asked.

"So that means that if you start spending more money on travel expenses, some of that money comes out of my percentage."

"Yeah? So?" I said.

"It means I'll be paying for part of your fancy hotel room," he said.

"Then get your own fancy hotel room," I said.

"I'd rather have the cash," he said.

"I'm the star here. Without me this whole thing goes splat," I said.

"I understand the situation," he said. "And I think that's reflected in the percentages we each earn."

He was being calm which just made me madder. "Either we stay at a nice hotel tonight or I quit!" I said.

I stayed at the Miami Beach EDITION that night and I ordered room service. It cost way too much money, but I deserved it. You don't get over a breakup eating at a Taco Bell.

———

The show that night was just outside of Miami so I had another day by the beach. I woke up late and went to the hotel gym. I'd never been an exercise person. When I first moved to New York, the gyms cost way too much. Now I could afford to get a hard body, and I wanted to show Bran what he'd passed up. As I pumped iron, I thought about how Bran was too skinny. I don't think he could do one pushup. Then that sad lump in my stomach started to grow—it was always there, only the size changed. Thinking about Bran made me sad, even when I was thinking about what a loser he was so I did my best to stop thinking about him completely. (Harder than it sounds.)

After my workout, I hit the pool, and by "hit the pool" I mean lay out in the sun, not do laps. There were a few kids splashing around in the water. A woman who I think was on a Netflix series laid out on a deck chair near me. I popped in my earbuds and created my breakup playlist. I'd listen to a couple sad songs, and then some pissy ones, then more sad ones... During the sad ones I'd cry and hope that the big black sunglasses I bought in the hotel gift shop hid my tears.

Seth didn't stay at the EDITION. He stayed at a Ramada in Miami Springs. He came over as a guest and sat out by the pool with me, because this pool was better than the one at the Ramada.

I shut off my pity/pissed playlist and checked out the people around the pool drinking brightly-colored drinks with umbrellas in them. I wanted one of those. Ten of those.

I needed someone to talk to, and I knew that Seth would never ask, so I just came out with it. "Bran broke up with me." When I said it, I could swear Seth smiled just for a second.

"He wasn't right for you anyway," he said.

"What do you mean?" I asked.

Seth shrugged. "Well, if he broke up with you, then he wasn't right for you."

I couldn't argue with that logic.

"I always thought he overplayed his role as an *artiste*," said Seth.

I don't speak French so I guessed that "artiste" was their word for artist.

"That guy was the sensitive singer/songwriter type straight out of central casting," said Seth.

I didn't know what Seth meant by "straight out of central casting." I guessed it was one of those movie terms he was always throwing around. I thought about it and, yeah, Bran was the sensitive singer/songwriter type. That's part of what I liked about him.

"He wasn't that sensitive when he broke up with me," I said.

"It must have been over the phone," said Seth. "That's immature."

"Yeah," I said. "I think I need someone who's more mature." Then I remembered that Seth had broken up with me and he was more mature. What was the difference if a guy was mature or immature? Suddenly I really, REALLY wanted one of those pink drinks with the umbrellas.

———

I told myself I wouldn't look at Bran's Instagram, but I couldn't help myself. Just before the show that night, I went out into the crowd and took a selfie with every cute guy in the place. (Okay, there were only, like, six, and some of them were missing limbs.) I posted them to my Instagram.

After the show I went back to the EDITION and Seth drove back to Miami Springs. I was up in my room, still coming down from the show, watching TV, and I felt bored. Then depressed. I started to freak out. Seth dumped me. Then Bran dumped me. I came to the terrifying realization that no one would ever love me. NO ONE! EVER!

I went out looking for a liquor store. It was Florida, so I found one within walking distance that was still open. I went in.

The place was huge, like an alcohol superstore. They had every kind of everything, but I didn't want to stay too long. I picked out a bottle of Jack Daniels and put it on the counter. The sales clerk asked for ID. I showed him mine.

"This is a fake," he said, like I'd insulted him.

Oh shit, I thought. "No, it's not," I said.

The sales clerk shook his head. "I can spot a fake ID a mile away."

"Okay, Sherlock" I said. "You got me."

I put the bottle of Jack back on the shelf where I found it and went back to the counter. "I need my ID back," I said.

"No can do," said the salesclerk. "State law requires me to confiscate this."

"Hey!" I said. "It's mine. I paid for it!"

"Doesn't matter," said the clerk. "If you don't like it, you can take it up with the cops."

I left mad. And embarrassed.

I started walking back to the hotel, but when I got a couple blocks away, I turned around and walked back to the liquor store. I wasn't going to give up that easily. I wasn't that kind of girl. I was a fighter. A winner!

I waited around the side of the building until a car full of college-aged guys pulled up. When they got out, one of them wore a University of Miami sweatshirt. I asked them to buy me the bottle of Jack.

"We're going to a party right now," said the driver. "Why don't you come with us?"

I knew better than to go to a party with a random bunch of dudes. "No, thanks," I said. "It's not that kind of a night." I gave him $25 and waited.

They came out with a couple bags, walking fast. They hardly looked at me as they got in their car.

"Hey," I said. "Where's my Jack?"

"Sorry," said the driver. "Not happening."

"Then what about my money?" I asked.

He got in the car and drove off.

I was so pissed I thought I'd explode. I screamed at the sky and went back to the hotel.

———

I made two amazing discoveries that night. The first is that you can slip one of the bellboys a hundred bucks and he'll bring a bottle of Jack Daniel's to your room. The second discovery was about where the mysterious voice was coming from:

As soon as I got back to my room, I twisted the cap off and drank straight from the bottle. Wow, did that burn. Fine. It fit the occasion. I took another swig.

That's when I heard the voice, just like when I drank the champagne. This time, I kept my cool. I took another swig and the voice said something else. I kept drinking to keep it talking, trying to figure out where it was coming from. It seemed to come from everywhere at once. Again, I heard the same language I heard when I was on DMT. That freaked me out, because I thought about having those faceless things surrounding me. I put the cap back on the bottle and put it on the dresser. Then I got in bed (with my clothes on) and turned on the TV.

your best life 17:

Haters Gonna Hate. Fans Gonna Email You Pictures of Themselves in Speedos.

Fame means that people know who you are. It also means that those people will have an opinion about you. The ones that like you are fans, and they're the best. They think as much of you as you do of yourself. Sometimes even more. Living up to their expectations can get to be too much. You can't please everybody all the time so don't make that the goal. You just have to try your best, and do what you think is right. Your fans will understand.

Sometimes fans do some stalky stuff and send you weird things. They're just trying to show you how much they like you. You can't get too creeped out by it.

Then there are the haters. These are the people who think you totally suck, you've always sucked and you always will suck. You'll never be able to do anything to get them to like you so don't try. Be proud of your haters, because they mean you're getting somewhere. If you weren't rising, no one would need to drag you down, right?

But why the hate? Like, why can't the world be happy for your success? It's because haters are people who feel crappy about their own lives so they have to make yours just as crappy. Once you understand that it's easier to ~~be nice to~~ ignore them.

seventeen

. . .

WE DROVE to Tampa the next day, stopping for breakfast at a Waffle House in Naples. Seth had the All-American Breakfast. I had two eggs over easy. (I'd only been on the road 10 days, and I'd already put on four pounds. I'm not one of those girls who obsesses about her weight, but I had six suitcases of clothes that I needed to fit me for the next couple of months.)

I was still thinking about what had happened the night before and what I saw while I was on DMT. I wanted to talk to Seth about it. I didn't, because it sounded too crazy and I would have had to admit that I tried to get drunk.

"Why didn't you stay at the EDITION?" I asked him.

"To save money," he said.

"We're making tons of money," I said.

"I told you. I only get twenty-five percent of it."

"Twenty-five percent is still a lot of money," I said.

"I'm saving," he said.

"For what?" I asked.

"To finance my feature film," he said.

I was impressed. Seth hadn't given up on his dream.

"How much do you need to save?" I asked.

"I'd like to have a couple hundred thousand," he said.

"Wow," I said. "That's a lot of money."

"It's barely anything if you're making a movie," he said. "Every dollar I save, I'll need."

I didn't want to control my spending. I'd done enough of that. That was the story of my life up until then. And I knew that would always be that gap between Seth and me. He could never understand what it felt like being poor. To him, watching every penny was something you did on special occasions. Not an everyday reality.

I remembered when I was like five years old, I saw an old couch by the side of the road. I looked between the cushions and found twelve cents. I gave them to my mom because I already knew that I was a poor kid and that my mom needed more money. She made a big deal out of thanking me which was sweet of her, because it was only twelve cents, and it didn't make that big a difference. I hadn't thought about that in years. It's weird all the memories you have in your brain that you hardly ever think about.

The show that night had a huge crowd. A TV news crew showed up. The story was that one of the Tampa Bay Buccaneers had been sidelined - Is that the right term for baseball? - with a knee injury and spring training was about to start. He wanted to be healed in front of the whole crowd. Sure. Why not?

I'll tell you why not. Instead of saying, "Expect a change in your life," like I usually did, I decided to go off script and said, "Go Pirates!"

Okay, in my defense I don't know anything about baseball and a buccaneer *is* a kind of pirate.

I got some boos and some laughter from the crowd. Then I

tried to recover with a loud "I mean, go Buccaneers!" I didn't watch the news that night.

———

I stayed in a hotel right on the bay that night. I didn't know if those things were watching me everywhere I went, or if they were just in hotel rooms. I looked at the bottle of Jack Daniels in my suitcase and thought about "making contact." *Bad idea*, I thought.

———

We kept going through the deep south. It was different from where I grew up and sort of the same. Seth felt uncomfortable outside of cities, like everyone who didn't live in a city wasn't just a hick, but dangerous. I was used to trucks with shotgun racks. I'd shot a shotgun before. A handgun too.

"I just don't see why anyone needs to own a gun," he said, while we had lunch at a seafood restaurant on Mobile Bay.

"Then don't own a gun," I said.

"I can't own a gun," he said. "New York has some of the strictest gun laws in the country."

"Okay," I said. "Then live in New York. But don't try to tell other people in other places what they can and can't do. It's a free country."

"Guns are dangerous," he said.

"No kidding," I said. "That's why people own them. Anyway, guns don't kill people..."

"People kill people," he said, like it was a dumb thing to say.

"Whatever," I said. He was making me mad, and I didn't want to talk about politics. Talking about politics seemed dumb to me. No one ever changes their mind anyway.

———

Some people sent me "before and after" photos of themselves. That was cool. I liked seeing how I'd made people's lives better. A few women promised to name their babies after me (if it was a girl, of course.) A guy had my face (the picture from the front of the Daily News) tattooed on his arm. That was a little strange.

A bunch of guys who'd I'd cured wrote me love letters afterwards. A guy who lost his nuts to testicular cancer sent me a marriage proposal along with a picture of himself in a Speedo. A guy followed us from show to show along the tour. He never asked me to cure him of anything; he just bought a ticket and sat in the back. He was with us all the way from Tampa to New Orleans. I never learned his name. He always wore a Hawaiian shirt so Seth and I called him "Hawaiian Brian."

And sometimes people would knock on my hotel door at night. That would creep me out. How did they find my room? I'd never answer.

One time, after I didn't answer, this couple sat down in the hallway and waited for me. I knew they were out there, because I could hear them talking. They went away eventually.

And I had my picture taken with a ton of people. (Y'know, when you think about it, a ton of people isn't that many people.) One guy I had my picture taken with, months later, killed his wife. The picture went viral and the Internet exploded with people saying they couldn't believe I had my picture taken with a murderer. Like I knew that would happen! I'm not a mind reader!

———

And I had a doctor come after me. He tracked me down to my hotel in Jackson, Mississippi. He must have been camped out in the lobby because, when I got off the elevator, he got right up in my face. He said that Gary Hendersen, one of his patients, came to the show in Miami and that Gary was missing his colon. I remembered that guy! "What's the problem?" I asked.

"The problem is that I removed his colon," said the doctor.

"You what?!" I said.

"Mr. Hendersen had severe colitis and the only solution was to remove the colon," he said. "Now it's growing back, and I'll have to remove it again."

"What sort of shitty doctor are you?" I said. "A guy comes to you with colitis and all you can do is cut out his freaking colon?"

"I'm not going to argue with someone who probably flunked high school health class."

"I got a C," I said.

People in the lobby were staring at us.

He made a pfft sound. "I don't know what sort of snake oil trickery you're pulling here but you don't know what you're doing. You're going to do more harm than good!"

"You're just jealous because I can heal people and you can't!" I said and I pushed past him.

I replayed that argument in my head, over and over, and I got three things out of it: 1. If Gary wanted his colon back; that was his decision. He knew the deal. 2. The doctor *was* jealous because he admitted that Gary's colon grew back. He knew I had power and that it wasn't "snake oil trickery." 3. What I should have said was, "Good thing you're not a cardiologist!"

I wanted to get to New Orleans, our next stop, in a big way. Mardi Gras was happening. I'd never been and it sounded like fun.

We arrived to find the party still going on. I got the feeling that Seth wanted to keep me away from it, like it would be too much of a distraction and that I would act up. As if I would show my boobs to strangers.

The venue that night was a football stadium out in the sticks. (It was a community college football stadium, but it was still a stadium!) I looked at the cars streaming in and checked the size of the field, trying to figure out how many people it would hold, how fast I could see everyone, and how fast I could be back in the French Quarter where I heard all the action was. (I didn't have my fake ID anymore, but I could try.)

I wasn't sure if the crowd could tell how impatient I felt. Sometimes it takes folks with serious medical issues time to move from point A to point B. I know I was looking at people on crutches and thinking, *get a move on!*

It took me three hours to get to everyone. I felt tired and my feet hurt. But it couldn't stop me from heading to the French Quarter.

When we arrived, it was still raging. Seth went out of curiosity and because he knew I wanted to go. I didn't have as much fun as I'd hoped because, with Seth there, I couldn't go into any bars.

So we just walked around, looking at the crazy people, trying not to step in puke. As we walked Seth wanted to talk business. "We're selling out everywhere," he said.

"Wow, cool," I said. I was a little distracted by four people walking past dressed like Satanic mermaids on Broadway.

"It is cool," he said. "But we need to step up," he said. "I'm talking to the organizers further along in the tour to see if we can do two events a day."

That jolted me. I'd just done three hours and I'd had

enough. Having to do six hours sounded exhausting. "One right after the other?" I asked.

"I'm thinking one in the afternoon and one at night, with a break in between," he said. "Of course, we'd be doubling our income. Do you think you can handle it?"

"You had me at 'doubling our income'," I said.

your best life 18:

Drugs.

Now a word about drugs: Don't do them.

Like, when you ask an old friend about someone you both used to go to high school with and the friend says, "She got into drugs..." You don't think, "and then she became an astronaut!" Hell, no. People who start taking drugs end up dead. Or in jail. Or at Burning Man.

eighteen

. . .

THE NEXT STOP was Baton Rouge. Seth drove me to another football stadium. It was the middle of the day and the crowd filled the field and the bleachers. Seth said that all the people who couldn't see me in New Orleans made the trip to Baton Rouge.

I worked for three whole hours with ten-minute breaks every hour. Some people wanted to chat, some wanted to give me a hug. I didn't have the time! And then I had to do it all over again that night. I felt seriously tired by the end. It would have been great if I could have done the whole thing sitting down, but that wasn't going to work. I'm sure it would be a lot easier for Beyonce if she could sit through all of her concerts. I gave serious thought to how I could make a pair of sneakers work with the rest of my outfit.

Seth said that the weak link in our operation was that it wasn't scalable, that we'd always be limited by the fact that there was only one of me. I was happy there was only one of me. If there were a thousand people out there with my abilities, I wouldn't be special.

———

Houston was only a few hours away. I had the time (and $$$$$) to buy that Porsche I'd promised myself. I could tell that Seth didn't like the idea, because it would make it harder for him to keep an eye on me. Well, tough. I was holding up my end of the deal and I deserved a few perks. He knew how hard he'd been pushing me and he had to cave.

We went to a dealership in West Houston. I could see the salesman trying to figure out what the deal was with me and Seth. I made sure the salesman knew that it was me paying for the car.

With as much money as I'd earned, I could get a Porsche Boxster. It had to be white, black or silver, because I couldn't wait for a custom paint job. I needed to drive it off the lot that morning. I settled on white and took every extra and option they had.

Seth took care of all the insurance blah blah blah through Hand of Destiny. I didn't want to wait for Seth and the pokey RV so I had him tell me the address of the hotel and I took off in a cloud of dust. I felt so excited to drive it off the lot. Woo-hoo! My first car and it was a Porsche! I was living my dream!

When I got out on the Interstate, I opened her up to 100mph. I don't think the speedometer dropped below eighty the entire trip.

And I felt like a BFD pulling up to the Grand Hyatt. I didn't want the valet driving my new car so I parked it myself way in the corner of the parking garage, away from all the other cars.

———

Houston was another college stadium and it was the biggest crowd yet! I had YouTube to thank for that. People who I'd visited at the beginning of the tour were posting before-and-after videos showing what I'd done for them. A fifteen-year-old girl with bad acne scars (I remembered her!) turned out to have model-good looks underneath. She had over 1 million views! I checked Instagram too. #destinyhealer had over 800,000 posts. I laughed when I saw that all the stadium concession stands had lines of people buying hotdogs and cokes. I was big business. I told Seth that we should start selling t-shirts and he liked that idea. He said he would get on it as soon as he had some breathing room.

I had to do two shows that day. At the afternoon show—or matinee, as Seth called it—a fight broke out. Someone thought that someone else cut ahead of them in line and decided to take it to the next level. A bunch of people got thrown out by security.

I had a couple hours break after the show while they cleared the field. I talked one of the school's janitors into giving me a foot rub. (This wasn't as creepy as it sounds.)

San Antonio was a repeat of Houston. Two shows with a break in between. Seth tried out us having VIP sessions. People who were willing to pay more (a lot more) could come see me before I headed out to meet the masses. I had to spend more time with these people and make them think they were getting their money's worth. I'm not outgoing by nature so I really had to tap into the reserve fuel tanks for the evening VIPs.

Back at the hotel, I collapsed onto the bed and stared at the ceiling. I thought about what Seth said about scalability. How would I ever go global, and reach millions of people, without killing myself?

Then, I had a plan.

I waited until a little after midnight, then I snuck out. I drove up the I10, looking for a truck stop.

I found one in Boerne. I parked outside and watched the parking lot. My mom used to complain about drug dealers hanging around the parking lot of the truck stop where she worked, dealing amphetamines to the truckers who needed something to keep them going through long hauls. I'd seen them a few times when I had to go visit her at work.

I saw a guy hanging around the parking lot who fit the mold. I got out of my car and tried to stay cool and casual.

Up close he looked ragged, like maybe he was getting high on his own supply.

"Hey," I said.

"Hey yourself," he said, sizing me up.

"I'm buying," I said.

"What you need?" he asked.

"Speed," I said.

"I might have that," he said. "How much?"

Crap, I thought. I had no idea how much I needed. "Three ounces," I said.

He looked a little shocked. "You got that kind of money?" he asked.

"Of course I have money," I said, suddenly worried if I had _that_ kind of money.

"That'll be $1,200," he said.

"Oh," I said. "Then, make that an ounce and a half." I only had $600 on me.

"I've got a couple of 8-balls for $500," he said.

I didn't know what an 8-ball was. "Sure," I said.

He nodded and walked off. I stood there worrying. What was I getting myself into? I wanted this to be over fast.

He came back a minute later with a bag. "Five hundred," he said again. I handed him a wad and he handed me two tiny baggies. It felt icky.

———

My friend, the Internet, suggested that I just do a quarter gram. I snorted it in my hotel room before I left for the venue.

I'd forgotten about my invisible frenemies. They were in my ear the second the speed hit my system. My mind raced, putting two and two together. They always had something to say when I drank or did drugs. Maybe they were saying "Just Say No," in that weird language of theirs. If that's all it was, a lecture, then I could ignore it.

I drove to the Paramount Theater. The Paramount was usually a concert venue. It was a beautiful old theater. Turns out, I didn't need the speed because it wasn't that big a place and we only did one show. While I walked around, checking the place out, Sierra came up to me. She was a tall, thin redhead.

"Do you need a headset mic?" she asked.

"A what?" I asked.

"A headset mic," she said. "You can talk to the audience with your hands free." The way she looked at me, I wondered if she could tell I was speeding.

I'd never used a headset mic before. I'd never even thought about it. Like, duh, it was a great idea. "Sure," I said.

Sierra led me to the stage. "You must have seen some amazing shows," I said, while she fitted me with a headset.

"I've only been here a month," she said. "It's been great so far." She turned to the back of the room and gave a thumbs up to a guy up in the sound booth. (Isn't it weird that you say "give a thumbs up, when it's only one thumb?)

"Headset mic check, please," said a guy's voice, in my ear. I jumped. It reminded me of the other voice in my head.

I didn't know what to say. "Testing, testing, 1,2,3," I said, like I'd seen people do in movies. Suddenly my voice filled the room.

"Could you keep it going?" said the voice in my ear.

"Check, check, 1,2,3" I said again, now feeling stupid.

"Okay, we're good," said the ear voice.

Sierra took the headset from me and I went back to my dressing room. I was so amped up, I didn't know what to do with myself. I checked myself in the mirror about a thousand times.

Seth popped in. "Great theater, huh?" he said.

"Uh, yeah," I said, trying to act normal. "They're giving me a headset," I said. "So I can talk to the audience. It's way cool. I can say, y'know, stuff."

"That's cool," he said. "Look, there's been a lot of demand. We're going to have to do two sets."

"Two sets?" I said. "No problem. I can do it. Really, it's no problem. Two, three, four, five...whatever." I was so wired, I felt like I could go all night.

"Cool," he said and left.

Then he popped back in again. "You okay?" he asked.

I thought I was busted. "No, I'm fine," I said.

"Okay," he said. "You just seem nervous."

Every other time, he took "fine," for an answer. Now he kept nosing around. I started to sweat.

"Maybe a little," I said. "The theater is so... It's great. I just want to do a good job."

Seth looked at me a little too long. "I'm sure you will," he said. And then he left for the second time.

But I got the feeling that he wasn't really gone. Like, maybe he was standing just outside of the doorway, listening to me. I stood up, super quiet, and tip-toed to the door. Then I peeked out into the hallway. No Seth. I wondered if the drugs were making me paranoid.

I charged out at 7PM sharp, my theme song pumping. "Hello, Austin!" I said as I hit the stage. "Who's here to feel good?!!"

The audience roared back. It was awesome.

At 10:30 I went back to my dressing room so they could clear the theater. I wasn't one bit tired. Seth popped in again,

"How you holding up?" he asked.

"Ready for round two!" I said, all chipper.

"You're quite the Chatty Cathy out there," he said.

"I'm just pumped," I said. "And the headset mic is... inspiring."

"Okay," he said. "Just try to pace yourself, y'know?"

"Got it," I said. "Pacing, yeah, I'll do that."

By then, the speed had worn off and I was losing steam. I probably could have gotten through the second show under my own power, but I had another bump in my purse, so I waited for a moment alone and snorted that one too.

After the show, it was 1AM and I was *still* wired, but not hungry. Sierra came to collect the headset that I forgot to take off when I left the stage. It was all sweaty when I handed it to her.

"Me and the crew are going out after we're finished up here," she said. "Do you want to ride along?"

"Yeah," I said. A night out was exactly what I needed to come down after all the excitement.

They showed me around Austin which was a great place, like a cooler version of Billings. We caught a couple of bands and talked to the rest of the stage crew who were all super cool. Bran's musician friends came with a lot of attitude. *Artistes* as Seth put it. The stage crew was more down to earth, even though almost all of them were musicians too. They told me all kinds of stories about the famous people who had played the theater and believe me, I wasn't the only one who had done drugs before going on stage.

As the night went on, I bonded with Sierra. She was super cool in every way. By the time she dropped me off at the InterContinental (around 4AM) she felt like the big sister I never had. I went up to my room and crashed. Hard.

———

Ecstasy was a form of speed. Who knew? (Okay, a ton of people. It's just an expression.) I was having breakfast the next morning at the Eastside Café, thinking that the speed was keeping me on my toes, but not doing anything for my mood. If I could do ecstasy *along with* the speed, I could feel good AND not get tired either.

Seth interrupted my thoughts. "I think we've grown too much to stay a two-person operation," he said.

No duh, I thought. "I agree," I said. "I need another hair and makeup person. And a personal assistant."

"A personal assistant?" said Seth, like I'd said something crazy, like "personal chef."

"Yeah," I said. "I'm tired of having to do my own laundry."

"The hotel does your laundry," he said.

"I still have to put it in bags and leave it out by the door," I said.

"I'm thinking *I* could use some help on the road," he said.

"So you need something like a personal assistant?" I said, sarcastic.

"An assistant," he said. "Not a *personal* assistant."

"I don't see the difference," I said. I knew what he meant, but there was no way he would get an assistant, and I wouldn't.

"Tell you what," he said. "How about we get you a hair and makeup slash personal assistant and I get an assistant?"

"Sure," I said. "But how are we going to find someone in the middle of a tour?"

"Believe me, I've asked myself the same question," he said, frowning. "I'll see what Tiara can do from New York. "Even if we fly someone out to meet us, it might be worth it."

All this talk of building up an entourage got me excited. I couldn't feel like a star without a posse.

I called Sierra (from the night before) as soon as I got back to my hotel room. After the night before I knew she wouldn't freak out if I asked her where I could score some E in Austin.

Eureka! She knew someone!

I drove out to a house in Tarrytown on my way to Dallas.

Sierra had phoned ahead and all I had to do was hand over the money. That was way better than a truck stop parking lot.

The deal done, I called her again.

"Hey, Sierra," I said. "It's me again."

"Hey," she said. "Did it work out?"

"Totally," I said. "Hey, do you want to go on the road with me for the next couple of weeks?"

"As what? A stage tech?" she said.

"Actually, I need someone to do my hair and makeup and, y'know, keep me supplied," I said.

She laughed. "You've seen me," she said. "I'm no hair and makeup expert."

It was true. She had a just-rolled-out-of-bed look, that was part of what made her so cool. She made it look effortless.

"Don't worry about that," I said. "I know how to do it. You can just help out a little. C'mon, you're a lot of fun, and I just need help. You see how crazy things have gotten."

She thought for a moment. "For how long?" She asked in a way that I could tell she was interested.

"Just a few more weeks," I said. "But it could become a regular thing. And I'll pay you way more than you're getting at the theater."

"I also have a waitressing job," she said. "Remember?"

I'd forgotten she'd told me about the waitressing job the night before.

"Okay, I'll pay you more than both of your jobs," I said, knowing it was probably going to be a big deal with Seth but, then, he never told me how much money his assistant was getting.

She thought for a few more moments. "Okay," she said.

"Great," I said. "Pack your bags and I'll come pick you up."

We drove up to Dallas together. She'd been there a bunch of times and already knew some places we could go hang out after the show.

"Austin's not like the rest of Texas," she said, as we drove up the 35. "But you probably noticed that already."

"Texas is a lot like Montana," I said. "It doesn't feel weird to me."

I introduced Sierra to Seth when we met him in Dallas before the show. I said she was my new stylist. (Seth didn't remember her from the night before and had no idea that she was a stage tech.)

I could tell that Seth was annoyed that I'd promised Sierra a job without checking with him first. That was part of my plan, so he couldn't say no.

"Look," I said. "I took care of this myself. It's one less thing for Tiara to do, and now you can put all your attention to finding your assistant."

It felt awkward, but Sierra and Seth agreed to her pay right then and there. I think Seth might even have been impressed with Sierra's negotiating skills.

That night was another stadium double-header and I wanted the headset mic again. I asked Sierra if she could hook me up. She had me drive her to the Guitar Center where she picked out everything we needed. She was a total pro talking to the sales dude. It cost a bundle and I put it all on my company card. I'd been in the business long enough to know that it was a tax deduction.

Sierra helped me get ready for the show. She also knew the balance of speed and ecstasy I needed to do. I never asked her where she learned all that. I guessed from working at the Paramount.

That night was even better than the Paramount. The E helped me connect with the crowd. They loved me. I loved them. About two hours into it, Seth asked me if I wanted to take a break. I shook him off and dove into a crowd of VIPs, all smiles and hugs. I didn't want it to stop. Not ever.

But eventually, it did. I left the stadium sweaty and dizzy.

your best life 19:

Fans and Haters: Part 2

Being famous is all about getting attention. That's it. You can get famous by doing good things, like making music, playing basketball or being amazingly beautiful. And you can get famous for doing bad things, like robbing banks and killing people. (There's a word for bad famous: infamous. The word famous is still in there. It's just a different kind of fame.)

And, like I said in Your Best Life 17, there are fans and haters and when a fan *becomes* a hater, he can get infamous for killing someone famous. That's what happened to John Lennon. The guy who killed him was a big fan of the Beatles, the band that made John Lennon famous. Then the guy decided that John Lennon was a sellout. Five bullets later, Lennon was dead and everyone knew his killer's name. He was infamous, not unfamous.

nineteen

. . .

I HAD the next day off. There wasn't much to do besides eat BBQ and relax by the pool, which is exactly what me and Sierra did.

"You need a spiel," she said. "While you're on stage."

"I must sound like a crazy person," I said.

Sierra laughed. "A little. I mean you're so... enthusiastic."

"I don't know what to do with my mouth," I said.

"That's what I'm talking about," she said. "You need a message."

"I guess," said.

"Do you ever listen to inspirational speakers?" she asked.

"No," I said. "Like who?"

"I don't know either," she said. "I just know they're out there and people pay lots of money just to come and hear them talk. If you could add something like that to your act, then..."

"That's a cool idea," I said.

"Let's see who's out there," she said and picked up her phone.

"Sierra, you're amazing," I said. "I couldn't do this without you."

"Thanks," she said, distracted by the phone. "Here we go: the top 10 inspirational speakers. Whoa, it's all dudes."

"Really," I said. "That sucks."

"We should listen to some of them to hear how they do it. But you need your own unique message."

"I'll have to think about that," I said.

I thought about how Sierra was a little further down the road than me. She just knew more and had more experiences. If only I'd had her around earlier. Maybe she could have spotted Bran as the loser he turned out to be.

———

Seth spent the day on the phone. He came down to the pool late in the afternoon after Sierra had gone up to the room we shared. (Sharing a room was part of the compromise of hiring her.)

"We're going to extend the tour by a week," he said.

Now that I wasn't amped up, the idea sounded exhausting. I think Seth saw my expression.

"Some of the cities we visited earlier on the tour want us to come back. The demand is there. And, I've negotiated the deals with more leverage."

"More money?" I said.

"Essentially," he said.

"Okay," I said. "And I need to be able to talk to the audience more," I said.

"Uh...," said Seth. "I wanted to talk to you about that."

"What's the problem?" I asked. I knew my rap wasn't as good as it could be but I felt annoyed anyway.

"You have a tendency to ramble," he said.

"I know," I said. "I'm going to work on it. I'm going to check out some inspirational speakers. I haven't found my message yet."

I could see Seth thinking about it. That's what Seth does

best: think. "I suppose," he said. "But really work on it, okay? I mean, have something prepared."

"I will," I said. "It's going to be killer."

———

We started back east again, toward Little Rock. Sierra downloaded some inspirational talks for us to listen to during the drive. We started with Bruce Eagleton, because, according to the Internet, he was the top inspirational speaker in America. It was amazing to see how successful (rich) he got by just talking. He had lots of advice about how someone could transform their life. *I really could* transform someone's life. If I had some inspirational words to go with that, I could make Bruce Eagleton my bitch. And a lot of what he said sounded like stuff I could get off the internet. Just take some quotes that were already out there and change a few words here and there. Sierra and I started making up our own inspirational quotes:

"Surrender to yourself and you will achieve victory."

"When your head and your heart are in agreement, that is the essence of you-ness."

"If you think someone is lying to you, check to see if that person is yourself."

"What you know is your past. What you don't know is your future."

"Find inspiration in failure."

See? Easy. I put some of those over pictures of sunsets and flowers and posted them on Instagram. Got tons of likes, too.

When I got to Little Rock, I did the same mixture of E and speed before going on. After the show Sierra brought a six pack of beer back to my room so we could relax and wind down. That's something else that big sisters do—buy the beer.

———

The next stop was Memphis. Sierra and I squeezed in a trip to Graceland. I freaked out when a I heard how Elvis died. OD'ing on the toilet wasn't how I wanted to go. I had to be careful with the drugs, just do them when I had to. It was like medicine, right? In the proper doses, it's good for you.

"What's the deal with you and Seth?" Sierra asked as we drove back to the hotel.

"He's my business partner," I said.

"I know that," she said. "But you're close, right?"

"He used to be my boyfriend," I said.

"Ohhh," she said. "Now it makes sense."

"What do you mean?" I asked.

"It's just the way he acts around you," she said. I must have made a face because next she said, "Hey, I didn't mean to pry."

"It's cool," I said. "I just didn't know it was that obvious."

Seth's new assistant joined the tour. Tom had graduated from NYU with some sort of degree in entertainment business something. He was the most hyper guy I'd ever met. When he was straight, he acted like me on speed. We started calling him the Flash because, if you asked him for anything, he'd have it done in under a minute. I guess that's what you want in an assistant. At least what Seth wanted. I liked Sierra because she was easy-going. Honestly, I didn't ask that much of her but she got it all done without a fuss. And her hair and makeup skills were getting better. She watched a ton of makeup tutorials and was really good at learning how to do things. "Beauty engineering," she called it, and she was only half joking. It was her idea to exaggerate my makeup for the stadium events, because most people were far away from me and we didn't have video screens on the side of the stage, at least not yet. My hair got bigger, too. Yay for Aqua Net.

––––––––

The venue in Nashville was huge. I tried to be inspirational.

"Hello, Nashville!" I said. "Who's here to feel good?!!"

That'd become my usual opening.

"I'm looking out at all of you and I'm seeing the love. I'm *feeling* the love! I know a lot of you came here tonight with problems. You feel broken. You feel like you need to be fixed. I'm here to tell you that there's a perfect self inside all of you. And it's just waiting to get out. Who wants to become their perfect self?"

The bumps I took before each show started to wear off earlier and earlier. I worked out a plan with Sierra to meet me in the ladies' room during my hourly breaks to get topped off. I'd learned to ignore the voice in my head. If it wasn't going to talk sense, I wasn't going to listen.

––––––––

Sierra was the most excited to be in Nashville, America's music capital. I told her she could skip the show that night and take off after my hair and makeup were done. I also let her snort a line so she'd have the energy to hit all the hot spots in town.

I missed her that night. I liked having someone to talk to after the show. I sat in my room and thought about Bruce Eagleton. He was a multi-millionaire. Why wasn't I? Maybe it was coming down off the speed, but I fell into a downward spiral. I started to wonder what was wrong with me that I hadn't bought a second home yet. I hadn't even bought a first home yet. And why didn't I have a tour bus? Then I wondered if it would ever happen, or if I would end up as a has-been who never was, working some crappy nine-to-five waitress job where, every once in a while, a customer would ask me if I was the girl who used to heal people? And then I'd say "no," because it would be too sad to admit what a loser I was and ...well, sometimes my imagination can get going that way. I watched TV and cried at the commercials. It was pathetic.

————

Seth was packing up the RV and Sierra still hadn't come back to the hotel.

"Where the hell is she?" he asked.

"Don't worry," I said. "She'll show up. And she's riding with me anyway. Like, what's the difference?"

"We need to run a tight ship," said Seth. "Things are getting real. If I have crew members going AWOL when there's only four of us, how are we going to keep it together when there's a dozen?"

I liked the idea of there being a dozen of us. That would mean I'd hit the big time. But I could do without Seth's worry-warting.

"She'll turn up," I said. "She always does."

An hour later and she still wasn't there. Seth was losing his shit. "We can't wait around for her all day!" he said.

"It hasn't been all day," I said.

Seth looked at his watch. "We have to leave. Now," he said.

"Go ahead and leave," I said. "We'll catch up with you."

"Did you call her?" he asked.

What a dumb question. Of course I'd texted her. "Yes," I said.

Tom came bouncing up to Seth. "Just got an email from the venue," he said. "They have to bring in a bigger security company for tonight."

"Okay," said Seth. "Thanks." He turned back to me. "We're out of here. And it's on you to get to the venue on time," he said. "You know how to get there, right?"

"I emailed her all the necessary info," said Tom.

"Yeah, I got it," I said.

Then the two of them drove off in a cloud of exhaust and pissiness.

————

Sierra pulled up in a cab about ten minutes later.

"Seth totally freaked out," I said.

"Sorry," she said, but she didn't sound sorry, and she didn't have to be.

"It's no big deal," I said. "Did you have a good time?"

"The best," she said, and she left it at that.

Sierra and I jumped in my car and cut back down to Birmingham, Alabama for another huge show. We listened to more inspirational talks, only this time we wanted to hear from the ladies. Can't say their message sounded any different from the dudes. It's all about having a positive attitude and taking action to get to the life you want. Success really is that simple.

————

Atlanta was going to be huge. We'd skipped it the first time we came through Georgia, and it's a BIG city. We were at the Bobby Dodd Stadium, where the Georgia Tech Yellow Jackets play.

It's always felt weird backstage at stadiums. There's so much space and it was just the (now) four of us. Like four BBs rattling in a tin can. Seth and Tom were off somewhere taking care of business. Sierra and I were finishing up my makeup. I wore a black jumpsuit with rhinestones. (Rhinestones looked good under all the stadium lights.) Sierra laid out a half gram of speed and a half gram of E for me. After I snorted it, we took a selfie and posted it on Instagram. (451 likes)

I jogged out onto the field. "Hello, Atlanta! Who's here to feel good?!!"

By now we'd figured out how to have the people lined up in groups to move things along. I gave my talk about everyone's perfect self and I had to hand it to me, I sounded good. Then I got into the main event.

Maybe an hour in I saw a guy in a long coat walking toward me. Some people thought he was cutting the line, and they shouted at him to go back to the end.

When he got within four feet of me, he reached into his pocket and pulled out a gun, a revolver, like a cowboy would use. I stood there petrified while he pointed it at me. I didn't even scream.

"Hey, buddy! There's a line!" shouted some burly guy who gave him a shove. (I don't even think the burly guy saw the gun.)

The gun went off. I felt the bullet hit me in the hip. I fell to the ground and heard two more shots, and a lot of yelling and screaming. Everyone was so concerned about the guy with the gun they forgot about me.

Seth reached me first. "Are you okay?" he asked. Then he saw the blood. "Holy shit!" he yelled. "Someone call 911!"

Then I blacked out.

your best life 20:

Stay Out of Hospitals at All Costs, Because Hospitals Cost a Lot.

Imagine a hotel where the rooms are small, kind of run down, and the walls are painted something not quite white and not quite beige. Now imagine that the hotel staff comes into your room at random times to ask you why you're staying at the hotel. Also imagine that room service finds its food left over in a high school cafeteria. Getting the picture? Okay, then imagine that you may have to share the room with someone you've never seen before in your life and that person wants to watch TV every time you want to sleep. Last, imagine that the room costs ten times as much as a suite at the Four Seasons.

That's what a hospital is, so drive safe, quit smoking, and don't put anything weird up your butt.

twenty

. . .

I WOKE up in a hospital bed. It was dark outside, and Seth was sitting in the room with me.

"What the hell happened?" I asked, feeling groggy.

Seth looked relieved to see me awake. "You're going to be okay. The doctors had to operate on you."

"Doctors?" I said. Then I drifted back to sleep and had dreams about my DMT frenemies. You know how in dreams you just *know* stuff? In this dream, I *knew* I was on their turf. Everything looked all melty and sparkly. The sky was a pale pink. All I wanted to do was get out of there and I knew a ship was leaving that could get me home, I just couldn't get to the ship. Not a nightmare exactly, more like creepy and frustrating.

I woke up later, not sure of how much time had passed. Seth wasn't there and it was light out. I stared at the ceiling for a while, remembering what had happened. I felt where I'd been shot. A nurse wearing purple scrubs walked in.

"Good morning," she said. "How are you feeling today?"

"Not good," I said.

"That's understandable," she said.

"What happened to the guy?" I asked.

"The man who shot you?" asked the nurse.

"Yeah," I said.

"He's with the police," she said.

"Good," I said. "Where's Seth?"

"That's the young man who came in with you?" she asked.

I hadn't thought of Seth as being a "young man." "Uh-huh," I said.

"I don't know," she said and then she went to checking on things. She didn't seem too concerned about me, maybe because I was going to be fine, maybe because she'd already seen a hundred gunshot victims and I was nothing special, just another person with a hole where there shouldn't be one.

————

Sierra came by with flowers a little after that.

"How you feeling?" she asked.

"That's what everyone wants to know," I said.

"Sorry," she said. "Stupid question." She pointed her thumb toward the door. "There's a horde of reporters out there waiting to talk to you."

"All publicity is good publicity," I said.

Sierra laughed. Then she got all serious. "We don't have to worry, right? You're going to be okay, right?"

"I'll be fine," I said. "I can heal myself, remember?"

"I assumed so," she said. "But that's a relief, hearing it from you."

Seth came in.

"Where have you been?" I asked. (Not in a mean way. I really wanted to know where he'd been.)

"Talking to the doctors," he said. "They found drugs in your system, amphetamines."

Sierra and I looked at each other. We were busted.

Seth glared at Sierra. "Were you part of this?"

I cut in before Sierra could say anything. "It was all me," I said. "She didn't do anything."

"What the hell, Destiny!" said Seth.

"Hey," I said. "I just got shot. How about a little sympathy?"

Seth took breath. "Sorry," he said, but I could tell he wasn't going to let it go. He was just putting it on hold. "How are you feeling?" he asked.

"I'll be okay," I said. "I still don't know exactly what the hell happened?"

"The guy who shot you thinks you're a witch," said Seth. "They're still trying to figure out how the guy got the gun into the stadium."

I remembered my talk with Cardinal Mulcahy and his warning about Satan's power. I should have known that some nut job would jump to that conclusion.

"We'll need more security," I said. "Metal detectors or something."

"We were lucky other people jumped in," said Seth.

"Did anyone else get hit?" I asked.

"Yeah," said Seth. "Some lady got hit in the shoulder. She's in a room across the hall."

"Really?" I said. Then I had a flash of brilliance. "Let's invite all the reporters in and I can go across the hall and heal her in front of the cameras?"

Seth thought about it. "That's a great idea," he said. "Let me go work on that." Then he got up and left.

"Whew," I said to Sierra as soon as he left. "That was close!"

"Thanks for covering for me," she said.

"No problem," I said. "But you'd probably get while the getting's good."

"I hear you," she said. "Looks like the tour's over, anyway."

"Yeah, pretty much," I said. "I hope you can get your old job back."

She shrugged. "I'm pretty good at landing on my feet," she said.

She caught plane back to Austin that night. I was going to miss her. Like I said, she'd become like a big sister.

———

My mom arrived that afternoon. Seth had called her and she'd flown down.

"Oh my god!" she said when she saw me.

"I'm going to be fine," I said, before she could ask how I felt.

"When Seth told me what happened, I couldn't believe it," she said.

"I couldn't believe it either," I said. "Lot of nut cases out there."

"You could've been killed," she said, like I hadn't noticed that yet.

"Mom," I said. "Calm down. It's over. I'm going to be fine."

"The doctors said you were on drugs," she said.

Shit, I thought, *she knows already*. I didn't know that doctors would snitch ion you. I didn't say anything. Instead, I closed my eyes like I was tired and needed some sleep.

But Mom wasn't letting me off that easy. "I can't believe you've gotten mixed up with something like that," she said.

"It's no big deal," was all I could think of saying, so I did. I felt terrible, disappointing my mom like that. It seemed like the worst thing you could do to your mom, other than getting arrested.

"It *is* a big deal," she said. "You know what happens to people who get into drugs. I see them in the parking lot every day."

"Okay, Mom, I get it," I said, losing my patience. "I wasn't using for fun. I needed to get through the shows, y'know? Like the truckers who need to drive all night."

She shook her head. "It's never a good idea," she said. "You're the star. You call the shots. If people need to wait, then they wait."

A lightbulb lit up over my head, like in a cartoon. "You're right," I said.

———

With my mom's okay, I checked out of the hospital that day. The room cost thousands a day and I had no health insurance. (When Seth created the company, he didn't get health insurance for either of us because why would he? *I* was our health plan. Besides, it didn't look good for the girl who could heal anyone to be in a hospital.) The doctors weren't happy about it, but I had to get out of there.

Seth worked it out so I could visit the woman across the hall before I left. Irene had a gunshot wound and an ankle that got crushed in a car crash years ago. I fixed both. (A two-fer!)

I took more questions from reporters outside the hospital. They didn't know anything about the non-prescribed drugs, and I didn't tell them.

"The man who shot you claims you're a witch," said the woman from the Atlanta Journal-Constitution. "Are you a witch?"

"Of course not," I said. "That's ridiculous."

"Are you going to heal yourself?" asked a guy from the Atlanta Georgian.

"Already am," I said. "That's why I'm checking out of here."

"But the doctors still had to operate on you," he said.

"That's just because I blacked out," I said. "They didn't have to. I could have taken care of myself. I've saved gunshot victims before."

"What do you have to say to the man that shot you?" It was a lady from the Atlanta Journal-Constitution again.

"I hope that he gets the help he needs, and becomes his perfect self."

I think I nailed that answer.

———

We went back to the Sheraton in Atlanta. My mom and I got a suite and I just stayed in bed, watching TV. I even saw a rerun of my Hoax Busters episode. It seemed like so long ago.

In the hospital, I had all kinds of prescription painkillers. Now I had to rely on Advil. The pain was THE WORST. The doctors told me exactly what the bullet had done to me, hit me in the hip bone and bounced off at a crazy angle. (It was a .22 bullet so it could have been more serious.)

Seth and my mom had flushed the last of my speed and E down the toilet. (Not that it would have done me any good in my present condition.)

After a few days, I thought I would lose my mind. The Advil wasn't doing the job. My bad mood became infectious. Within a couple of days, Seth was grouchy too. Still, he checked in on me every few hours.

It took a week before I could get out of bed.

Having my mom around was too much stress. She tried to make me feel better which was somehow annoying. Then I'd start to feel guilty about getting mad at her when she was only trying to help. I fell into a downward spiral.

As soon as I could get myself to the bathroom by myself, I sent her home. I could tell how much it hurt her, but it was for her own good. I wanted to be alone in my misery.

With time to myself, I took the opportunity to think about my future. I was definitely done with the drugs. I didn't need them anymore. My mom was right, I was the star. Everything would have to work around ME. I would tour when I wanted to tour. There was no rush. About 16,000 car accidents happened a day in the U.S. My audience would never disappear. And there was the rest of the world. This wasn't a sprint. It was a marathon. No, it was a walkathon!

I had to change my relationship with Seth. I'd be taking over the company in a year and he'd be my employee. He needed to get used to that now. I called Seth to my room and told him the new rules, about how I was going to set a slower pace.

"Okay," he said. "That makes sense." I think he needed a break too.

"And how are we coming on my TV show?" I asked.

"Um," said Seth and I knew from the look on his face that he hadn't been working on it at all. "We can look into that," he same, lamely.

"Haven't we heard from Jas!?" I asked.

"No, nothing," he said.

"I need you to get on it," I said.

"I'll see what I can do," he said.

"Not good enough," I said. "I need you to Make. It. Happen."

"I can't make Jas! give you a TV show," he said.

"Yes, you can," I said. "And, if you can't, I'll find someone who can."

I could tell he wanted to come back at me, but he didn't. "I'll call Jas!, and see what the deal is," he said.

your best life 21:

Of the People, by the People, and for the People? Don't believe it.

I'm as patriotic as the next American. This is the greatest country on Earth. Ever. From sea to shining sea, every American has an equal opportunity to life, liberty and the pursuit of happiness. The American Dream is written into our Constitution. No matter where you start in the Land of the Free, you can make it to the top. I'm living proof of that.

But don't trust the government. I don't know how it happened but, somewhere along the line, the government forgot who they work for. I'm not even talking about the politicians either. I'm talking about unelected people who don't have to answer to anyone. Like the NSA. They can look at your phone records, track you with your phone, even hack into your computer. Facebook, Google and Apple will gladly hand over your information, just like that. And it's not only them. The IRS, EPA and a bunch of other initials can come after you any time they want.

It's not what the Founding Fathers intended; that's for sure.

And there's not much anyone can do about it when the SWAT team knocks down the door. All you have is your lawyer, (See Your Best Life 9) and your gun. Until they take those away, too.

234

twenty-one

· · ·

SOON I WAS ALL BETTER! We checked out of the hotel. I didn't look at the bill. I'm sure it was huge. (The room service bill could probably have bought my mom another trailer.) Still, cheaper than the hospital.

Seth took off in the RV and I got into my Boxster for the drive back to New York. I felt like I'd been sprung from prison. I hopped on the 85 north and gunned it.

I was thrilled to see the Empire State Building again, even if the temperature was only in the 40s. Traffic into the city was insane as usual. It's like the closer you get to New York, the harder it is to get there, like trying to drive through quicksand.

My decision. I could have taken time off, but I wanted to get back into it. I had the car. Now I wanted the penthouse apartment.

I told Tiara the story of the tour. She couldn't believe it. "You should write this all down," she said.

"I have," I said. I'd been keeping kind of a diary since I got to New York.

The day started out okay, but I kept thinking about the guy who shot me. I gave every client the once over when they walked in. I told Tiara I wanted to interview potential bodyguards.

———

Seth and I had a meeting at Laura's office to talk about my dad's legal action. (I had almost forgotten about that BS.) I had to retell Laura the story of the tour. (Of course, I left out all the drinking and drugs, and especially my frenemies.)

She came back at my dad's lawyers with the message that we were going to fight. Then they got back to her with a dollar amount that would make them go away.

"Hell, no!" I said. "Not one penny!" I couldn't believe what an asshole my dad was being.

"I'm not saying we're going to accept it," she said, calm as usual. "I'm letting you know what they said to me."

"How much will it cost to take it to court?" asked Seth.

"Hard to say," said Laura.

"More than the settlement amount?" he asked.

"Again, hard to say," said Laura.

"I don't care how much it costs," I said. "He's not getting anything."

Seth looked at me. "I tend to agree with you, but we need to consider all our options."

"Nope, not an option," I said. "No way."

"Destiny," said Laura, "Seth is the owner of Hand of Destiny. Ultimately it is his decision."

I knew she was right and that made me even madder. "If you make a deal with him, I quit," I said.

Seth looked at Laura like he wanted her to tell him what to do.

"I agree with Destiny," said Laura. "Let's tell them to go stick it where the sun don't shine."

————

Jas!'s people got back to Seth. The good news was that Jas! was "thinking about what she wanted to do with me next." (A direct quote!) She didn't use the words "TV show" but, if there were a couple steps in between, I could live with it. The only thing in the way was that she had already committed the first half of the year to building 100 schools in Africa. Six months was more than I wanted to wait, but I'd been patient before. I could be patient again.

————

I spent a morning at the local Starbucks, interviewing potential bodyguards. The biggest guy was a 350-pound ex-college football player named Solomon. The smallest was Tae-Won Choi, an ex-R.O.K. commando.

Two of the candidates scared me. "Kong" looked like he couldn't wait to hurt someone. I swear the whole time he talked to me he was scanning the room for someone to give a beatdown to, not even as a demonstration, just to do it. A guy named Simon seemed scary because he was the opposite, ice cold. Like a killer robot. No human emotion AT ALL.

I settled on Chris, a middle-weight boxing champ, because I felt comfortable around him. He had a crooked nose and arms like Popeye. I ran it by Seth too, because I wanted him to feel included. Seth gave Chris the thumbs up.

On Chris's first day at work, Seth disguised him as an office employee. Clients would come in and Chris would do a greet-and-seat which was really a chance for him to do a threat assessment. If they looked cool, he would send them into the back to see me. (Everybody looked cool.)

―――

Seth called me at home. He got an email from the Department of Defense inviting us to Langley Air Force Base in Virginia. I would heal a bunch of wounded soldiers they would fly in from around the country.

"How much are they paying?" I asked.

"Nothing. This is your patriotic duty," he said.

No friggin' way," I said. "Doesn't the military have, like, billions?"

"We can't exactly say no to the Department of Defense," he said.

"What are they going to do, bomb us?" I said.

"I mean that it's for the troops," he said. "We can't say no to wounded veterans. You of all people should know what it's like to be shot."

"Thanks for reminding me," I said.

"You know what I mean," he said. "Until we seal a deal with Jas!, we need all the good PR we can get."

That made a lot of sense to me. "When's it supposed to happen?" I asked.

"At the end of the month," he said.

"And Chris is coming with," I said.

"If you want," he said.

"And we stay at a nice hotel," I said.

"The Department of Defense is putting us up," he said.

"Where?" I asked.

"The Marriott," he said.

"We can do better," I said.

"It's Hampton, Virginia," he said. "There aren't any trendy hotels."

"Okay," I said. "For the troops. Sure."

your best life 22:

The Truth About Honesty.

On the way back to New York, I tweeted out: "The truth has no wisdom."

I just thought those words looked cool over a picture of the moon rising above some Aztec pyramids. Only later did I realize what it meant. The truth might be a stupid thing to tell people, because a lot of people can't handle the truth. Dropping truth bombs on their Fantasyland will only make them hate you. And, of course, they'll lie about you to try to destroy you. You can see why some people keep their mouths shut. The truth can sound even crazier than a lie. Like, if you didn't know that dinosaurs were real, would you believe it?

But sometimes you run out of comfortable lies, and you have to be honest, even though it's going to ruin everything.

So let me try another quote (and try to imagine it with a picture of a tiger charging right at you): "When you're desperate enough, only the truth will do."

twenty-two

. . .

I DROVE DOWN THERE with Chris. Seth flew, because it was faster for him and what's the point of a bodyguard if he's not right next to you?

It took all day to get there, more time than I'd spent with Chris before, just the two of us. He wasn't as much fun as Juan or Sierra. We talked about our lives and I could relate to him, because he never went to college. He had some stories about growing up in Southie which is part of Boston. He said that he went into boxing so he could have a fight without someone pulling a knife on him.

Both of our butts ached by the time we got to the Marriott in Newport News—That's a weird name for a city!—and Seth met us. The three of us had dinner at a nearby fish restaurant. Seth said I'd meet the Secretary of Defense.

"Why couldn't they send the Chief of Defense?" I asked.

"What do you mean?" asked Seth. "She *is* the chief of defense."

"You just said it's just his secretary," I said.

"The Secretary of Defense is the head of the Defense Department," said Seth. "She's second only to the President."

"Oh," I said. At my high school, you didn't take Government until senior year, so I'd missed that bit of trivia.

The morning of, a car came and picked us up at 0600. (That's military time for way too early.) Chris stayed at the hotel because, if I wasn't safe on a military base, I wasn't safe anywhere. On Laura's advice, I wore something less flashy, a skirt suit with a pair of high heels. I thought I looked like a real estate agent. Seth wore a suit so we both had to suffer.

The base was a town in itself. The car drove us right out to where the hangars and runways were.

Colonel Barry "Boom Boom" James from the Air Force greeted us. He looked like someone's uncool uncle. "Thank you for coming," he said. "We've got a big event planned for today," he said. "You hear that?"

"That" was the sound of transport planes landing, one right after another.

"We're flying in over 4,000 veterans today," said the Colonel.

"Four-*thousand*?" I said to the Colonel. That seemed like an insane number. I'd be there all day. All night, too!

"There are 1.1 million veterans with a disability rating of 70 percent or higher. I wish they could all be here," said the Colonel.

I gave Seth my what-the hell-did-you-get-me-into look. The Colonel didn't seem to notice. "We're going to get started at 0700. There's a news crew here already. First you'll meet some men and women who are back from Iraq and Afghanistan with serious injuries."

"A little positive P.R.," said Seth.

"That's right," said the Colonel. "It's an important component in any military endeavor." He turned to me. "I read that story about you in the Washington Post. At first, I thought it was a bunch of malarkey so we sent one of our veterans to see you down in Miami, just to see if you could deliver."

"You did?" I said. I felt like they'd been spying on me.

"That's right," said the Colonel. "Young man by the name of Chester Buttonwood. His hand got mangled in a piece of construction equipment in Iraq back in 2009."

"Oh, yeah," I said. "I think I remember him."

I didn't remember him at all.

"His hand grew back good as new," said the Colonel. "None of us could believe it. That's when we said we had to get you up here."

"Well, here I am," I said, hoping he would stop talking. He didn't.

"I was particularly interested in the story about your encounter with the Native American gentleman," said the Colonel.

"Oh, that," I said.

"One of the veterans you're meeting today is Corporal Cliff Beaumont," said the Colonel "He's from the Crow reservation outside of Billings. Maybe he can tell you something about who that man was."

I didn't look at Seth because I didn't want to see his I-told-you-so face. "I'll be sure to ask him," I said.

I was NOT going to ask him.

The Colonel led us to an airplane hangar that had been filled with what looked like a thousand folding chairs. A few hundred veterans were already there, along with the news crew the Colonel had told me about. I started to think about how my feet would feel after standing in heels all day.

Next, as promised, we met Janelle Morris, the Secretary of Defense. She wore a dark suit and pearls. She was all smiles and thank yous.

Looking around, I had a sudden rush of panic. I was at the center of a military operation. This wasn't my show. What did these people expect me to do? What did they think I could do?

Stay calm, I told myself. *You can do this.* I'd face challenges before, and I'd always risen to them. I'd do it again today.

As promised, at 0700, the TV cameras moved in. No introduction or theme music. The soldiers were all in uniform and it looked like they put the worst cases first. Everybody was missing some combination of arms and legs.

I did my best to put on a show for the cameras.

The first guy rolled up to me. Both his legs were gone. "Where're you from, soldier?" I asked.

"Lubbock, Texas," he said.

"That sounds like a good place to be from," I said, because I couldn't think of anything better to say. I put my hand on one of his stumps. (By then I had gotten used to touching stumps.) "Expect a change in your life. And thank you for your service."

The next soldier was missing both his arms below the elbows. "What's your name, soldier?" I asked which was a dumb question because he had it right there on his uniform.

"Reed Crandall," he said.

I touched both of his arms. "Reed Crandall, expect a change in your life."

As Reed walked off, I looked over to see the Colonel and the Secretary of Defense (second only to the President) watching me like hawks. This was going to be a long-ass day.

Next was another guy missing his legs. "Where are you from?" I asked.

"Montana," he said.

"Really?" I said, "I'm from Billings!"

"Yeah," he said. "I grew up on the Crow reservation."

I looked at the name on the soldier's uniform. It said Beaumont. This was the guy the Colonel told me about! I felt like a deer in the headlights, on camera. "I know where that is," was all I could say.

"You said you met one of my people, a medicine man," said Beaumont. He looked at me like I was full of shit.

Uh-oh, I thought. "Yeah," I said. It was Hoax Busters all over again, but somehow worse.

"I never knew of any medicine man on the reservation when I was growing up," he said.

My heart sped up to a mile a minute, like it would burst out of my chest and run away. "Actually, he never said he was a medicine man, he just... y'know, said what he said." I didn't want to argue with this guy, I wanted him out of there. I reached toward his legs.

He slapped my hand away. "I don't want any of this white woman's magic!" he said. Then he turned his wheelchair and rolled away.

I felt everyone in the room staring at me. All the cameras, too. I froze, like a statue. I took a breath, shrugged and forced a smile. "Can't please everyone," I said.

A guy missing a leg hobbled up to me. I didn't talk to him. I just went to work.

Good: another hour passed and no one yelled at me. Bad: All the seats were full now.

As yet another soldier hobbled up to me, I held up a finger and said, "Just a second."

I walked over to the Colonel and Seth. "I need to use the ladies' room," I said.

The Colonel nodded. "Sergeant!" he said.

"Yes, sir!" said a woman who'd been standing in the back of the hanger, by the door.

"Escort Miss Wallace to the ladies room!" he said, so loud that everyone in the room could hear.

"Yes, sir," said the Sergeant and she waved me over. I felt so embarrassed. Then she walked me to a port-a-potty in the corner of the hangar.

Really? I thought.

At least I had my own personal port-a-potty and it was clean. While I was in there, I felt everyone waiting for me to come back out. I kept it quick.

By midday my feet were killing me. (Why did I have to wear new shoes?) The Secretary of Defense had taken off, but the Colonel was still there. He looked like he could go all day. Seth stood right next to him, looking worried. "When's lunch?" I asked.

"1300," said the Colonel.

"Which is when?" I asked.

"That's 1PM in civilian time," he said.

I looked at the clock on the far wall of the hangar. It said 12:15.

"Could I have some water now?" I asked.

The Colonel nodded and a soldier took off. Actually, that's an exaggeration. A soldier ambled off.

I didn't get the water for another 15 minutes. I knew because I was watching the clock constantly, counting down the minutes until lunch.

At exactly 1300, I turned to the Colonel. "Lunch time," I said.

The Colonel did a "right this way" thing with his hand and Seth and I followed him. What I hadn't noticed was that they had set up a table for two behind me while I worked. Seth and I exchanged looks. This felt too weird.

We both sat down and a soldier brought us lunch: a deli sandwich, bag of chips and can of coke each. They hadn't asked us what we wanted either. My sandwich had mustard on it. I hate mustard.

No one else broke for lunch though. Hundreds of soldiers were still sitting in their seats, staring at us. Even the Colonel. AND NO ONE SAID A WORD!

"What the F?" I said to Seth, super quiet and trying not to move my mouth.

"Something's wrong here," he said only loud enough for me to hear.

"No shit," I said. I felt super self-conscious about eating in front of that big an audience, but I was too hungry. "How many troops did he say were coming?"

"Four thousand," said Seth.

"And how many have been in here so far?" I asked.

"I don't know," said Seth. "I wasn't counting. A thousand?"

"A thousand?" I said. I still couldn't do math in my head, but I knew it meant I'd have to do what I just did three more times. "Did they tell you any of this was going to happen?"

"No!" he said. "I'm as surprised as you are."

I scarfed down my lunch in minutes, I was so hungry. Then I just sat there with everyone staring at me. "The sooner I get this done," I said to Seth, "the sooner we can get out of here."

I stood up and my dogs started barking. I kicked off my shoes and went back to it.

I looked at the clock. It was only a little past 1PM. If I started at 7AM, that meant I'd been at it for... (I had to do the math in my head) ...six hours! That meant dinner break would be at...7PM!

I had seen all the troops with obvious injuries by then, the ones missing big parts. Now came the ones where I couldn't tell just by looking. That was a huge pain in the ass. I had to ask them what the problem was so I could touch them in the right place. It seriously slowed me down.

And the troops kept coming. As soon as a seat emptied, someone else would take it. Some of the troops smiled and thanked me, and some just walked away, like I was a ticket taker at the movies.

My mind started to drift: What if I had died when I got shot and this was Hell? What if this was my eternal punishment? What if the Colonel was a demon? I glanced over at him. He was still standing there, watching me. He didn't look tired. Demons don't get tired, do they? What had I done to deserve this?

Seth brought me a bottle of water. "How you holding up?" he asked. That made me feel better. If Seth was there, it couldn't possibly be Hell. I mean, no one gets a manager in Hell, right?

"God, this sucks," I said. The soldier standing in front of me heard me, but I didn't care. I was THAT far gone.

"You're doing a lot of good here," he said. "Concentrate on that."

"Okay," I said. And I concentrated on that. For about five minutes.

We broke at 1900 for dinner. Again, Seth and I sat at a table and ate with the entire room watching us. Seth looked at the dinner – some kind of beef over noodles – and frowned. "What did we ever do to the Department of Defense?" he asked. "Someone didn't get the aircraft carrier they wanted?"

"What's the Colonel been saying to you?" I asked.

"Nothing," said Seth. "He keeps telling me how important this is and how much good you're doing for the soldiers."

"Remind me never to join the Army," I said.

"No kidding," said Seth.

"This can't go on for another 12 hours," I said.

"The Colonel says we're going until 0100 tomorrow," said Seth.

"Tomorrow!" I said.

"That's 1AM," said Seth.

As crazy as it sounds, I felt relieved. I thought I'd be working all night. "I think I can make it," I said.

"Really?" asked Seth.

"Yeah," I said. "Now that I know where the finish line is, I can do it. And if I work fast, maybe we can be out of here sooner."

"Please, let that be true," said Seth.

After I'd finished eating, I took a bathroom break and took my place at the head of the line.

The hours crept by, but with every one that passed, I got closer to the end. By 2200 (10PM) I could see the light at the end of the tunnel. My whole body felt sore from the waist down. I was dreaming of what I would do when I got back to the hotel: I'd take a bubble bath, then get in bed. A foot rub sounded like heaven. Could I find a professional foot massager in Newport News in the middle of the night? Probably not.

A little before 2400 (midnight), troops stopped coming into the hangar. The seats emptied and didn't refill. The end was in sight. I felt a sudden burst of energy. I started to feel good about myself. Another challenge conquered!

At 2351 there was only one soldier left. Sergeant O'Neal had partial loss of hearing in his left ear. "Expect a change in your life, O'Neal," I said as I touched him. "And sorry about the wait."

He smiled. "No problem, ma'am," he said, and he walked off.

I turned to the Colonel and Seth and pumped my fist. "Mission accomplished!" I said.

The Colonel gave me an awkward smile and said, "This way to the debriefing."

I didn't know what a debriefing was. As long as I could sit while it happened, it sounded great. I picked up my shoes and followed the Colonel. Seth started to follow, too.

"You'll have to stay here," the Colonel said to him.

Seth didn't look happy about that, but he didn't say anything. You couldn't argue with the military. They had nukes.

The Colonel led me outside and a couple of armed soldiers joined us. I walked for what seemed like a mile in my stocking feet (which had holes by now). *When will this be over?* I asked myself.

We ended up at an office building and went inside. The Colonel led me into a windowless room and there it was: A CHAIR! I sat down.

I took a moment to feel the relief. <u>Foooooooooot maaaaaaasssssssaaaaaaage!</u> was all I could think of. Then I noticed a desk in front of me. I wanted to put my feet up on it. Would that be rude? I turned to see that I was alone in the room. The two armed soldiers were standing outside on either side of the door. I kept my feet on the ground.

The room looked weird. It didn't have anything in it besides my chair, the desk and two chairs on the other side, facing me. I'd seen rooms like this before, on cop shows.

The Colonel walked back in with the Secretary of Defense. She wore the same dark suit and pearls she wore earlier in the day. They went to the other side of the desk and sat down. Neither one smiled.

"Miss Wallace," said the Secretary. "You never picked up a Native American hitchhiker, did you?" The way she said it, it wasn't a question.

"Uh, no," I said. I couldn't think of why that was a big deal.

They both kept staring at me, like they were waiting for me to keep talking. "That was a story I made up for the press," I said.

"Along with the story about your mother," said the Colonel.

Something felt definitely wrong here. I felt like I was in my high school principal's office, only my high school principal didn't have guys with guns by the door. "Well, yeah," I said.

"Then you admit that you've been lying about the source of your abilities?" said the Secretary of Defense. Again, not a question.

"I wouldn't call it lying," I said.

"Miss Wallace," said the Secretary. "Where did you get these extraordinary abilities?"

I was too tired to deal with this. Too freaked out. I couldn't think straight. Before I could think of anything to say, I heard Laura's voice behind me. "Destiny, don't say anything!"

I'd never been so happy to see anyone before in my life.

The Colonel and the Secretary glared at her.

"And who are you?" asked the Secretary. This time it really was a question.

"I'm Laura Seaberg, Miss Wallace's lawyer."

"This isn't a legal proceeding," said the Colonel.

"Don't care," said Laura. "My client will not be interrogated."

"We're merely asking her a few questions," said the Secretary, trying to play innocent.

"I believe Miss Wallace has given you enough today," said Laura. "We'll both be leaving now."

I stood up. I felt happy to get the hell out of there, but not about having to be back on my feet.

———

"How did you know what was happening to me?" I asked Laura as soon as we got out of the building.

"Seth texted me earlier today," she said. "He thought something wasn't right. I flew straight down,"

"Wow," I said, "Thanks."

"What *is* going on here?" I asked.

"I don't know," she said. "And I don't want to talk about it here. Let's get you back to your hotel."

We found Seth and walked all the way to the entrance of the base. A car waited for us outside the gate. I braced myself for some soldiers to come and capture us, but none did.

———

I had a million questions on the way back to the hotel, but Laura didn't want to get into it. "Get some rest," she said to me. "We'll pick this up in the morning, when we're all fresh."

When I got back to my hotel room, I collapsed on the bed. As tired as I felt, I had trouble going to sleep. I couldn't figure out what I'd done to piss off the military. Or why they cared if my story about the medicine man was fake. In a lot of ways, this freaked me out more than being shot. That I could fix. This was something else. Thank God I had Laura. She could handle this.

Eventually, I drifted off to sleep.

———

I was so busy the day before, I didn't think about making the news. But I did. And I'll give you one guess what for. That's right: Corporal Beaumont slapping my hand and calling me a "white woman." Hardly anything about all the servicemen and women I'd helped. I hated the media.

That hardly seemed a big deal compared with the other dump truck of bullshit heading for me. Me, Laura and Seth had a meeting in my room around 11AM. I sat on the edge of one bed. Laura sat on the other. Seth sat in a chair in the corner. My stomach tied itself into a knot.

———

"Do you have any idea why the military wanted to interrogate you?" That was Laura and she was asking me.

"I don't know," I said, and I shrugged.

Seth and Laura looked at me like I was full of it.

"Really, I don't!" I said.

"Is there something you're not telling us?" asked Laura.

I didn't say anything. I mean, I wanted to. I just couldn't get my mouth to move and make the sounds that I should.

"Destiny..." said Seth, but Laura held up her hand, like he should shut up.

"Let me handle this," she said. "Destiny, I understand the Colonel and the Secretary were interested in your story about the Native American medicine man."

"I never said it was a medicine man," I said. "Everyone just assumed that."

"Okay," said Laura. "Whatever the details, they didn't believe your story."

"The story's not true. I told Seth," I said, exasperated. I fell back on the bed and looked at the ceiling. "For god's sake! I can heal people! Why does everyone want to look a gift horse in the butt?!"

"How did you get your powers," asked Laura.

I didn't say anything. Like maybe if I sat there long enough, she'd give up and go away.

"Destiny, I'm your lawyer," she said. "Anything you tell me is protected by attorney/client privilege. I can't tell anyone."

"You're not going to believe me anyway," I said.

"If it's the truth," she said, "I'll believe it."

I sat up and took a breath. It was time to come clean.

"The first part of the story *is true*. I was driving home from a party. I saw a flash of light across the sky, like a shooting star. It hit the ground, and I heard a boom. It didn't seem like it was that far off.

"I didn't feel like going home yet and I thought maybe I'd see something – I don't know – cool, like a meteorite. I found a dirt road that headed in that direction and took it.

"When I got closer, I saw a glow. When I got closer than that, I saw the glow coming from some burning scrub brush. I got out of the car and looked around. At first, I thought it was a plane crash. There was junk everywhere. It freaked me out. I wondered if there were bodies out there.

"Then I heard a voice calling for help. The weird thing was, I didn't hear it in my ears, I heard it in my head. And it wasn't even the word help, it was more like the feeling that someone needed help. I know that sounds weird, but that's how it felt. And I could sorta tell what direction the voice – or whatever it was - was coming from.

"Okay, now here's where it gets really weird. But I swear it's true. When I found where the voice in my head was coming from, it was coming from an alien."

I stopped the story to look at Laura and Seth. I expected them to call bullshit, laugh, or roll their eyes. But they didn't.

"Keep going," said Laura.

"It sort of looked like a person but was definitely not human. And I could tell it wasn't a guy in a suit or anything. This was real. And it was lying on the ground, and it looked hurt.

"Next I had this thought in my head that I need to go find something. It wasn't like it explained what to look for, I just knew. It was the ship's first aid kit.

"So, I started searching for it. I knew exactly what it looked like, but it was dark and - like I said - there was junk everywhere."

"I found two other aliens, and they were both dead. Then I found what I was looking for. It looked like a glove. I put it on as best I could. The alien's hands were different from ours. Their fingers were a lot longer. Then I went back to the alien and pressed the glove to him. Suddenly, I knew that he would be alright.

"Then I heard another sound, kind of a humming. I look up, and there's *another* ship coming down, only this one didn't crash. It looked like a silver disc, and it didn't have as many lights on it as you see in the movies."

I looked at Seth. "What's that movie where the aliens come to Earth?"

"That could be a bunch of them," he said.

"The one where they land at Devil's Tower," I said.

"Close Encounters of the Third Kind'" said Seth. He was so good at remembering movies.

"Yeah," I said. "Not as many lights as that. Anyway, it looked like it was going to land. Next thing, the alien disappeared from out of my head, like he'd forgotten about me. That's when I got scared. I backed away and hid behind a bush while the ship landed. They picked up the hurt alien and the two dead ones and took off.

"As soon as they were gone, I ran for the car and got the hell out of there. I was back on the road when I realized I was still wearing the glove. And that's how I got my power. It was in the glove."

"Wow," said Seth. "The story about the medicine man does sound more plausible."

"I said you wouldn't believe me," I said.

"I believe you," said Seth. "So that's why you wore gloves when I first met you?"

"Yeah," I said. "Those weren't from the crash. I figured out that there was a metal disc inside the glove, about the size of a quarter, that did the actual healing. I cut it out and stuck it into another pair."

"But you're not wearing gloves now," said Laura.

"After the *HoaxBusters* show, I knew people would be after me about that – the gloves I mean – so that trip I took to Mexico? With my mom? I had a doctor down there surgically implant the disc into my hand."

Laura looked shocked. "Destiny, that could be dangerous. You don't know what that thing is made of!"

"The doctor put a coating of silicon on it," I said. "It's the same kind of silicon they use for boob implants. He said it would be okay." I looked at my hand. "It seems okay to me."

"Wow," Seth said again. "Now what about the military?"

Laura thought for a moment. "Are there any Air Force bases in Montana?"

"Sure," I said. "Malmstrom is up by Great Falls."

Laura nodded, like she'd figured everything out. "It probably took them a while to get to the crash site," she said. "If, as you say, the aliens left the crashed ship, they must have recovered the debris and maybe some advanced technology. Then when someone started to exhibit extraordinary abilities, they investigated it. The fact that Destiny is from the area of the crash site must have drawn their attention."

That made total sense. Laura was smart.

"What do we do?" asked Seth.

"We'll have to talk to them," said Laura. "And I don't think we can avoid giving them what they want."

"What? No!" I said. "This is mine!"

"I agree with Destiny," said Seth. "And not just for reasons of self-interest."

"The greater good would be served if this technology could be understood by all and not merely in the hands of one person," said Laura.

I didn't know how to answer that, but Seth did. "Have to disagree," he said. "Since the crash, we haven't heard of any other breakthrough technologies. That means either the military is sitting on what they've found or – most likely – they can't make heads or tails of it."

"Right," said Laura. "And that's why this is so important. This is the first piece of tech where they know its function. It could be the Rosetta Stone for everything else."

I didn't know what the Rosetta Stone was so I couldn't see her point.

"What if, though," said Seth, "they take it apart, try to reverse engineer it, and fail? Then we have nothing."

"That's an assumption," said Laura.

"This is all assumptions," said Seth.

"I thought you were on my side," I said to Laura, feeling mad.

"I am on your side," she said. "Part of my job is to be honest with you."

"Suppose we say no?" asked Seth.

Laura sighed. "That's an uphill battle. But the burden of

proof is on them. They have to make the case that Destiny has the tech in the first place before they can take it from her."

"Cut it out of me," I said.

"Right," said Laura. "Forcing a teenage girl into surgery could sound Big Brotherish."

(Hey! I got that reference!)

"It would be a media circus," said Seth. "Do they want that kind of publicity?"

"Don't know," said Laura. "But the more I think about it, the more I see how that event yesterday was supposed to work. Healing all those veterans was a demonstration of this technology as a public good. It's just another step to it not being something that should be – quite literally - in the hands of an individual who's using it for personal gain."

I started to see how truly screwed I was. "What do we do?" I asked again.

"We need to talk to them," Laura said.

"Fine," I said, I felt so pissed. I couldn't believe the goddamn government wanted to take this away from me! It just wasn't fair! It was...Big Brotherish!

Laura stood up. "I'll need some time to prepare. We need to have every contingency worked out before we sit down with them." And then she left.

"This sucks," I said.

"Yeah," said Seth.

"I can't let them take this from me," I said. "It's all I have." I started to feel panicky. "What am I going to do? I can't go back to Montana!" I looked at my hand. "Without this I'm just another high school dropout. A nobody!" I started to cry.

Seth came over and sat on the bed next to me. He put his arm around me. "You're not a nobody," he said, lying to be nice.

"You two don't get it!" I said. "You have lives...futures! I can't go back to living with my mom in a shitty trailer!!"

"It's going to be okay," he said, lying again.

I shook his arm off. "Just get out of here, okay!!!"

He got up and left, leaving me by myself. I didn't know what to do.

Then I knew what to do.

I grabbed my suitcase and threw in my toothbrush, toothpaste and some clothes. Opening my door, I checked the hallway to make sure the coast was clear. I didn't check out of my room. I just went downstairs and had the valet bring me my car. I hopped in and gunned the engine.

Canada was closer but I thought I'd have an easier time hiding in Mexico. If I took I85, I could be at the border in 25 hours. Less than that, if I drove over the speed limit.

At least, that was the plan. There was an accident on I64 West and traffic slowed to a crawl. Really, people. Learn to drive.

Seth called my phone. I ignored it. I'd explain later.

It took three hours just to get to Richmond! I was running low on gas, too. I stopped to fill up (using the company credit card).

While I waited for the tank to fill, I checked my messages. There were six:

1."Hey, Destiny it's Seth. Do you want to go out for lunch?"

2."Hey, Destiny, Seth again. Where are you? Call me when you get this."

3."Hey, we really need to know where you are. Laura is starting to freak out."

4."Destiny, it's Laura. You need to come back to the hotel. We can talk about this when you get here. But, please, call us and let us know where you are."

5."Destiny, we need to know if you're okay. Call me, please!"

6."Destiny, I know you're listening to this. You need to call me. We're worried. It's going to be okay, okay?

————

I felt crappy about them worrying about me, but what could I do? They would only try to stop me.

I looked at the directions again: I95 to I85 then the I65 to Montgomery, Alabama. I could remember that. I turned off my phone. I'd call them as soon as I was south of the border, where the US government couldn't touch me.

As I drove, I started to think. What would Seth and Laura do once they knew I'd flown the coop? Would they tell anyone I was missing? I remembered that someone has to be gone for 48 hours before you could report them as a missing person.

Would the government come after me? Thinking about that got me paranoid. What if the government was following me already? I looked in the rearview mirror for black SUVs. That's what federal agents always drive in the movies. I didn't see any. Then I checked the sky for drones. I didn't see any either. What if they were tracking me with my phone? (They can do that, you know. Even if it's off!) I thought about throwing it out the window, but I needed it for directions.

It was already 3:30 in the afternoon when I got to the I85 in Petersburg. I felt too wound up to be hungry but I needed some caffeine. I stopped at a Starbucks.

"Hey, you're Destiny Wallace!" said the barista. His name tag said Daevon.

"That's me," I said. It wasn't a good time to be famous.

"I saw you on the TV this morning," he said. "Man, what was that guy's problem?"

I knew that he meant Corporal Beaumont. "Some people," I said.

"No kidding," he said. "Me, I would have been, like, thank you for the legs!"

"Yeah," I said. "The whole thing was weird." Then I looked around to see if anyone else was looking at me. No one was. I paid cash and got out of there.

I found a Walmart nearby and stopped in to buy a hat and sunglasses. I put them both on the company card. I didn't have much more cash on me.

By then it was 4PM and I was still in Virginia. I got back on the road.

I thought about what I'd do once I got to Mexico. I wouldn't want to draw too much attention to myself. I'd find a sleepy town by the coast and set up shop. I'd only take as many clients as I needed to get by. I'd tell call myself a *bruja*. (That's Spanish for witch.) I kicked myself for not having tried harder in my Spanish class in high school. Maybe I'd learn how to surf. That sounded cool.

I gassed up again in Greenville, South Carolina.

I got to Atlanta a little after midnight. I hadn't been there since I got shot. I passed the Sheraton, where I stayed while I healed up. It was weird. The feeling, not the hotel. It looked the same.

It'd been a long day. I wanted to stop for the night, but I couldn't. I stopped for more coffee. And to pee. Drink coffee. Drive. Pee. That was my life that day.

I gassed up again in Montgomery and got on the I10 which would take me all the way to Texas. I'd been worrying about Seth and Laura. What if the government had them? What if they were being interrogated? Tortured even? I knew the government did that if they wanted to know something really bad.

I listened to my phone messages and heard more of the same. It didn't sound like they were being held by the government. But what if they were being forced to make those calls?

It sounds crazy, but I was stressed, tired and caffeinated. It was around 2AM.

A line of speed was exactly what I needed to get me through that long haul. I found a cash machine and took out $300. Then I found a truck stop.

I waited in my car, looking for someone who might be selling. I eased the seat back and closed my eyes.

I woke up at dawn. *Shit!* I thought. I looked around the parking lot to see if anyone had caught up with me. No one had.

I felt like garbage. I looked like garbage. And I was a little hungry. I put on the hat and sunglasses and went into the diner. I had the All-American breakfast: eggs, bacon, home fries and toast. I paid with the cash I hadn't spent on speed.

I gassed up in Baton Rouge, again paying cash. I figured I had enough money in the bank to get to Mexico and start a new life. Buying the car had almost cleaned me out but there was still enough.

I remembered it was the end of the month, the time when Seth would usually give me my paycheck by way of direct deposit. *He'd better have paid me*, I thought.

I got to San Antonio at 8PM that night. Laredo and the border were only two and a half hours away. *This is it*, I thought. I knew that once I crossed that border, there would literally be no turning back. I could never step foot on US soil again. That freaked me out. I loved America. I was a patriot. America was the greatest country on Earth. The land of the free and the home of the brave.

And Mexico? It was a nice place to visit.

I had no choice. I turned my car south onto I35 and drove.

Laredo is one city in two countries with the Rio Grande running through the middle. The border was closed. I thought it would be open 24/7. But it wasn't. It was almost 11PM and the border wouldn't open until 8AM the next morning. Seriously, this sucked.

I went looking for something to eat. It would be my last American meal, so I had to pick carefully. No point eating at Chipotle, there would be plenty of that where I was going. The Chick-fil-a was closed. I ate at Jack-in-the-Box.

I tried to sleep in my car, in front of the Greyhound Bus Station. Another night of sleeping in the car was beyond uncomfortable. And I was on edge, waiting for Blackhawk helicopters to swoop in. So, like I said, I *tried* to sleep. It was a long night.

your best life 23:

When Your Career Is in the Toilet, Some Things to Think About Before You Flush.

Careers get derailed for all kinds of reasons. Sometimes it's you: You get distracted by personal stuff, like a divorce where your ex accuses you of being abusive. Or you get pulled over on a DUI, make an ass of yourself, and have to go into rehab. Or you stop paying your taxes and, when the IRS notices, you have to sell everything you own. Or you get some bad plastic surgery that makes you look like a fish.

Or you make some bad career moves, like singing when you're an actor, or acting when you're a singer. And I can't say this 100%, but it's probably not a good idea to star in a movie with a computer cartoon Kangaroo.

Sometimes your career fizzles and it's not your fault, like if you're a sports star and you get hurt. Or maybe you're as amazing as ever while the world loses interest in whatever you're so amazing at, like playing saxophone, figure skating or break dancing. And maybe you're still all that but there's someone new coming up who does what you do and, even if they're not any better at it than you, they're just a fresh face. Unless you've reached legendary status, you can get replaced.

When the phone stops ringing, you'll have to jump start your career. There are a bunch of ways to do this.

If you got run off the road by a scandal or personal problems, you can just remind the world of how good you are at doing that thing you do. Put those five months in prison behind you, get back on that horse and ride. Or you can try doing something new, like, if you're a movie star and you always play heroes, you can try playing a bad guy or, if you're known for writing books for kids, you can write a book for grownups.

And you can try doing what you've always done, just somewhere else. Leave all that baggage behind, and get a fresh start in greener pastures. You'll already have experience so you can avoid all the mistakes you made the first time around. And it'll give you a new perspective. Maybe you'll start to see and do things differently.

So don't call it a comeback. Call it a go to.

twenty-three

. . .

I CROSSED the border at 6AM. I hit some red tape, and my heart was in my throat when the border guards looked at my passport. I imagined that the US government had called up Mexico and told them not to let me escape. (I know it sounds silly, but I hadn't gotten much sleep.) The Mexican's didn't give me a hard time. To them I looked like another tourist.

Bienvenido a México! Nuevo Laredo was instantly different and not just because all the signs were in Spanish. I couldn't put my finger on what that difference was. I just knew I was in another country.

Monterrey—where I'd stayed with my mom and had my surgery—was three hours away. It was a big city. I headed there.

When I got there, I found the hotel that me and my mom had stayed at. I was low on *dinero*. Luckily, my corporate credit card still worked.

Seth called as soon as I got to my room. "You're in Mexico?" was the first thing he said.

"Yeah," I said. "How did you know?"

"Because I just saw the charge made to your credit card," he said. "What are you doing there?" he asked.

"I just needed a break," I said. "That's all."

"You need to get back here," he said. "The IRS contacted Laura. Hand of Destiny is going to be audited. And they're coming after you personally, for all that cash you collected at the beginning. You never paid taxes on any of it."

None of that sounded like a reason to go home. It sounded like a reason to stay in Mexico. "I need more time," I said.

"We don't have time," he said.

"Yes, we do," I said. "When Jas! gets back from Africa, we'll..."

"Jas! dropped us," said Seth, cutting me off.

I felt the rug come right out from under me. "She what?" I said.

"The bad publicity from Corporal Beaumont torpedoed the deal," he said.

I hated Corporal Beaumont. And what was Jas's problem? (No way I was going to write her name with an exclamation point now.) "Whatever," I said. "We'll find someone else."

"Okay," he said. "Get back here and we'll start working on it."

"I'll be home soon," I said. "Promise."

"Not soon," he said. "Now."

I didn't like being bossed around. This was my life and my career. "I'll be back when I'm ready," I said. Then there was a pause.

"Destiny, Laura and I talked it over and either you play by our rules, or we'll have to cut you loose."

I couldn't believe what I was hearing. "You can't do that!" I said. "You both need me!"

"No, we don't," he said, and it felt like a punch to the stomach.

"Okay, fine," I said. "Have a nice life as a wannabe movie director!"

"I'm calling the credit card company now and contesting the hotel charge," he said. "Financially you're on your own."

"Go ahead! I don't care!" I said/yelled. "You think I can't take care of myself? I started with *nothing*! I can do it again!"

"That's your prerogative," he said. The way he could stay calm made me *so mad*! I threw the phone at the wall. Then I stomped around the room, trying to calm down.

It was true, I told myself. I had started with nothing. I could do it again, this time with more experience. I would be bigger and better than ever. It would just keep calm and carry on. I picked up my phone to find the screen shattered.

I heard a knock on the door, and I thought it was a noise complaint. Instead saw the guy from the front desk telling me that there was a problem with the credit card. I got mad at Seth all over again. I told the guy, *no problemo*, I'd pay in cash. I just had to go to an ATM.

I could still see the screen well enough to find an ATM a couple of blocks away. But the money didn't come sliding out like I expected. I didn't know why because, of course, the message was in Spanish. I tried another machine nearby and got the same message. That totally freaked me out. Had the government shut off my bank account? Had they figured out I was in Mexico? I went back to the hotel and packed up my suitcase.

———

I parked my car on the street and got out. I still hadn't slept properly, and I was hungry. The smells drifting from the street food carts called my name. I needed money immediately. And I knew exactly where to get it.

Monterrey had panhandlers at NYC levels. Even more so. Many of them needed my help more than they needed the pesos they'd collected that morning. Of course, I had no way of explaining the fantastic deal I had to offer. They'd just have to find out later.

It was broad daylight, and the sidewalks were busy. A guy

on crutches stood under the awning of a jewelry store shaking a paper cup. I came up to him and touched his arm, saying *"Espera un cambio en tu vida."* (I got that from a translation app on my phone.) Then I flipped over his cup and took whatever was in there. The guy started yelling something I couldn't understand, and everyone was looking at me. I couldn't explain to him, or anyone, what I was doing so I started walking. Fast.

Where the policeman came from, I don't know. He appeared right in front of me, asking a question in Spanish . The guy on crutches caught up to me surprisingly fast. The two of them started talking and I could tell from the way the panhandler waved his empty cup around and pointing his finger at me that things weren't going my way. I tried to play dumb. *"No comprende,"* I said, looking at the panhandler like I'd never seen him before in my life.

And that's how I wound up in a Mexican jail.

———

I'd never been in jail before but, if I had to do a Yelp review of this one, I'd give it two stars. My cell had bars, like from the wild west, and it smelled like disinfectant. A drunk slept it off in the cell next to me.

I was up Shit's Creek without a paddle, headed for a waterfall. The creek was the Mexican justice system. The paddle was Laura. My only hope was to explain to the cops who I was, not someone who steals spare change, but a good and special person who needs a break. Lucky for me, one of the cops, Luis, spoke pretty good English. Better than that, one of the other cops had heard of me! His niece had come to see me in Houston! I'd cured her of something that couldn't get translated. Something about an arm? I just smiled and nodded as the two cops sorted out the situation. I could see some light at the end of the tunnel.

"Like, y'know, maybe I could help you guys out and you could let me go," I said. Luis, translated that to the other cop. (I think.)

An hour later, a crowd of people who needed healing filled the police station. The cops never let me out of the holding cell. The people came in and I cured them. Luis never told me what the deal was, and he ignored me when I asked. I could only guess that they were charging everyone who came in. This was turning into a nightmare. Was this human trafficking? Was I their slave? After a few hours, I stopped working. Luis came in and told me I just needed to work a little while longer to "pay off my debt." I didn't totally believe him, but I went back to work anyway.

I wasn't saying my catch phrase, or anything. I'd just wave people in and out. I heard *"gracias"* a lot, but I wasn't even sure if I helped some of these people. I couldn't ask what was wrong with them and Luis never asked me about the limits of my powers.

The parade ended that night, and I asked about being let go. Luis said I could go in the morning. This was worse than being interrogated by the U.S. Military. I felt scared. More scared than I'd ever been before in my life.

I started working on an escape plan. If I could just grab Luis's gun. Even if I got shot by the other cop, as long as I wasn't killed instantly, I'd be okay. I went over the plan a thousand times until I fell asleep from exhaustion.

Luis woke me up the next morning. He didn't look happy. An *hombre* in a gray suit stood next to Luis, smiling. He was short, with a comb over and a mustache that looked like it was drawn on with a marking pen. "Miss Wallace," said the short guy. (And the way he said it, it sounded like "Gwallace.")

I hoped this guy was here to rescue me, but I wasn't sure yet. "Yeah, that's me," I said.

"My name is Ernesto Moreno. I'm from the IMSS, the

Mexican Social Security Institute, he said. Then he nodded to Luis and Luis opened the cell door.

I didn't know what the Mexican Social Security wanted with me but, if it was my ticket out of jail, I had to give him a chance.

———

I followed Ernesto out of the police station onto the street. It was still early morning. I literally breathed easier once I stepped outside.

He handed me my phone and my car keys. "Sorry about that," he said. "I hope this unpleasantness doesn't give you a bad impression of Mexico."

The "unpleasantness" definitely gave me a bad impression of Mexico. I didn't say that. I still felt like another hole was about to open up underneath me.

"When we became aware you were in Mexico, we had to find you," he said.

"Thanks," I said. "It was getting scary in there."

He nodded, like he wasn't surprised. We walked to a street food cart, and he bought me breakfast and coffee. Then he launched into his speech: "The Mexican health care system is different from the United States. Here, the IMSS runs the country's hospitals."

I started to connect the dots, but I was too busy stuffing my face to talk so he kept going.

"Someone with your abilities will be very helpful to us." he said. "You will find that there's less resistance to traditional medicine here. In Mexico, you'll be accepted by doctors."

"Okay," I said. "So, you want me to work in a hospital?"

"Partly," he said. "All over Mexico. There is much work to be done."

This wasn't what I'd imagined for myself. I didn't see how this was going to make me an international celebrity. Maybe

Ernesto could see that in my expression. If there was one thing, I'd learned about myself, I had a hard time keeping my thoughts off my face.

"The government is ready to make you quite comfortable," he said. "Either here or in Mexico City. You will not have to compromise your standard of living."

I didn't know how much he knew. Did he know the barrel I was over? That I couldn't go back to the US? I had to play my cards right. "I need to talk to my lawyer," I said, bluffing.

He gave me a smile that I didn't trust. "What I'm proposing isn't that complicated. But I understand." He nodded to my phone.

"She's not in her office yet," I said.

"Of course," he said. "Please, consider our offer. There are tens of thousands of Mexicans who need your help."

"I'll think about it," I said.

––––––––

Ernesto put me up at the Westin Monterrey Valle, a fancy place. (They found my car too and parked it in the hotel garage.) I went up to my room - a suite- to weigh the pluses and minuses.

On the plus side:

1. The Mexican government didn't want to take my power from me.

2. I could be Mexican famous.

3. The food was good.

4. I could help thousands of people.

––––––––

On the minus side:

1. I couldn't get American rich and famous.

2. I couldn't understand what anyone on the TV said.

Ah, what the hell, I thought. Then I went down to the pool.

———

I met Ernesto that night at the rooftop bar. The music was chill, there were mountains all around and everyone was dressed for success.

"Okay," I said. "You've got a deal."

Ernesto burst out grinning.

———

After that I became a caged bird. I got a big house with marble floors in San Pedro Garza García, the fanciest part of Monterrey. The mountains reminded me of Billings. I never thought I could have missed Billings, but I did. I had a house-keeper and government cars drove me everywhere I needed to go. (I never got a Mexican driver's license.)

Most days, I'd be at the local hospitals. The doctors didn't give me side eye. I had my turf, and they had theirs. I spent a lot of time in the E.R. and I wore a white coat with my name stitched on it.

Some days they'd drive me way out into the sticks to visit a *pueblo* that didn't have a doctor. Sometimes I'd meet the town *curandero*. That's Spanish for healer. The curanderos would have fit right in at the Global Wellness Summit. The locals respected the *curanderos,* and the *curanderos* were cool with me. It wasn't anything like the stadium visits I'd done back home. No music. No spotlights. I didn't even bother to dress up. Sneakers and jeans, that was it.

I dressed up for when I met *El Presidente de los Estados Unidos Mexicanos* and I did a lot of photo ops with other politicians.

This went on all summer.

About two thousand times, I thought about calling Seth. I wanted to know how he was doing and what he was up to. I didn't call because I didn't want him to know how I was doing or what I was up to. I needed to return in triumph. Bigger and better than ever. I still hadn't forgotten my dream. This whole south of the border detour was just that: a detour. I told myself not to get too comfortable. I thought about all the places I could go next... London... Tokyo...

Seth called when I was coming back from China. Not China the country. China the town northeast of Monterrey. When I saw his name, I grabbed the phone. My finger was an inch from the screen before I thought better of it. I threw the phone back down on the car seat. Then I stared at it, waiting to see If he'd leave a message. He did:

"Hey, Destiny, it's Seth. Good to see that this number still works. Because, uh, I have some bad news. Your mom was in an accident, and I thought you should know. Give me a call, okay? Hope you're doing okay. Any time, okay? Alright, thanks, bye."

Of course, I called him back.

"What happened to my mom?" was the first thing I said.

"There was a gas explosion at the diner where she works. Blew out the entire kitchen. She's lucky to be alive."

That got my attention. "So, she's okay?" I asked.

"Not really," said Seth. "She's alive. But it's touch and go."

I felt mad at Seth. I knew it wasn't his fault. He was just the messenger. Still, I felt mad. "I guess you want me to come up there," I said.

"I don't want you to do anything," he said. "I'm just telling you about what happened."

"Yeah, sure," I said. "Well...message received." We said our goodbyes and I ended the call.

Like I needed this bullshit.

I had to think this through: If I stayed in Mexico, <u>maybe</u> my mom would die. If I went back to the US, *for sure* I'd have my power taken away from me. And how did I know if the story was even true? Had Seth seen my mom? What if the government had made the whole thing up and were using him to do their dirty work?

I called my mom.

No answer.

I left a message for her to call me back.

———

By the time I got home, Marta, my housekeeper, had dinner ready. I was too distracted to enjoy it. I had my phone next to me, waiting for mom to call.

I thought about everything I had. I was the Florence Nightingale of Mexico. I was doing a lot of good. A nation depended on me. How disappointed would *El Presidente de los Estados Unidos Mexicanos* be if I bolted?

And what would my life be without my power? I'd be useless to the world. An Adele who couldn't sing. A Steve Jobs who couldn't program a computer. A Michael Jordan who couldn't sink a three-pointer.

———

The next morning was a hospital day, and I was in the E.R. Everyone I saw made me think about my mom. I'd given up on my mom calling me. A gas explosion. What would that do to someone? I saw what a car crash had done to Laura. An explosion sounded worse. Even if my mom lived, what would she look like? And what if Seth called me again to tell me that my mom had died? I was a wreck, and I had no one on Earth to talk to about it.

———

When I got back home that night, I sent Marta home. After she left, I went to the kitchen and got a cooking knife. Then I went out on the back patio and dragged a chair out under the stars. I sat there for a while staring up, wondering which one of those little dots of light the thing in my hand had come from. I kept staring, trying to clear all the thoughts out of my head. Then I took the knife and stuck it in my forearm.

See, I'd figured out something about the voice in my head. It was coming from the thing in my hand. Looking back at all the times I heard it; I realized it happened whenever I needed to heal myself. Like when I stubbed my toe, or when I had a drink. (Alcohol is a poison, folks.) Sometimes I just couldn't hear it, like if I was at a party or a dance club, because it got drowned out by all the other racket. That part I was 100% sure of.

And I had a hunch that it *was* trying to tell me something, that it wanted me to do something. And maybe, *maybe*, we could learn to talk to each other, the way I'd learned to talk to Mexicans.

As soon as the knife went into me, Dr. Alien spoke up. As usual, I didn't understand it. The pain of the knife in my arm distracted and I did my best to concentrate.

"C'mon bro," I said "I've been in Mexico for a few months and my Spanish has gotten way better. You've been with me for years and you can't speak a word of English?"

I wiggled the knife a little bit and it said some more Alienese. It was beyond frustrating.

"Don't talk, then," I said. "Just listen."

I told the aliens all about the jam I'd gotten into. How the U.S. Government wanted my powers. How lonely I was in Mexico. What had happened to my mom. What would happen to me if I went back to the U.S. All that. And y'know, just hearing myself saying it out loud helped. That's why people go to see shrinks, right? Not for answers, but just to get it out of their heads. Only my shrink was from another part of the galaxy.

When I finished singing my soap opera, I knew what I had to do. I mean, it was pretty obvious. I took the knife out of my arm.

your best life 24:

Caught Between a Rock and an Even Crappier Rock.

In Your Best Life 13, I talked about some of the theories of how to make the right decision. And that's what they are: theories. Philosophy is great for when you're getting stoned with your friends and you've already talked about what you'd want your superpower to be but, eventually, the rubber will meet the road, and you'll have to make a choice that matters in your life. Let me break it down for you.

Most choices in life are easy, because they don't matter much. The easiest are the everyday decisions: Cap'n Crunch or Cocoa Puffs? Slip-ons or lace-ups? Blonde or brunette? Tomorrow is a new day, and you can order the kale salad instead of the cheeseburger so no biggie.

The next level up is what's called life decisions, things like your career, getting married and buying a house. These still aren't that hard to make, because they can all be undone. Some people get married two or three times, have two or three careers and live in two or three houses.

None of these ask for you to give up anything. Becoming an actor doesn't mean you can't also be a model. Marrying

Matt means you can't marry Ben. (And Ben's not asking anyway.) Buying a house doesn't mean giving up all the other houses. It just means getting more money so you can get one in the city, one at the beach and one in the south of France.

You'll probably get through your entire life never having to make decisions bigger than these.

Other decisions are about right and wrong and these are pretty easy to make, too. Every day you decide not to rob a 7-11. You don't even think about it. And it's not just because you'll get caught and thrown in prison. It just wouldn't be right. And what's right is better for you, too. Pay for your Slurpee and everyone goes home happy.

Tough decisions are where the hardest thing and the right thing are the same thing. You know what you have to do, and it's going to suck. My advice is to never have to make any decisions like this.

twenty-four

. . .

I BANDAGED my arm and got a couple hours of sleep. It was still chilly and dark when I hopped in my Boxster, put the top up and headed north. I felt just as nervous leaving Mexico as I felt entering.

Sure enough, Nuevo Laredo was on the horizon when I saw flashing lights behind me. There were a few other cars on the road, but I knew the lights were meant for me. I'd wised up enough to know the deal. I was valuable to the Mexican government. They weren't going to let their caged bird fly.

I stepped on the gas until I was doing over 150mph. (That's about 240kph for my Mexican readers.) Cars started moving out of my way. It was a scene.

I hit the Nuevo Laredo city limits in no time. The Mexican police had set up a roadblock across the highway. It was time for the Plan B that I hadn't thought of yet.

The Rio Grande was only two miles away on my right. I slowed down, like I was giving up then took a hard turn off the highway onto a dirt road. A few police trucks broke from the roadblock to come after me. They were 4x4s. They didn't need a road.

As they bounced in my direction, three helicopters appeared in the sky on the U.S. Side of the river. I aimed straight for them and floored it, leaving a cloud of dust behind me.

I slid to a stop where the road ended, maybe a thousand feet from the river. I got out and ran. I was too pumped to be scared. I looked over my shoulder and saw the 4x4s closing in. It felt just like a movie. And just like in a movie, I tripped and fell, scraping my hands. The voice said something. "Not now!" I said.

I got up and ran again and I reached the river when the trucks did. Mexican police jumped out, holding M16s. They pointed them at me. I stopped, not sure if they'd shoot me or not. I was breathing hard.

Across the river, a helicopter had landed and there were American soldiers with their M16s pointed at the Mexicans. The other two helicopters hovered over the river. I saw soldiers with M16s in those, too. M16s all around.

It was literally a Mexican standoff. I didn't know what to do. Was I about to start Mexican-American War II? I took a step toward the river, and no one shot me. I took another. Still nobody shot me. Then another step... Then another... Until I reached the riverbank. It looked about 100 feet across the river and one of the helicopters came down to right above the water. I guess that none of the helicopter dudes were going to help me until I got halfway across.

I waded out into the river; it got deeper with every step. Did I mention that I don't know how to swim? When it got neck deep I just pushed forward and flapped my arms and legs as best I could. I felt a hand grab my wrist and pull me upward. Next thing I knew, I was in the helicopter with a bunch of burly guys wearing camo and Oakley sunglasses. They strapped me in, and the helicopter shot up into the air so fast I got that roller coaster feeling in my stomach.

Internationals crisis over.

———

Out of the fire, into the frying pan.

It only took a half hour to get to Lackland Air Force Base near San Antonio. When I got off the helicopter, Colonel James was there waiting for me, like some dad who'd been up all night, waiting for his daughter to come home from a date.

"Good to see you again, Miss Wallace," he said. Yeah, sure.

They gave me some breakfast in an empty mess hall while the Colonel laid out the deal. The disc in my hand was "an issue of national security" and was now property of the U.S. Government. Out of the kindness of their hearts, they'd let me use my power one last time to heal my mom. None of this surprised me, but it still pissed me off.

"So, about this 'accident' my mom was in," I said, using finger quotes on "accident."

"It *was* an accident," said the Colonel, like he was disappointed that I would suggest anything so crazy.

I stared at him hard for a few seconds, waiting for him to crack. He didn't.

"This is all for the good of the country," he said. "I think you know that."

"You really think you can figure out how this thing works?" I said, holding up my hand.

"Maybe you can start by telling us everything you know about it," he said.

"It talks," I said.

"Talks?!" The way he said it, I could see that really put him back on his heels.

"Yeah, it talks to me sometimes," I said.

Now he looked at my hand like he wanted to grab it and rip it off my wrist. "What does it say?" he asked.

That's when I saw that I had a little leverage. "I heal my mom; you get to cut this thing out of me. You want anything more; you have to sweeten the deal."

He raised an eyebrow like he couldn't believe I was pushing back on him. But I'd been in a Mexican jail, and I'd had machine guns pointed at me. I didn't scare easily now.

"What else do you want?" he asked.

"I lost a perfectly good Porsche getting here." I said.

"Fine," he said. "We'll take care of it."

Of course they would. What was the cost of a new Porsche? One one-millionth of a fighter plane? I felt proud of myself for totally burning the U.S. Government.

"What does it say?" he asked, still looking at my hand.

I shrugged. "Don't know exactly. It speaks whatever language they speak on whatever planet it's from." Then I told him everything I figured out about the voice, how I only heard it when it was healing me.

"Probably alien AI," he said.

"Probably," I said. (I googled AI later and found that it means Artificial Intelligence.) "How about we chat about this while you take me to my mom?"

———

We took a plane to Malmstrom Air Force Base outside of Great Falls, Montana. It was a huge plane for just me, the Colonel and a couple of soldiers in blue berets. I don't know what they were there for. Did they think I would grab a parachute and jump out?

I told the Colonel the whole story about the UFO crash. The Colonel recorded the whole thing and wanted a lot of detail about what the alien looked like. I told him what I could remember. It had been a while, and the details were fuzzy. (I mean, my memory was fuzzy, not the alien.) I wanted to know if they'd already seen an alien like it, or if there were different kinds visiting us. Colonel James wouldn't tell me anything.

I didn't get a window seat (there weren't any) so all I could do is stare at the Colonel. He had a bunch of medals and ribbons on his suit jacket. Did he have a closet full of uniforms with the same medals? I didn't ask.

your best life 25:

Keep Your Eyes on the Prize and Your Feet on the Ground.

All the money in the world doesn't make you better than everyone else. It just means you have money. (And owe a shitload in taxes.)

Fame doesn't give you superpowers. It doesn't make you a genius and it doesn't mean everyone wants to hear your political opinions.

A rich and famous person is still a person. Celebrities put their Gucci pants on like everyone else, one $1,800 leg at a time.

And no one's perfect. We all make little mistakes every day. We've all pushed the door with a sign on it that says, "pull." We've all talked smack about someone only to find out that they're standing right behind us.

It's not just little mistakes. We all make big mistakes, too. There's no reason to feel bad about your first marriage or buying that land in Florida. Truth is, if you get to the end of your life and you've never screwed up *big time*, then you haven't taken any risks. Or had any fun.

So, you have to cut yourself some slack and stay humble.

Being humble shows strength, not weakness. When you start with nothing, you know you can survive with nothing, and there's something to be said for getting down off your high horse and walking a few miles in somebody else's shoes. It keeps you in touch with your roots, and the best roots are the humblest. Turning ten bucks into a million is way more impressive than turning ten million into a billion.

Best advice: Don't let your success go to your head. Instead, take your success and put it in the stock market.

twenty-five

. . .

I TOOK another helicopter ride to Billings and a car trip to the hospital where my mom was. Being back in the US was a relief. It was easier being able to speak the language and just being able to read the billboards felt good. I saw a bunch of fast-food places I looked forward to eating at again.

I didn't get to the hospital until after visiting hours. When the nurse at the front desk tried to put me off until the next day, the Colonel stepped in. Phone calls were made, arms were twisted. I got in to see my mom.

They had Mom in the ICU. I went into her room alone while the two soldiers in blue berets stood outside by the door. (It was the same two guys that'd been glued to me since we left Lackland Air Force Base, and I didn't think either of them had gone to the bathroom the whole time.) Mom was asleep and she looked in bad shape. Even under the bandages I could see that parts of her face were missing. Machines hooked up to her, beeped and blinked. There was no time to freak out. I put my hand on her head and said, "Expect a change in your life," one last time.

Colonel James appeared at my side like magic. "Miss Wallace," he said, and I knew what he meant.

———

I went straight back to the car and on to the airport. On the helicopter ride back to Malmstron, I couldn't stop thinking about my mom and how she looked. I reminded myself that she would be as good as new.

As soon as the helicopter landed, they took me to an airplane hangar with a big white tent set up in the middle, all lit up, bright as day. Inside was an operating room with a doctor and nurse, ready and waiting. I felt so special.

(I'm being sarcastic.)

They stuck a needle in my hand, and I felt it go numb (which is a weird thing to say, because how can you *feel* something *go numb*?) When the scalpel sliced my palm, I didn't hear the voice, I guess because of the Novocain, or whatever they'd stuck in me. In less than a minute, the disc sat on a metal tray and, *damn*, did they get it out of there fast. Colonel James disappeared along with his Precious, and the Air Force instantly lost interest in me.

As they stitched me up, it hit me that I'd have to heal like any other person. I was Iron Man without his suit. Thor without his hammer. Bruce Banner without... I was just Bruce Banner.

No, I was Destiny Wallace, a girl from a trailer park outside Billings, Montana who took a flying jump at the brass ring and ended up making more of herself than anyone would have expected. And, for the first time in my life, I was okay with being me.

———

The guys in the blue berets escorted me out of the base and left me by the side of the road like a rusty B-52. It was pretty late at night, but I could still get a car to the Greyhound Bus Station in Great Falls. I never thought I'd have to ride the

Dirty Dog again, but it was 200 miles back to Billings and they had a bus leaving at 1:30AM.

Buying my ticket was a little complicated because all my money was in Bancomer, a Mexican bank, but it got done. I took my seat, and the bus rolled out. Around Armington, a guy claiming to be a professional skateboarder tried to hit on me. I still wore the clothes I'd had on when I jumped in the Rio Grande and my hand was freshly bandaged. Like, how horny was this guy?

I got off in Billings as the sun came up. It was a new day, and I felt just a little bit optimistic. My neck was sore from trying to sleep on the bus. I hadn't appreciated how many of life's everyday aches and pains the aliens had taken care of for me.

———

When I got to the hospital, the nurses at the front desk let me back into my mom's room. A nurse came in to check on my mom. "You must be Patty's daughter," she said, all bright and chipper.

"Yeah," I said. "How's she doing?"

"She'll need to be sedated for quite a while," said the nurse, then she squinted at me, sizing me up. "Can you do all the things they say you can?"

I guessed that after last night's dust up with the Air Force someone had gotten curious and done some checking. "Not anymore," I said.

"Easy come, easy go," she said.

"I guess," I said, even though *none* of it had been easy, coming or going.

My hand hurt. The pain started while I was riding the Dirty Dog. "Do you have an Advil or something?" I showed her my bandaged hand. "This kind of hurts."

She rustled up a couple which was totally cool of her. Nurses really are heroes.

After she left, I thought about Seth and Laura. Did they know I was back in the US? Did they care? It was already two hours later in New York. I called Laura.

"Destiny," she said in her professional voice. I'd heard that tone before, when she talked business with other lawyers. This call wasn't going to be as easy as I'd hoped.

"Hey," I said. "I thought I'd call. I'm back home, in Montana." Then I gave her the rundown of what happened with me and the Colonel.

"Do you need legal representation?" she asked.

"No," said. "I think the government is done with me. They got what they wanted, y'know."

"That was inevitable," she said, and I couldn't help but pick up a little I-told-you-so in there.

"I guess," I said. "I mean, you're right. I should have listened to you the whole time."

"That would have made things easier," she said.

I couldn't argue with that, so I didn't. "Is the IRS still coming after us?"

"It's not really 'us' anymore," she said. "I haven't been keeping up with Hand of Destiny. You'll have to talk to Seth."

"Yeah," I said. "He's going to be my next call. Anyway, it was fun hanging out with you. You were my favorite room-mate." She laughed at that, not in a bad way.

"It was fun hanging out with you too," she said, and I could tell she was smiling as she said it. "I don't think I'll have another client quite like you,"

"Probably not," I said.

"I wish you only the best in your new life," she said.

"You too, " I said.

"And if you're ever in New York...," she said.

"Maybe we can go to that burger place on Seventh Avenue," I said.

"Maybe," she said.

Then we said our goodbyes and I ended the call. It felt weird. Laura had been like my other mom for so long. Now she was... what? An old friend? Anyway, it was cool. I had a mom. I didn't need a second one.

I knew I should call Seth, but calling Laura felt like enough for one day. I'd get to him tomorrow.

———

I hung around the hospital all day. I couldn't stay there overnight so I went to Castle Creek, the trailer park where I grew up. I'd promised myself I'd never set foot in the place again. Ever. Technically, I still hadn't as I stood on the side of the road looking down on the place. It hadn't changed much since the morning I slipped out of there on the way to the Greyhound Station.

What the hell, I had to pee. I went in. It had been almost two years so I hoped that maybe, if I kept my head down, no one would recognize me.

I didn't get 100 feet before I heard, "Destiny!"

I looked to see Emma Thune waving at me. She'd gone to my high school and we used to take the school bus together. "Hey, Em," I said, realizing how crappy I must have looked.

"Oh'm'god, I heard about your mom," she said.

"She's gonna be okay," I said. "I was just at the hospital."

"She's lucky to have you around," said Emma.

I knew what she meant by that. "Yeah, I'm around," I said and, before I could get away, Emma's mom came out of her trailer. She looked at me like she couldn't believe it.

"Hey, Missus T," I said, and she just kept looking at me, like I was a ghost. I started walking again and Emma walked with me.

"I was following you on Instagram," she said. "Then you just disappeared."

"I was in Mexico," said.

"Mexico? Really?" she said.

"I had to take some time off," I said. I didn't want to talk about myself, so I changed the subject. "How are things at North?" That was the name of my high school.

"I don't know," she said. "I graduated over a year ago. I'm working now."

"That's cool," I said.

"Sometimes it sucks but, y'know..." Then she shrugged. "They put up a picture of you in the cabinet of fame."

I knew what she meant. In the main entrance of North, they had a glass case with pictures of "famous" graduates. It was kind of a joke. One guy in there played a few seasons with the Washington Redskins and there was the girl who became the county sheriff.

"Oh, wow," I said. "I'm honored, I guess."

Mom's trailer came up on the right. Her old Ford was parked out front and there were some potted plants on either side of the front door that hadn't been there before.

"Can you help me break in?" I asked Emma.

"Sure," she said. "What do you need me to do?"

"I think I can get in through the back window," I said, because I'd done it dozens of times as a kid. "I just need you to give me a boost."

"No problem," she said.

We went around back and, lucky enough, the lock on the window was still busted. I climbed in. After I was inside, Emma just stood there, like she wanted me to invite her in. I wasn't in the mood.

"If you want, I can hang out later," I said. "Right now, I gotta get some sleep, okay?"

"You must be exhausted," she said.

"Totally," I said.

"Same phone number!" she said as she walked away.

"Cool," I said. I'd deleted everybody's phone number when I left for New York.

After I peed, I went into the kitchen and opened the refrigerator. It was new. I guessed my mom bought it with some of the money I sent her. That made me happy. The milk was still good, and I found a box of Rice Crispies in the cupboard. While I ate, I looked around the trailer and noticed all the familiar details - the fake wood laminated cabinets, the red and gray checked curtains, the framed paint-by-numbers of a deer I'd made when I was 8.

With breakfast/dinner completed, I took a shower. It was the best shower of my life. After that, I went to my old room to get some (desperately needed) clean underwear. My room was exactly as I'd left it. My blue North High School sweatshirt was still where I'd dropped it the night before I ran away. It felt too weird being in there. I slept on the couch.

———

I woke up the next morning when someone knocked on the door. I threw on a robe and answered it. It was Craig Marks from a few doors down. He apologized for waking me up and asked if I could help him. He broke a bone in his hand years ago without knowing it and later found out it hadn't healed right. He wanted to know if I could fix it.

"Sorry, I can't do that anymore. I lost my power," I said, and I held up my bandaged hand. He looked at my hand, confused. I didn't want to tell him my life story, so I said, "Easy come. Easy go."

He left disappointed and I figured I'd get a lot of that for a while.

I found some clothes I could be caught dead in and walked over to Emma's place. She gave me a ride to the hospital on her way to her job at Costco. When I got to the

ICU, Mom looked pretty much like when I left her. It was hard to tell with all those bandages.

A doctor stopped by, one of the surgeons that'd operated on her. He told me they had to remove a spoon and a salt-shaker from Mom. He also said that, when her condition stabilized, they'd need to do more surgeries.

"Nah," I said. "You won't need to do that."

"Much of her body needs to be reconstructed," he said.

"I get that," I said. "But you won't need to do any more surgeries. She'll be fine."

He made a frowny face and left. Fine with me. I was done arguing with doctors.

———

That afternoon, I went and got a Diet Coke out of a vending machine. As I popped the top, I thought about how I'd have to be more careful about what I put into my body from now on.

When I got back to Mom's room, I saw Seth standing by the doorway. I hadn't called him yet; I was going to do that later. None of this was easy and I needed to pace myself. I felt relieved to see him. I didn't say anything. I just gave him a hug for, like, a minute.

"How's your mom?" he asked after I released him.

"She'll be okay," I said.

"Gotta love the alien tech," he said, then he looked at my bandaged hand. "Looks like the Military Industrial Complex got what they wanted."

"Yep," I said. "Laura said there was no other way it could have gone."

"She's right," he said. "Then I assume you spoke with her."

"I called her yesterday, I said. "I think she was mad at me, but we made up."

"She was pretty pissed," he said, and he laughed. "She kind of cut me off too."

"I think she said something like that," I said. "But we're good now, I think."

"That's good," he said, and we looked at Mom for a few seconds.

"Did Colonel James put you up to this?" I asked.

"He had me call you when your mom got hurt," he said. "He didn't tell me to come here."

"Of course not. He doesn't care about us now," I said.

"I think this'll all be for the best," he said. "And, to Laura's point, it was inevitable."

Seth had been a lot of things to me since we met. First, he was my boyfriend, then my business partner slash manager. No matter what, he always looked out for me.

"I think I screwed this up," I said. "I mean between us."

"It's complicated," he said.

"I know, and it didn't have to be, y'know? If I'd just been honest with you in the beginning, maybe we wouldn't have started dating."

He smiled. "That part wasn't so bad," he said.

"Yeah, but it made it harder when you were my manager," I said.

"True," he said. "But if I hadn't started dating you, I would never have been your manager."

"I can't imagine going through all that with anyone else," I said.

"Me neither," he said.

"Anyway, thanks for being there for me," I said.

"No problem," he said. "It was an amazing gift you had," he said. "I think we did some good in this world."

"Yeah, I guess we did," I said.

He stayed with me for the rest of the day, and we ate at Fuddruckers that night. I needed the company, and it felt like when we used to hang out together on the road. We talked business, about how Hand of Destiny LLC was no more. Technically I'd been fired. (Not the first time in my life. Technically I was fired from Hardee's but, *really*, I quit. I just never told Todd, my shift manager, because he was the reason I quit.) Seth couldn't get out of the lease he had on the office space, so we lost a bundle there. Still, enough money was left over so that I wouldn't end up on the street.

"Hey, can I talk to you about something?" I asked, because it seemed like the time.

"Sure," he said, so I told him about the DMT trip and what I'd seen.

"Wow," he said when I finished my story. "That's weird. And that's coming from someone who's met extraterrestrials."

"I know," I said. "But if there's life on other planets, do you think there's something beyond all this?" I nodded toward the dining area, but I meant all of the universe.

Seth knew what I meant. "According to string theory, there're supposed to be ten dimensions," he said.

I didn't know what string theory was, but the "ten dimensions" part I got. "Maybe that's what I saw."

"Or you were just hallucinating," he said.

"Or that," I said. "I'm not going to try it again; that's for sure."

"I would advise against it," he said.

———

He drove me back to Castle Creek and we said our teary (for me) goodbyes in the rental car. The next day he flew back to New York.

———

A ton of my mom's friends stopped by, and they were all as nice as can be. A lot of them brought flowers. I couldn't talk to them about everything that happened, so I kept my half of the conversation short and asked them a lot of questions about their lives. I got all the Castle Creek gossip and everything that happened at the diner, before it went kablooie.

———

After a week or so, the nurses couldn't help but gawk at how my mom was getting better. Parts of her that weren't there before started to grow back. They called the doctors who stood around in their white coats, scratching their heads. I asked if Mom could be taken off the sedatives and got more scrunched faces and "hmmms." I kept bugging them until they finally agreed to let Mom wake up.

After they disconnected a couple tubes, I sat watching her face, waiting for her eyes to open.

It happened late in the afternoon. It took her a second to realize where she was and, when she did, I could see how freaked out she felt. (Hey, I'd been there myself.)

I jumped up from my chair. "Mom!" I said.

She looked over at me, still trying to figure out what was going on.

I held her hand, the one without a bandage. "It's okay, Mom. You're going to be alright," I said. "I took care of everything."

That seemed to calm her down a little, then she got that confused and scared look again.

"I know," I said. "You can't talk. Your jaw got hurt in the accident." I was sugar coating it. Most of her jaw was still missing. It would grow back though so a white lie right then and there wasn't going to hurt. "I have my phone so you can text me."

I put the phone in her good hand.

"What happened?" she typed.

"There was a gas explosion at the diner," I said.

"??????!!!!!!"

"Yeah," I said. "Blew up the whole place."

"What about Gus and Pedro?"

I'd heard about those two from Mom's coworkers. "They didn't make it," I said. Mom stared up at the ceiling, looking lost.

"The doctors say it's a miracle you survived," I said. Mom dropped the phone, and I didn't say anything after that.

The next day, Mom and I watched some TV together. I think she wanted to get her mind off everything that'd happened. After a couple of game shows, she turned on Jas!. Guru Nusbaum was on, talking about a visit he made to a town that'd been flattened by a hurricane. The guru's message was basically "shit happens," and "whatcha gonna do?" wrapped in an orange robe. The show was tough for me to sit through. It was impossible not to think that it could have been me, riding to the rescue at disaster sites all over the world. But, like the guru said, shit happens and whatcha gonna do?

Soon Mom got off all the monitors and drips. Every few days, another set of bandages would come off and the doctors popped in to be amazed at Mom's progress. Sometimes I'd catch the doctors looking at me sideways. What was with these people? The doctors in Mexico didn't have their stethoscopes up their butts like these guys did.

I had a lot to talk to my mom about and had to wait until she could talk too. I guess it was good that we could just be together without having to get into any issues. She was so happy to see me. I remembered how much she irritated me when I was recovering. (In my defense, Mom did have prescription painkillers to lighten the load.)

It was days later when she said, "Destiny."

"Mom!" I said. "You can talk!"

Actually, she could only sort of talk. She was still missing the tip of her tongue and that made certain sounds impossible to say, like Destiny came out "Dechigy." Here's what I said and what I'm pretty sure she said:

"How do you feel?" I asked.

"Much better," she said. "I can't wait to get out of here."

"Me too," I said. "I don't think the doctors want to let you go anytime soon."

"I see the way they look at me," she said.

"They don't know what the hell is going on," I said. "It's like a miracle to them."

"It is a miracle," she said. "You don't need to stay here with me every day."

"I don't know where else I'd be," I said.

"You need to get back to your work," she said.

"I'm all done with that," I said. Then I explained the whole deal to her, about the Air Force. I didn't leave anything out, because it was my mom, and I could tell her the truth.

It took her a few tries to say, "That's bullshit!" because the letters b, l and t were almost impossible for her to say.

"Total bullshit," I said. Of course, then I had to tell her the story of how I got the disc in the first place.

"I knew it!" she said, meaning she always knew that Earth was being visited by aliens. Mom had always said they had alien bodies at Area 51.

"I should have told you about it when it happened," I said. "I was afraid that, if anyone found out about how I got my power, they'd take it away from me."

"You were right," she said.

"I guess, but I don't know," I said. "I could have told *you*."

"And I would have told you to do exactly what you did," she said.

"Really?" I said.

"Hell, yes," she said. "You had to make the most of it. Everyone wants to get out of here and you had your ticket. You would have been crazy not to use it."

"Why didn't you ever leave?" I asked.

"Couldn't afford to," she said. "Maybe I could have when I was young and had nothing to lose. But I got married. I got stuck. That's what happens to a lot of people. They don't escape when they can and, next thing you know, they can't."

"It's not too late," I said. "You can still get out."

"Oh, I'm not leaving," she said. "This is where I belong. Maybe that sounds crazy."

"Everyone says they're going to rebuild the diner," I said.

"It could have used a redo," she said.

"So, you're gonna go back?" I asked.

"Probably," she said. "What about you?"

"I don't think I can go back to New York," I said. "I don't want to have to start over in the same place. I don't know where I'll go." That was true. I'd been all over America and it wasn't like any one place seemed perfect for me. Well, maybe Austin, Texas.

"There must be a reason why we're both here right now," she said. "We both almost died."

I hadn't thought about that before. "Yeah," I said. "That is weird. Why do you think that is?" I asked. I really wanted to know.

"You needed to be here to save me," she said.

"That makes sense," I said. I wasn't sure if it did make sense. I just couldn't figure the whole thing out right then and there. "I guess you'll have to save someone now," I said.

"I don't know about that," she said. "I'm happy just to be

here with you." It was a totally mom thing to say, and totally sweet.

"You're not sorry you had me?" I asked.

"What? No!" said Mom. "Why would you ask such a thing?"

"Because of what you said before," I said. "About how you could have gotten out when you had nothing to lose, how you got stuck."

"I didn't get stuck with you," she said. "You were always a bright spot. That's what got me up and out the door in the morning."

That seemed like another totally mom thing to say. "But having to support me," I said.

"That's not a bad thing," she said, "living your life for someone else."

That made sense to me. Now that it was all over, I could see that all the good I did helping people was going to last longer than the money or the fame.

All that talking was too exhausting for Mom, so we watched some more TV.

epilogue

. . .

I STARTED at the University of Montana in January. (Go Griz!) My major is Business Administration. I picked U of M because Missoula is like the Austin of Montana; they let me in with a GED because of my real-life experience; and the tuition was cheap.

Laura ended up marrying some guy who works in finance, and they moved to South Carolina together. I saw it on social media and gave it a like.

Seth went on to make his independent movie, and I say movie because it was fun to watch. Remember it was about the guys who steal the fake painting? It's called "Portrait of Hubert van Losser" because that's the name of the stolen painting. He even got a sort of famous actor to be in it.

They rebuilt the diner and gave it a new name, the Phoenix. My mom went back to work feeling better than ever.

My dad gave up on his lawsuit, and I haven't heard from him since.

Another part of the deal with the government was that I had to make up a story about how I lost my powers. They wanted to keep a lid on the whole alien angle, after all. My made-up story – which came from one of the President's speechwriters – was that by leaving Native American lands and using my ability for financial gain, I corrupted it, and they left me. I felt stupid saying it on the couple of interviews they set up for me, but it worked. Journalists will believe anything.

Meanwhile, the government said that the Walter Reed National Military Medical Center was working on some revolutionary medical technologies to benefit wounded veterans. (Eye roll emoji.)

I got my Boxster back from the feds, the same one I abandoned at the border. They didn't even wash it, and it had a flat tire.

What a bunch of dicks.

one more thing

If you've been paying attention, you're probably wondering how I can write about all this stuff if the whole alien landing business was such a big secret.

Well, remember the alien glove I took the disc out of? Yeah, somehow that found its way to some people at MIT. (That's the Massachusetts Institute of Technology.) Don't ask me how the glove got there. I lost track of that old thing before I even moved to New York. Anyway, the nerds/geniuses at MIT did some tests and said it was made from alloys that would be impossible for a Type I civilization to make. (I won't go into the details of the Kardashev scale here. Just know that we're not even a Type I civilization yet so there's no way we could have made that glove on Earth.) People started to connect the dots and, next thing you know, the cat was out of the bag: we had already made contact. It wasn't a huge shock. Most people were, like, "Duh, of course we've been visited by aliens," and, because they weren't trying to conquer us, everybody just went about their normal business. The government still keeps all the alien stuff under wraps for "national security reasons," and we still don't have flying cars so I guess Seth was right, the military couldn't make heads or tails out of the technology they had.

your best life 26:

Final Thought.

We think of our lives as a movie starring ourselves and everyone else in the world is a co-star, a bit player or an extra in the rom-com, buddy film or kung-fu flick playing in our head.

Of course, that isn't how it is at all, even for a movie star. No one person is the center of the universe. That's pretty obvious.

Admitting that it's not all about you isn't easy. Who wants to feel like a nobody doing a bunch of stuff that doesn't matter one way or the other? Not me.

Well, you don't have to, because what you do *does* matter to the people around you. Shovel the snow off your neighbor's sidewalk, cat sit for a friend, or bake your mom a cake for her birthday, and you're making the world a better place just a little. And all those "just a little" things add up.

What's in it for you is that when you stop being the center of the universe, the pressure is off. All your mistakes, all your shoulda, woulda, couldas, shrink to where you'd need a microscope to see them.

It all comes down to this (and imagine this written over a picture of a mountain climber looking up at a snow-capped mountain): If you live your life thinking about yourself, you'll never stop worrying if you made the right decisions. If you live your life thinking about other people, you'll always know you're on the right path.

THE END

acknowledgments

Thank you to the Brooklyn Speculative Fiction Writers, who have been with me every step of my writing journey.

Special thanks to the Rad Files Novel Group for beta reading this book and helping make it the best it can be.

And, of course, a big thank you to everyone at Stag Beetle Books for picking this story out of the submissions pile.

- Fred Stesney

from the publisher

Thank you so much for reading Saint Destiny!

We hope you enjoyed the journey and characters as much as we loved bringing them to you. **Please leave a review on Amazon** and Goodreads while the story is fresh in your mind. Reviews are writing fuel for authors and help their books get into the hands of other hungry readers. If you're a big fan of speculative young adult and middle-grade fiction, we invite you to join our street team. Get copies of our books in advance, early access to covers, and other freebies!

Stag Beetle Books
  www.stagbeetlebooks.com